I0699682

SILENT ORCHIDS

A Brief History of *Alandria*

Alandria—a realm of Elves, Faeries, and Shifters—was once a land of great beauty and magic. A place filled with mountains and forests, all vibrating with mystery and life. However, the origins of this great land were actually borne of desperation to escape a terrible evil. This evil was known as the Droch-Shúil, and its power was unleashed by the race of Elves called the Ónarach.

The realm was the result of co-creative forces of magic. Birthed from the joined energy of its most powerful beings and fused with the natural life forces of a nearby realm referred to as Earth. At its very essence it was made of natural magic. The realm of Alandria rests atop Earth—with specific, but limited, points of interception—as a cloak covers a sphere. They are parallel, and yet individual, sharing an ebb and flow of the very natural energy sources essential for each to survive.

For two thousand years, Alandria was a place of peace and beauty, and its inhabitants lived in harmony. But the darkness would find them again. With great subtlety, the Droch-Shúil would implant itself in the hearts of a small band of weak-minded beings of each race, eventually separating and dividing Shifters, Faeries, and Elves and creating hostility between and even within their respective territories. As a result, after so much peace, the seeds of darkness that had been quietly growing came to maturity and there was war. Many were lost, but it appeared that after months of bloodshed, the power of the Droch-Shúil had failed. With celebration, the king and queen of Feraánmar, the domain of the Faeries and mighty Ferrishyn, greeted the king of Lumari, the territory of the Elves, to sign the final articles of peace.

As the celebration began in the Faeries' capital city of Elnye, the power of the Droch-Shúil aimed a surprise final assault. The king of Lumari escaped badly wounded, but there was no escape for the leadership of Feraánmar. The king, queen, and their daughter were all killed. The king of Lumari returned to his dominion to find it overrun. His son, the prince, had run out to battle and never returned, his body never found. The king was forced into hiding, taking with him only one: a small child not yet known to the people of Alandria.

Thank You...

It has been almost 15 years since I began envisioning and sharing the journey of Kaeleigh, Daegan, and the crew's adventures in Alandria. This special edition is to celebrate 10 years of being published!!

Writing can be a very solitary experience, and yet there are so many people I want to thank who have been a part of my journey, bringing this story to life from beginning to present. From author friends offering support, advice, encouragement, etc. along the way to the technical support of editors and graphic designers to beta, ARC, and proof readers... my book wouldn't be what it is today without you. This edition is what I have always imagined this story could be and it finally is!!

To my husband, Steven, you inspire me, challenge me, and encourage me to be the best version of me I can be even when I wasn't sure who that was, thank you. And to my beautiful daughters, I continue pursuing my dreams so that you know you can pursue yours. I love you. Also to the rest of my family, you have been an incredible support and encouragement. Thank you for believing in me and cheering for me. Especially my momma: I can't tell you how much it has meant over the years that you liked my story, believed in it, and invested in it...me.

As in life, we grow, evolve, and take on new iterations of ourselves to become the best version of ourselves, so has this project...

From the foundations of this book, I want to thank the creative team: Claudia at for her creative genius with the cover art and Ashley at The Bookish Brunette for her beautiful fonts and layout. Thank you both! Your art has been a part of this journey for over 10 years.

In this edition, I want to give credit and thank Evelyne Paniez at www.secretdartiste.be for her amazing cover design, all created by her human layering process (no AI used see resources below)!

All good fantasy stories need a map! (At least I think so). And Alandria has gone through several versions when it's come to the map. From my scratchy drawing to Donna Dull with Sharp Covers who brought it visually to life to then Bill Morgan's edition, giving it that extra push to Gerralt at Dimension Door's (https://www.dimensiondoor.nl) current spectacular version... I thank all of you!!

Thank you to Amber Beuschel—the wordsmith!—who took my story and my characters and helped me discover their greater potential all whilst getting crazy with ALL "there was" to highlight ;) the 2nd time around. You have made me better and for that I will always be grateful. Christine LePorte, you took a novice writer and helped shape my story in the very beginning, thank you.

Also a special Thank You to Steven James Wylie and Blair Masters for your beautiful original soundtrack *Silent Orchids* inspired by this book.

I would most especially like to acknowledge you, the reader. For it is with you that my story has wings. Thank YOU for 10 enchanting years and here's to many more!!

<u>Cover Art Resources Used By Secretdartiste:</u>
FONTS: Lucy Rose (Title) and Athelas Regular (Author name and
    tagline)
Leaves: depositphotos 419916432
Orchids: depositphotos 15750191
Sword: depositphotos 60411679
Particles: depositphotos 157239980
Texture snakes: depositphotos: 230230888
Magic effects and fireflies: www.neostock.com
Branches and crown elements: www.fantasybackgroundstore.com
Vines and leaves: www.hwwostock.com

MORTAL REALM
ARY'THN
CAVES OF VULDÜN
FOREST OF DUL-ISTEACH
BRIDGE OF REVEALMENT
HUNTERS COTTAGE
THE STONE FOREST
RIVER OF RANCIER
LAK
MANDÜ TRÉ LAN
SHADOW RIDGES

Author's Note

There are several new terms and locations in this novel. To better assist your reading experience, I've added a few of the initial terms with their identifiers and definitions that you will encounter. Please see the map and full glossary in the back of the book.

Alandria: A realm parallel to our mortal realm inhabited by several races of magical beings and creatures. Created by the Originators also known as The Orchids.

Feraánmar: The territory mainly inhabited by Faeries and the Ferrishyn.

Elnye: The capital city of Feraánmar.

Ferrishyn: (fair-i-shin) They are the warrior race of Faeries, mostly male, in the territory of Feraánmar. They serve as hunters, guides, and guardians. Elite members become a part of the royal guard for the Paladin.

Earth Faeries: The most common race of Faeries. They are cultivators and growers for Alandria, their magic strengthened from the earth itself even as they give back to it.

Lumari: The territory mainly inhabited by the Elves.

Adettlyn: The capital city of Lumari.

Elves: At one point were the majority race in Alandria. They have a base magic as most do in Alandria, but some are gifted with more abilities than others. Their magic is strengthened from the light of the sun, moon, and stars.

The Orchids: An illusive collective of heads from various races united together originally to flee darkness thus creating Alandria. Considered the Originators and make up the group considered the Elders. Their goal to unite Alandria against the darkness that stirs upheaval against the kingdoms.

The Droch-Shúil: Is an evil entity. It is an ancient host collecting souls that went bad—the unforgiven dead. It grows with the strength and magic of the souls it consumes. Also considered a kind of demon.

Paladin: The governing rulers of a territory, specifically Feraánmar territory of the Faeries, that took reign when the King and Queen died.

The Sol-lumieth: A new power, a new magic, that was foretold in an ancient prophecy to return the light and life—the hope—of Alandria.

* Several races that are present, or created, in The Age of Alandria series are inspired from various mythologies throughout history.

PROLOGUE

Darkness had fallen, but the stars refused to shine. Dulled light shone softly from two reluctant moons hanging, bloated with grief, reflecting the heart of Alandria. The king and queen of the Faeries had been slain, along with the princess, the remaining heir of Feraánmar. Her love and partner in rebuilding the treaties between the races, the prince of the Elves and heir to the throne of Alandria, was lost—presumed dead. As was the hope for a united Alandria.

In the depths of the Forest of Dul-Isteach, the Elders carried out their last act before they disbanded. Some would diminish with time, cloaked in glamour to live out their days. Some would go into hiding to preserve what remained of the ancient magic for another life.

Floating balls of fire along the periphery lit the clearing. There were no additional witnesses but for the forest and the creatures that lay within; their cries and calls were the only sounds to be heard in the vast silence. At the cry of the raven, seven figures hooded in ancient tradition walked ceremonially from the forest, each stopping at one of the seven points indicated on the star burned into the ground. Robes colored in blue, purple, brown, dark green, crimson, light green, and white each represented a different tribe. They carried in one hand a single candle with a purple flame flickering in the stillness of the night. In the other, a small silver dagger carried by the hilt, pointed toward the sky. The light from the flames reflected off each of the blades, dancing onto the trees and creating the illusion of a greater light. The hooded figure in green at the top point of the star said something in a very low, monotone voice. A single word in an ancient language.

"Drachmot."

Everything went silent: all the creatures of the earth and sky. Simultaneously, the flames extinguished. Darkness.

Two heartbeats of silence. As suddenly as all fell into darkness a sound arose so primal, so ancient, it seemed to come from the depths of the earth. Flames ignited with a burst of life, permitting the creatures to release their cries, their sorrows for the tragedy that had befallen them all. In the center of the star, where there had been only a large, flat-topped boulder, stood another hooded figure, this one cloaked in black. His head was bowed, his stature humbled, wrists bound in front of him by shackles alight with a fire that did not burn.

The green-hooded figure spoke out with a voice that carried power. "Your crime of murder upon the Ferrishyn innocents and royals in hiding is worthy of the soul you cherish to be torn away from your body and fed to the parasite that is the land of the condemned." His voice—even filled with the power of his authority—shook with despair and heaviness. There was a moment of pause to let the gravity settle.

Responding to a silent cue, each of the hooded beings walked toward the center, toward the figure on the rock. Surrounding the boulder, they extended their hands, palm to palm, symbolically closing the circle, their reverent chanting creating a low hum. Then once again, there was silence, this time weighted with anticipation and something tangible in the air... magic, old magic. The hood in the center dropped to his knees. The candles were raised to the sky, then brought down and placed along the edges of the rock's platform where the flames illuminated the earth. Stains of past sacrifices opened the ears of the earth and beseeched the rocks to bear witness. The green hood that opened the ceremony once again uttered a single word in that same monotone voice.

"*Rudan.*"

The hoods reached with their left hands, simultaneously grabbed their daggers by the blades, and swiftly pulled the hilt down, slicing into the meat of their hands. They uttered not a single expression or sound. Palms squeezed tightly and blood trailed down wrists to fall on the ground and rock.

Another word spoken: "*Rroonda.*"

The white hood released the bindings of the black-hooded being in the center with a simple touch of his hand. The black hood held out his left hand, palm up, waiting for the sting of sliced flesh as his turn had come. He closed his eyes and smelled the coppery scent of his own blood before registering the pain. He refused to flinch or utter a sound. He wouldn't dare. He deserved this, and more. This was the commencing of his punishment.

More ancient words were uttered: "*Brachtah. Gallten. Kollaque.*"

Then the white hood spoke so all present could understand. "Earth, receive this blood, hear our petition. Rock, take this offering and bear witness to this sacrifice."

The blue-hooded figure to the right looked up at the black hood on the rock and said, "The blood spilled here tonight is not only an offering, but represents what will happen to the one who breaks the vow. The boulder is the strength of the bond created and serves as silent witness. The earth absorbs the secrets of the vows; it is ever present and will execute punishment as it deems necessary, even if all others are unaware."

The Elder in the purple hood spoke. "Due to the desperate circumstances of all of our people, mercy has been extended to you as you were in the service of the Orchaedia at the time of your failure. You have been spared and commissioned with the guardianship and protection of a blessed child. Let it be known..." He paused, looking at the accused straight on. He gripped his blade against his palm once more. The open wound released a greater flow of blood and dripped freely from the wound, pouring out like a pot of old tea, hitting the earth in thick thuds and pools of dark sweat. "You are hereby banished!"

The hood in the center, head already hung with shame, dropped his shoulders, his final stand of pride stripped, wishing for death instead. The purple hood continued, "Do you agree to the conditions of your pardon?"

For the first time, the condemned in the circle's center looked up and spoke. "I do." As ceremonially required to seal a vow, he squeezed his hand as the others had onto the ground and again onto the rock, adding his stain among those who had stood before him, whether for ritual or retribution, but almost never for a pardon from such a sin. The burden for carrying the knowledge of what he had done would be more than he deserved. He deserved to be sent to a place far worse than death; a place that would, over time, slowly strip his soul from his flesh to be absorbed into the land. He deserved to be sentenced to Exhile.

His thoughts were interrupted by the monotone voice reverberating behind him.

"Bring the child," the dark green hood spoke.

The child, barely old enough to walk, was carried from the forest into the clearing by a young woman. Blue iridescent tears streamed down the woman's face. She possessively gripped the child, infusing every ounce of love she had to give, hoping that some day the child, though not her own, would understand, and that forgiveness could be found. With slow sure steps, her arms quaked with tremors of uncertainty. She leaned down and bestowed a kiss on the forehead of the innocent in her arms. The woman, her whole being, on the edge of a storm of tears, released a choked sigh of grief as she handed the sleeping child to the black hood in the center. She looked deep into his eyes, eyes pained with the weight of his deeds. When she was satisfied with not only the regret, but the spark of hope she saw, she gave him a frank nod and ran back into the cover of the forest.

Awkwardly, the figure in black cradled the child. Looking upon her innocence and frailty, recognizing her as his personal savior, he tenderly stroked a lock of her dark hair aside. Resolved with his mission, he then looked to the green hood, who now stood in front of him and waited.

"You have been given a great gift, but one that will weigh on you for as long as you live," the green-hooded figure spoke. "Take care of her. She has been marked... the last of *The Orchids*," he whispered, his voice choked. Lowering his head, he then uttered in that same ancient language, "*Lan du hasen ie.*"

There was instant darkness. When the flames burst back to life, the black-hooded figure and the small child were gone.

CHAPTER ONE

SIXTEEN YEARS LATER. PRESENT DAY. MISSOULA, MT.

"Oh no! Not again," Kaeleigh said, gripping her head as the faint buzzing grew louder. She reached out unsteadily with her other hand, searching for her six-drawer thrift-store-find dresser. Though steady with its support, she couldn't stop the flash of white light that was blinding her. She tensed and a cold sweat broke out along her forehead. "Stay calm," she coached herself, but, her breathing escalated. To anyone else, this phenomenon might have driven them to seek help. But to Kaeleigh, this was a part of her life and always had been.

For the briefest second, she could actually feel the ghost of a hand engulfing her own; a masculine hand rough with callouses, but warm and safe. Kaeleigh's skin tingled with the slightest increase in pressure from his hand, sending waves of calm deeply needed energy throughout her body. Once she could calm herself and stop her body from panicking, she could receive the vision with greater ease.

The calm fell thick, and this time...

She could actually smell the damp moss and fresh cedar fragrance of the forest. She could *feel* the ancient trees and the life energy flowing in them. She could feel his calm, soothing presence, making it all seem *alive* and real, even in the split second she had experienced it all. Then the images began, once again of places she had never been, people she had never seen. They began slowly at first, but then sped up as if she was zooming in on a particular image.

A never-ending, dense forest. Trunks the width of cars or larger, sky-scraper tall as they stretched for the sky. Trees of all kinds, some enshrouded with ivy that would consume everything in its path. Ancient. Healthy. Strong. Alive.

A clearing, lit with shimmering rays from the bright of day sneaking through the canopy of leaves above.

"Look," a sing-songy voice whispered through her mind, sending shivers down Kaeleigh's spine.

An empty clearing no longer empty, but filled with a small gathering. Not people, but a variety of beings. Disjointed images flashed from one feature to the next—pointed ears, inhumanly proportionate bodies, features more animal in nature—wings!—beings small and tall, butterflies, dragonflies, and creatures likely from a fairy tale. A man, a being, upon which all were focused seemed to be speaking to two other beings—a man and a woman, both smiling. They kissed. There was clapping. Orchids! Orchids blooming all over and out of nowhere, tendrils climbing down from the trees alive with the magic of the moment.

A new image flashed, this time more like a succession of still photographs:

A young man... being. A partial silhouette, though mostly to the back. Tall with hair black as night. Another image: *his head about to look over his shoulder, but stopped.* Another: *the same man poised with a sword in one hand and a knife in the other.* Another: *a tattoo; a small flower—an orchid.* Another: *a different marking on his wrist—tribal? Another: her hand laced in his.* Another: *close-up of their hands... his ring.*

The images of the man's silhouette flashed over and over again, faster and faster until they seemed to move with life of their own. As he was about to turn and look back at her, she saw his dimpled and sexy smirk just before she was ripped involuntarily from the scene, and thrust back into her apartment bedroom.

Gripping her dresser so hard her knuckles turned white, Kaeleigh held still, breathing several deep long breaths, letting her body catch up with what had just happened mentally. Getting her bearings took minutes, but this was nothing new. She had learned to cope with the onslaught of images that unpredictably flung themselves at her throughout her life. Still, and no matter how careful or focused on relaxation she was, they always took her breath away.

The buzzing finally left her ears, and slowly her bedroom came back into focus. Then the color faded, and a small depression followed.

Compared to the vibrancy of the forest scene she had just witnessed, her own surroundings were drab and despairing. And after each time, her heart broke with such a sense of familiarity and longing for something or someone she had never known. Kaeleigh couldn't understand her intense reaction or why these episodes happened at all. They just always had. And the orchids! They were always present in some way during these visions—just as in her real life. She felt as though the orchids were some signature in her life, quietly signing its way through dreams, visions and commonly, her every day experience in Missoula. Although, lately, the images had started to change. What was disconcerting, however, was how much more intense they were becoming, how much more... *real*.

CHAPTER TWO

Today was Kaeleigh Johnson's eighteenth birthday. But to her, it was just another day. Another day in which she attempted to find something she was good at. Another day to find somewhere she belonged in the workforce community of Missoula, Montana. There had to be something out there for her; at least, that's what she kept telling herself. But there wasn't anything significant about her that she was aware of, nor was there any great meaning to her daily life. Kaeleigh simply existed.

Thoughtlessly and by habit, Kaeleigh clutched the delicate, honey-gold locket that hung from her neck. It brought her comfort. The necklace was the only thing she had of value, sentimental or otherwise. It was delicate, yet uniquely shaped and the only thing identifying her when she had been brought to the orphanage at the age of two. It was the only visible sign proving she had belonged to someone; that someone had loved her or cared at least enough to name her. Turning it over between her fingers, she recalled how the many jewelers that she had gone to had never seen anything like it or the material used to forge it. She had hoped to find out where the locket might have come from, but without success. Each jeweler had made offers to purchase it or sell it on consignment. She definitely could have used the cash, but the locket was worth much more than money to her. It was special, and she needed special.

Singular among lockets, it was the shape of an orchid, with two connecting points at a petal's end. The front was inlaid with a much smaller orchid in a white iridescent material that baffled the jewelers. Opal? Ivory? A rare amber hybrid? None could determine its stone—if indeed it was a stone. On the back, a simple inscription reassured her of her name *Kaeleighnna*. No middle initial, no last name, just *Kaeleighnna*. It was the foster agency that had given her the last name Johnson.

She hadn't had much choice at the time, but the name felt wrong like a tight pair of shoes your feet longed to be free of, or an itchy sweater you were dying to rip off. The interior of the necklace wasn't hollowed out for pictures like most lockets, but simply flat and smooth with two foreign symbols etched into each side.

Years of searching had yielded no information to tell her what the symbols meant, if anything at all. Yet they were important though; she just *knew* it! Kaeleigh could feel a faint resonance of heat and slight vibrations of energy at times, either through her hands as she held it, or against the skin of her chest where it rested. It wasn't just another piece of jewelry; it identified her, had become a part of her.

Growing up "in the system," the foster care system, that is, she had lived with several different families. Some were passably okay, sufficiently loving and some made it obvious they were just in it for the monthly check. And then there was the one that she had no other choice but to run away from. No matter how bad it got, there always seemed to be that constant reminder—in the form of a simple orchid—that she once had a family out there and that she was not alone. A source of strange comfort, the orchid would speak to her. At times an orchid showed up randomly, for seemingly no reason at all. Other times it taunted her, a silent re-minder of what she didn't have... family, people to call her own, a place she belonged. Sometimes orchid appearances were more significant, as if someone knew just when she needed guidance or encouragement.

Like today, the single-stemmed orchid in a small, but beautifully ornate antiqued pot appeared out of nowhere on her dresser. She knew that things like that didn't just *appear*, at least not to normal people. But Kaeleigh had never been normal and things like that didn't bother her. She knew it to be a message, but what that message was, she simply couldn't discern. Deep down, she wanted to believe the lovely white or-chid on her dresser today was significant. After all, it was her eighteenth birthday.

Her best friends of many years, Chel and Finn, wanted to celebrate the traditional milestone, but Kaeleigh didn't feel like festivities. She felt raw and empty. Her heart hurt and it felt like part of her was missing, but she couldn't seem to get her feelings into words. Embarrassed and ashamed of what she did not know, but inside an ache pulsed on—she didn't know who she came from or who she was supposed to be.

Do other teenagers with real parents wonder about these kinds of things?

Celebrating would make her just feel worse, would make her dwell more on the "what ifs" and "whys," when in reality, it was just another day. She felt that sticking to the normal, going to her new job at the restaurant down the street was more likely to help her find that "thing" she was searching for.

It didn't matter that this was her fourth job in the last several months.

Did it?

Or even that before this one, she had multiple kinds of jobs in the last couple of years varying from fast food to front desk office work to holding signs waving at cars on street corners.

I need to try different things to find what I'm good at. I just haven't found it—whatever "it" is, she tried to convince herself.

Maybe going from home to home, with an inconsistent upbringing, had influenced her more than she'd realized. She was now noticing the effects it had had—the most unsettling one was the most recent insight from today—that she not only didn't know who she was or where she came from, but that she had no idea where she was going in life.

Alas, this is too deep for today.

Rolling her eyes at her introspection, she stretched her arms toward the ceiling. Out of the corner of her eyes, she noticed her beautiful little orchid suddenly began to droop as if saddened. Kaeleigh gently placed her hand under the bloom, cradling it like the fragile flower it was.

"I just got you," she whispered longingly to the flower. "Please don't leave me yet." She closed her eyes and pictured the orchid strong and healthy, vibrant and more beautiful than it had ever been.

When she opened her eyes, to her shock, the orchid had not only straightened once more, but had grown and its petals were shimmering like nothing she had seen before on a flower. Kaeleigh gasped, sucking a huge heave of air right back into her lungs and stepped back from the potted plant before knocking it over.

"Well, that's new," she said with awe as she examined the little flower. Kaeleigh then looked at her fingertips, studying her own hands searching for what she didn't know. When she saw nothing had changed, she watched the flower again as if it might grow two heads next. After a minute of no other changes, she simply sighed and resolved it was time to get dressed. A new job with new possibilities awaited her.

After her long, relaxing shower, Kaeleigh quickly got ready, putting on the required black slacks, black shoes, and black button-up blouse that Antonia's, the restaurant and her new employer, had given her to wear. The all black was very different from what she would have chosen to wear. Kaeleigh loved color... all colors. She even craved color. Some days she would *feel* certain colors for the day and had to wear them together even if they didn't match. She felt the colors impacted her day. In turn, Kaeleigh felt they impacted others' perspectives and moods, bringing at least a smile or even a giggle from those around her. She didn't care what other people thought about how she looked because *she* liked how she felt and that seemed important. Plus, it was fun to watch the expressions on the faces of strangers, more than once wishing she had a camera phone and not her old piece of junk that hardly worked.

Kaeleigh often had impulses to dye her hair with the different colors, but she loved her rich blackish-brown hair with red highlights streaked throughout—completely natural— so she refrained most of the time. Every once in a while, though, she would use those temporary dyes that squeeze into your hair like a paintbrush, choosing colors like pink, purple, and blue. She even added green once, which she surprisingly loved.

Her hair had loose, unruly curls that reached her lower back when left down. She had moments of "hair hatred," as Chel called it, just like any girl, but mostly she thought her hair rocked! The different stylists she had gone to for haircuts were always shocked that she didn't do anything to maintain her color. It apparently wasn't something "normal," as they would tell her. She'd always been able to wave them off, assuming that they of course just meant *natural*, until the very last stylist she had gone to made a little too big of a deal about it and caused a scene. She had walked out with a not-so-polite hand gesture before she had broken down in tears, feeling, not for the first time, like a freak. Chel's mom began cutting her hair not long after that.

With time for a quick pause on her way out the door, she looked briefly in the mirror to make sure everything was in its proper place. The black shirt was a little big on her slender frame but not too bad; maybe if she had more going for her in the chest department she could have filled it out. Even puffing up her chest didn't help. She wasn't flat, but she definitely wasn't curvaceous. Chel, on the other hand—that girl had some curves and she knew how to accentuate them. According to a body type quiz in one of the fashion magazines, Kaeleigh had an "athletic build." At least the pants fit well. It would have really sucked having to yank her pants up constantly while trying to serve food. Not the first impression she wanted to leave. However, her creamy complexion and deep emerald-green eyes—eyes that could appear a touch eerie if her mood went bad—were, in her opinion, her greatest attributes. Overall, she couldn't complain. Kaeleigh smiled, grabbed her bag along with a bagel for the road, and headed out the door.

✻✻✻

Missoula autumns were unmatched by any others. Leaves competed with her own hair's vibrant tones, the brisk air with her cool and calculated tone. But most of all it was the immense and vast Glacier National Park which compelled her heart, soul and mind into the outdoors, her heart falling in love with fall all over again each year. She belonged there, and yet still she felt like there was more out there for her. Living in an area with the variety and diverseness of the seasons spoke to the very core of her essence, but fall spoke the loudest. It allowed for the dying of those parts that needed to be trimmed away, and the resurgence of new life and growth.

Living on the third floor of the old brick Altadena apartment building, which the girls had affectionately named "Old Dena," wasn't so bad. They liked to say that they lived in one of those old brick buildings with the newly renovated apartments in the more eclectic art district—minus the renovations and the eclectic art. Instead, it was just an old brick building with old apartments in a decent neighborhood just outside the art district near the college. It was affordable and not too far a walk from her new job so she wasn't complaining. Plus, her two best friends lived in the same area.

Chel—like the sea "shell"—Marzén had been her bestie since junior high, her hiking buddy, confidant and most recently her roommate since they'd graduated from high school since months prior. Chel, however, had recently moved out of their quaint "girl apartment" into her boyfriend Samuel's "man-pad" against both her parents' and Kaeleigh's better judgment. He seemed like a good guy, but there was just something about him Kaeleigh couldn't put her finger on that made her uneasy. Maybe it was that it had happened so fast. In any case, she knew she didn't want to lose her friend over it so she tolerated him... for now. At least it was just a couple buildings down the street from her. To add to that Chel was now in college, they didn't get to hike as often as they liked or talk as much either. Plain and simple, Kaeleigh missed her.

Her other friend—her only other friend—Finnlan "Finn" Talaín, she had only known the last few years but seemed like she'd known him her entire life. He was loyal and caring, though to some his closed off and somewhat affrontive demeanor kept them away. But he had always been there for her when she needed him. He lived right across the street above the little bakery they loved to frequent, and she could see his window from her little balcony that opened to a fire escape.

Where Chel could be spontaneous and artistic, Finn was punctual and moody. Kaeleigh couldn't even remember how the three of them ended up together. For as long as she could remember, they'd been the only family she'd known. They accepted her for who she was, eccentricities and all. They didn't know about all the visions she got or even the orchids—just that she was extremely interested in the flowers and very loyal as a friend and sometimes extra needy, extra flighty, and extra emotional. Grateful for them both, she smiled as she thought about her good friends and headed to Antonia's. On more occasions than this one, she thought she should tell them about her "flashes," but they already thought her obsession with orchids was strange. Telling them she thought these flashes were from "the great beyond" would probably put her on the crazy list. So for now, though she hated keeping things from them, she decided she would keep them to herself just as she'd been doing for so long anyway.

Chapter Three

PRESENT DAY. ELNYE, THE CAPITAL
CITY OF FERAÁNMAR IN ALANDRIA.

The slam of his fist against the marble wall echoed as he marched
down the hall leading to where High Court was being held. Daegan didn't even register the pain in his hand until seconds later.

Summoned!? I am family*! Can they not simply request my presence?*

Clenching his fist then shaking it out to relieve the pain that was now
throbbing, he grumbled under his breath, "I do not know how much
longer I can do this. I guess it no longer matters, though, does it?" He
would comply no matter the request. He always did, even when it went
against his better judgment. His expression tightened as his memories
grew dark.

Daegan Waethní, nephew to the Paladin and third in line to the
throne, resigned himself to his current fate as he strode angrily toward
the chamber. He had been trained by the Ferrishyn elite guard—the Ferrishyn being the warrior race of the Faeries. As the most skilled warrior,
with the addition of his "gifts," he was invaluable as both protector of
the family and executioner of their dark justice.

The only slight differences between him and the Faeries of the earth
were his larger and stronger build, his more dominant nature (earth
Faeries were more of a peaceful race), and his slightly darker skin. The
Ferrishyn were bred to fight and to protect, whereas the Faeries were
made to grow and cultivate the earth. Daegan, with his raven black-blue
hair that fell to his ears, sharp facial features, and chiseled jaw, exuded a
dominance and an energy that when unrestrained made bystanders cow-
er where they stood. Thick, dark eyebrows punctuated the dark-choco-
late color of his eyes. Eyes that were deep set and held an intensity that

could see into the depths of the most guarded. Eyes that had seen too much despair and not enough hope. His strength and confidence came not only from years of training as a warrior but also from the center of who he was as a Ferrishyn.

Daegan was very young when his parents had fled with him from Feraánmar to the outlying lands. It wasn't long after that they had died. In fact, he hardly remembered them at all. Wren and Maleina, the current guardians of Feraánmar—called the Paladin—had found him. He was their great-nephew or great-great nephew; he couldn't remember. When they had found him, he had been in fairly bad shape, having had survived for over a year by himself roaming like a nomad and hiding in caves or whatever shelter he could find—or create—at the ripe age of seven or eight. He couldn't remember many of the details now, except to be reminded of the one event he couldn't escape in his dreams—the night his parents died. A long many years had passed since they left him alone to fend for himself, though not their fault. It terrified him, but his father had taught him to use every experience for his own gain; he allowed it to strengthen him, shape him, and even scar him.

He had been orphaned by the devastation and tragedies of the Uprising that began many years ago. The Paladin were now his only family. His anger and bitterness at having lost his parents when he was young had colored how he viewed everything growing up. He chose the path that brought him to his current station with not many other choices that he could foresee. He had dedicated himself to become the best warrior possible and he had succeeded. He was a warrior... the finest. And everybody knew it.

The Paladin were the guardian rulers of Feraánmar, the dominion of the Faeries. It consisted of only two—Wren and Maleina Endíl. They had stepped in after the last great battle—the siege at Elnye—when the king and queen, along with the princess of Feraánmar, were killed, leaving no heir to the throne. The Paladin had grown in power in the years since. This power gave them life, and they always craved more of it. However, as leaders they were weak. Wren had lost much of the ambition he'd had in his younger years.

Many would say Wren and Maleina should have been dethroned, but no one had yet tried—maybe because of Daegan himself, because he stood in the way whether he wanted to or not. Change was coming, however. Daegan could feel it deep within. He knew it was a time for planning and seeking opportunity... for what, he could not yet say. It was just a feeling, but he would be waiting.

❉❉❉

High Court was held in the throne room of the kingdom in Elnye, the capital city of Feraánmar. The surrounding walls were a beautiful ivory marble with veins of red threaded throughout from floor to ceiling. Eight giant marble pillars, four on either side of the room, escorted Daegan to the opposite end of the room. He had barged in, not waiting for the servant to "announce" him. He felt a bit bad thinking of the poor Faerie trying to keep up with him enough to make an official announcement.

Two oversized high-back ornate thrones set up on a stage covered in the lavish burgundy fabric stood ominously before him, their very expense and shine mocking him or anyone that would wish for any-thing different than what the Paladin would so "generously" offer. Two plush, brilliant-blue velvet pillows lay on the floor at the base of the stage for those entreating with the court to kneel. It gave a false sense of casual openness, as if one's petition might actually be heard, which, unless it benefitted Wren and Maleina—well, mostly Maleina—certainly wouldn't be.

Lush greenery surrounded the hall. Crawling vines with small white and purple blooms ate their way throughout the room. Thin-trunked trees with perfectly shaped leaves of all shades of green with roots that grew from underneath the marble floor were landscaped behind the thrones. Wren and Maleina were earth Faeries with a natural-born con-nection to the land. Not so much presently but in the past, earth Faeries had felt a responsibility to cultivate and nourish anything that grew in Alandria. Unfortunately, Maleina felt their magic was better used within their domain. As a result, everything beyond the borders of Feraánmar suffered. Alandria was dying and not just from a lack of magic. Inside High Court, however, there was something sinister lying within its nat-ural beauty. Something in the trees made them feel dangerous.

Daegan was announced, albeit a bit weakly, by the breathless Faerie that had followed him in.

I have been summoned. But I do not play these games. Let us talk and be done with it.

He strode in with strength and confidence straight toward them. He saw the briefest flash of shock in Maleina's eyes as she adjusted her posture, choosing to ignore his insolence. Daegan's attitude belied his belief that he was not their inferior—their position had not been granted, but taken. He usually hid it better. Not today.

Wren, a Faerie and one of the Ferrishyn, still looked to be in his fifties compared to a human's standards of age. The only physical evidence of his aging were the few streaks of silver highlighting his dark hair on the sides and the matching spattering throughout the crown. Still handsome, he had kept himself in the shape a seasoned warrior should be. He was tall and carried the ghost of someone used to commanding, but over time he had let it slip away. His flat gray eyes spoke defeat, as disconnect was the only means of getting through the next event he was dragged to, dressed in fine linens and attending the most important events and meeting with the leaders of other tribes. At first glance, Wren appeared to be wise beyond his years, ruling in splendor and glory, but the reality was he was diminished to the shadow of his wife.

Wren greeted Daegan with a slight nod. Deep down Daegan believed Wren actually cared about the people, but he hadn't stood up to her for them. That was where Daegan lost respect for him... and for himself.

Maleina was ever smooth, manipulative, and enticing, but her authority was absolute. Wren now deferred to her ambitions and all Feraánmar feared her. She was beautiful, with long autumn-red hair cascading down her back. Her hair was adorned in jewels, thick spools of it unwinding and twirling around sapphires and emeralds. Her dresses were flowing and colorful, always revealing a touch less than what was really wanted, pulling heads for a second look. She could seduce with false humility and charm, but at her core, she was arrogant and vengeful. The same fire in her hair flamed within her and was ready to consume anything that got in her way, often doing just that.

Daegan sensed the time of this horrific beautiful woman was coming to end. Her reign?... Her life?... He wasn't sure, nor did he care. Watching her grow more threatened by others, possessive of what she held dear, and more restless as the days went on, he had to believe she could sense it too.

Maleina and Wren's son, Halister, not much younger than Daegan, was lighthearted and sanguine; a show-off just trying to be seen and heard by his parents. Their daughter, Rheina, second in line after Halister to the throne, though younger and more docile, shared an ego and attitude with her mother. She was about to come of age and felt she was entitled. Rheina could be loud and spirited one moment, then grow moody and sulk in the shadows in another. What not many saw, however, was her quietly good heart as she struggled with her own complications at the depths of who she was against the position of rulership her family—specifically her mother—had taken.

Daegan refused to kneel on the floor pillow before them. Maleina bristled at his boldness, but he waited for Maleina to speak first. Hands clenched at his sides, he lowered his eyes in a show of subtle submission, enough to ease her infuriation in order to procure answers. It worked.

"Daegan, my dear boy," Maleina said in her most unnatural maternal tone as she rose from her throne and walked behind it pretending to admire a purple flower on the vines. "Tomorrow is your scouting day in Anise, is it not?" she asked. Her back was now to Daegan but she turned her head to the side just enough to see him nod in confirmation. "While you are there, I want you to listen for whispers of a new power—the Sol-lumieth. I have heard rumors circling about. Have you heard of it?"

"I have," he answered, glaring at his aunt's spectacularly jeweled hair. "Do you believe it is something we should fear?" he asked, even though he knew the answer.

"Of course we do not *need* to fear this new power," Maleina spoke, her voice sickly sweet, "whatever it may be. However, we should not be ignorant. Since no one will oblige us with the information we seek, we must search it out for ourselves."

Though her words were defiant, in her eyes he could see the fear of a potential threat as she spoke, and he wondered what that could be about. Daegan had decided against telling her that not only had he overheard the people whispering amongst themselves in a hushed frenzy, but he too had sensed something unknown stirring.

"I will see what there is to be learned in Anise," Daegan said thoughtfully, hiding the unease about the rumors he'd heard. "My visit may require a couple of days—May I request Halister to accompany me to cover more ground?" This last question he tacked on as if he'd suddenly been inspired with the idea. In truth, Daegan didn't need him to assist; it was that he enjoyed his company and he knew Hal liked to get out and explore the frivolity in other cities.

"That is a splendid idea!" Wren said, speaking with unexpected fervor as he broke his own silence. His enthusiasm was a contradiction to the subdued persona he had been giving off. Maleina accordingly shot daggers at him with her eyes, to which Wren acknowledged, but leaned forward anyway, declaring with a grin, "It's a shame I have so many boring duties to attend. I'm half tempted to go along with you boys." Then winking, the older man sat back and smiled at Daegan knowingly. Though silence persisted for a few moments, Maleina was decisive. "Yes, that seems like a good enough idea," she answered "I will inform Halister that you will be departing at first light and let him know that he is to meet you in the stables."

Despising the fact that her statement had to follow Wren's comment, she then gathered up the abundance of fabric from her dress and turned to leave. Turning back to look at Wren, her eyes commanded that he depart with her. Daegan half nodded, half smiled toward the only father figure he'd known, appreciative of the broken man, and that much more divided against the tumultuous woman.

***

The Forest of Lumei was the oldest of those in Alandria. In fact, the forest itself was aware of who or what crossed its border. It had friends. It had foes. Lucky not to have been ensnared, as many times as Daegan had passed through, he considered himself a friend. Those found to be enemies had not passed through to the other side.

A thick ground cover of moist, green moss blanketed the forest floor. It even climbed the trees covering their branches, making the earth and the growth a seamless transition to the trees. The trees were thick and strong, ominously towering over and protecting all they chose to within their bounds. Younger, smaller trees of all kinds, including many that bloomed, thrived in their care. Lumei had a mystical, enchanting energy. The tangible wisdom that permeated this forest was centuries old. Some... were among the Ancients.

The ground was not only covered by growth but by roots that had emerged from below like creatures from the depths of the earth clawing their way to the surface for air. Daegan and Hal would have to lead their horses on foot to navigate them through the barely visible path that had been worn over time.

At first light, Daegan had been in the stables across the field from the main house, which resembled a small medieval castle that he had seen in the mortal realm. With his horse almost prepared to leave, he heard Halister practically running down the pathway humming a familiar lighthearted tune. Daegan looked up and sighed. Finely attuned hearing was another of his rare and secretive gifts which was why he was being sent into Anise. The *family*, unfortunately, knew of his gift and used it for their gain. Daegan finished tightening the saddle on his beautiful stallion, Mayfair, just as Halister sauntered inside.

Hal, a few inches taller than Daegan, had a similar build: warrior style with defined, chiseled muscles all over. Daegan's shoulders were wider, allowing for the bit more bulk that he carried. Hal's ropy, often disheveled, blond hair gave others the illusion that he was one of the commoners until they realized who he was and repented with appropriate respectful murmurings. His hazel eyes were everything eyes should be; clear, bright, and inviting with warmth. Rumors tended to label him a philanderer and that might have been, but he wasn't a bad guy, a little immature with an air of expectation, much like many in "royal" positions. The truth was that for being brought up by Maleina and Wren he had a pretty decent head on his shoulders. Hal had been a fair "brother." He had a good nature and was one of the few that Daegan could easily be around. He was also Daegan's closest friend and a trusted warrior.

"You ready to go?" Daegan asked him as Hal walked in the stable doors.

"Well, good morning to you too, Daegan. Yes, I'm ready, just got to make sure Dolly's ready. I had Fritz shoe her last night." Sighing, Halister ran his hand down the back of his head. "I'm glad to be getting out of here for a couple days. I owe you one, brother." Hal smiled at Daegan as he saddled up Dolly, his beautiful chestnut-colored Arabian, then gave the horse a kiss on the nose and stroked her shiny black mane as she whinnied her own greeting.

With a simple nod, Daegan led Mayfair out of the stables. Halister followed on Dolly. Daegan gathered the reins, grabbed the horn of the saddle, and mounted his own horse with the practiced ease of a seasoned rider. Turning their backs to their home with the rising sun as their companion, they headed toward Anise. Riding swiftly and fluidly together, they didn't stop to rest until they reached the entrance to the Forest of Lumei.

Within the borders of Alandria, there was a succession of forests one after another threaded together by open fields and rolling hills and woven by the common bond that was the land, strong and alive. Along the vast edges of the realm, there were treacherous mountain ranges, some peaks capped with blankets of snow and others shrouded with shadows of mystery. Beyond those borders were lands yet to be explored. The Forest of Lumei gave respectable definition to the borders of Anise just outside Adettlyn, the capital city of the Elven territory, and its surrounding cities and villages.

It was always a bit of a risk traveling through the forest as there were many rogues—those who stood in opposition to the current rule—in these lands. Fortunately, Daegan had many "friends" and had never had any issues traveling through Lumei.

Except that one time.

Hal was mostly liked by those within their tribe and even outside of their tribe, but he was also the son of the most disrespected and feared leaders—namely his mother—in all of Alandria. If the Paladin had offended or angered any of its inhabitants lately, they were likely to take it out on Halister for the sake of convenience and revenge. For that, they would need to take extra caution.

Just outside the vast border of the forest looming before them, Daegan breathed deeply, inhaling life into his expanding lungs. He reveled in the crisp, clean air provided by the oxygen-enriching cedars, able to almost taste the sweet aroma of the aged forest. Daegan and Halister each scanned their surroundings, but today seemed to find only the peace such a forest could bring. Daegan had always found deep beauty in the mysteries that lay within all forests, but especially the ancient grove in front of him.

Rays of sun pierced through the canopy of trees, streaking down as they collided with a faint and eerie mist, rising from the ground. It was mystical. Quiet. Daegan's sensitive hearing allowed him to hear more than the gurgling of the small creek running nearby. He could hear the creaking of old wood as it swayed gently in the breeze. It sounded alive. They had been quiet, almost reverent, since arriving at the borders of Lumei. Ready for the adventure, and what possibly laid ahead, Daegan and Halister proceeded cautiously into the great Forest of Lumei.

Chapter Four

Daegan's Journey to the Territory of Lumari.

Before total nightfall, they passed into the borders of Lumari, the territory of the Elves. Anise was a small village just outside the capital city of Adettlyn. Daegan took a grateful breath of relief, the pressure of being watched within the forest having taken a much bigger toll on him than he'd realized. He wasn't particularly keen on moving through "foreign" territories, especially in these times. Over time, Daegan had learned to move carefully, adept in the art of both watching and knowing when he was being watched. The last thing he wanted was to spend the night in the forest.

Lortuna, the night house in which they stayed when in town, was a welcome sight. Lortuna housed less than an average inn, having only ten rooms. The beautiful, narrow, three-story stone home suited with white shutters on each of the front windows was beginning to be swallowed by climbing ivy between each of the windows. Illumination from inside each of the rooms softened behind sheer curtains gave the house a warm glow as night drew close.

They were invited in by the night clerk, an acquaintance from previous stays. Even though they were Ferrishyn, she greeted them as if old friends, reuniting with warm hugs and cheek kisses on either side, the customary greeting for the city dwellers. Daegan instantly stiffened, uncomfortable with displays of affection even as innocent as this. Hal patted him on the back as he stepped around him to get inside.

"Hello, boys," she welcomed as she released Daegan. She was an older Elf with a matronly heart. "Oh relax, Daegan, you are to stay in this comfortable home free from worries of whether you will be welcome here or not." She laughed good-naturedly. Even though there had not been peace in Adettlyn for quite some time, there were still a few inhabitants in Anise that lived with hope for a better future for Alandria.

Giving her a small but genuine smile and a gracious nod, he acknowledged the truth of what she said. Not everyone would be so welcoming of two elite Ferrishyn staying at their inn. Though he tried, Daegan could not relax, his inability to let himself trust anyone, even this sweet natured woman.

Halister was much more comfortable with this type of affectionate greeting. Releasing his pent-up energy from the journey, he lifted the innkeeper up and swung her around.

"Hal, put me down," she screeched as she swatted him.

"Hello, it's good to see you!" he said enthusiastically. He gave her a peck on the cheek as he put her down and sent her one of his notorious grins that could melt the heart of any girl of any race and any age.

Daegan shook his head at Hal's ease with others. He knew Hal had been seeing a girl in the city on and off—she was obviously not the one, but perhaps she knew who it was. *If Maleina knew this, there would be trouble for Hal.* But he kept those thoughts to himself.

Apparently, he and Hal were sharing a room this time due to full occupancy. The two twin beds in the very small cramped room indicated it belonged to the youngest children of the residence. Knowing who Daegan and Hal were—or with whom they were associated—the keepers of this night house made the extra room for them. It wouldn't be the first time this had happened to either one of them; sometimes it was a perk and other times a hindrance, as it tended to interfere with anonymity. Both full of pent-up traveling energy, they decided to go out. It would be a good opportunity to listen for any interesting news regarding the Sol-lumieth.

The Drunken Boar, their favorite establishment to eat while in Anise, was a welcome sight after a long day of travel. As they opened the creaky door, casual chatter escaped into the night, a beam of light chasing behind it to the street. Inside, the low light from oil-burning lanterns made for a stark contrast against it—its soothing ambiance casting shadows of the patrons onto the walls. An eruption of gruff laughter echoed from the dark corner as several Elves enjoyed their evening meal. Most of the company here kept to themselves. Daegan eyed a shady-looking character hidden beneath a dirty and tattered traveling cloak. He sat at the bar appearing to mind his own business, savoring his beverage. After several failed attempts from the traveler at inconspicuous interest in a particular Elf on the other side of the room, Daegan steered them in a different direction. In another corner sat a small ensemble consisting of two Faeries and an Elf playing quiet music that set a peaceful atmospheric tone. Several of the waitresses knew them, waved a hello, then went to ready their drinks. They made their way to the observation post, a back-corner booth from which they could see everything going on. Neither of them remembered who first named it thus, it just had been what they'd always called it. And it made for a great place to quell any paranoia that might be nipping at their feet—there were always those looking for trouble with the Ferrishyn, especially among the royally "aligned."

Hal waved at the three waitresses—two Elves and one Faerie—who were huddled behind the counter together whispering amongst themselves, not knowing that Daegan could hear every word they said about them. They pretended to be shy in that annoyingly coy way girls do, turning more boys away with disinterest than otherwise. *Mortal realm or Alandria, that approach does not seem to reveal anything to be desired.* Daegan's thoughts turned to irritation.

"What are they saying about us?" Hal whispered.

Staring down at his drink he told him under his breath, "They think you are cute, they think I look mean, and the Faerie with the brown twiggy hair wants to try to get you to ask her out... they now have a bet going." Hal laughed as Daegan slid him a sideways look. "She didn't know who you were, then the other girls told her but she still doesn't care," he added. "She's unusually forward... for an earth Faerie."

"Let's see what she's got. I like ballsy," Halister said with a smirk on his face, sitting back with his hands laced behind his head.

"Well, here she comes," Daegan said as he crossed his arms over his chest, purposefully trying to look intimidating—as if he needed to try—even though he was amused to see the outcome.

"Hello, gentlemen," the waitress said, looking only at Hal with a hand on her popped out waist, the same which was flirtatiously jutting out to the side. It wasn't unusual for Faeries to live or work in the Elven territory of Lumari, especially in Anise as the village bordered the territories. Daegan openly and blatantly studied her as she paid him no attention. Tall and slender, a pretty average build for most Faerie women, most of whom had long legs that looked disproportionate to their bodies. Her dark brown hair mingled with twigs—not unusual for earth Faeries—was tied up on top of her head, keeping it out of her extremely pale but not unattractive face. Hal's eyes followed her every curve in the mindless game of flirting, almost convincing Daegan that it wasn't an act. He had seen Hal play this game many times. Hal hadn't had many relationships; more often he just had fun.

"I am going to walk," Daegan said flatly as he got up, throwing a dark gold coin on the table to cover his drink. Most places they went didn't charge them out of fear of the Paladin. A time early on in the new reign of the Paladin, Maleina had been in the market on a rare occasion. She found a beautiful bracelet inlaid with gems and stones, surrounded by pale rose gold. Maleina wanted it for Rheina, but refused to pay the price the vendor was asking for it. In fact, she made such a spectacle, belittling the poor woman who had made the trinket, the woman simply handed it over to Maleina. Since then, the vendors feared what Maleina would do to their business—or possibly their lives—and did not charge her. Word spread quickly. Daegan always paid his bill.

"See ya back at the room in a bit," Hal said, not taking what Daegan said personally, which was a part of his charm. The Faerie—Janel she had said her name was—seemed offended for a moment, but without another thought slid into the booth Daegan had just vacated. Daegan eyed her suspiciously but trusted Hal. He gave him a nod then headed out into the dark night.

Anise was a small town with only one real main street. Lined on either side were quaint little shops stacked one to another like pieces individually created to fit together—all closed for the night. Daegan glanced each way of the road, peering into the mostly dark night before deciding which way to go. Not many street lamps were positioned to light the way, but he made out the restaurants and cafés from the mercantile, the clothery, and the currency exchange. As he walked, rubbing his hands together, he noticed above one of the tall, narrow stone establishments, wafting into the clear and brisk evening sky was a continuous puff of white dust. Curious, he paused as the scents of fresh baked bread poured out from the small bakery, flooding his senses and stirring his hunger.

Nights in Anise were getting colder and Daegan's breath escaped from his mouth in an opaque cloud. He wore a simple, yet sufficient, traveling cloak; the material flapping openly as he continued to walk unaffected by the light breeze. Suspiciously watching each corner and open alleyway, he clenched the hilt of his knife strapped at his upper thigh, but the only life tonight came from the pubs.

Just past the shops, the street headed toward the forest. The land became more wooded and the buildings became sparse. There was very little light this time of night closer to the trees. Tonight not even the stars or the different blues of the moons shone through the clouded sky. A somberness that hinted of loneliness and fear slithered on the air. The only ones out this far were a few stragglers walking off their brew before headed home or those with intent to cause trouble.

A bird took flight, causing the rustling of a tree, and small nocturnal creatures sang their songs, but it was the hushed words whispered on the wind that caught his attention. Instinctively, he drew his knife, but kept it low at his side. Slowly he crept down the alley next to a tall brick building that not only stood in the darkness but created it. A rodent made the mistake of crossing his path. Though any other time Daegan would have kicked the creature off to the side without thought, instead he waited for it to pass so as not to give any indication of his position. Stealthily he continued toward the voices.

He hugged the shadows that clung to the building as he prowled toward the end of the alley. The dark mouth of the narrow lane opened to reveal a simple stone building in disrepair with a steeple at the top. Adjacent to it nestled a small, but very old place of burial for final rest as the souls departed for their determined beyond. At the base of a dark and sickly ancient oak, bearing charred marks and lifeless limbs, stood an altar of sacrifice. Postured in awful majesty, it stood as if it had survived a great feat long ago. The structure was marked by a lone crack that ran top to bottom, a silent witness accepting the release of unspoken desires and untold evils, feeding death and destruction to the land around it.

Just beyond the small cemetery, were patches of bushes—the direction from which he heard the whispered words. Daegan snuck around the stone building, creeping in between the ancient oak and the bushes, getting as close as he could without being seen. Not sure what he had stumbled on, he focused on the whispered words.

"What are we going to do?" a slightly panicked masculine voice said in hushed tones.

"What *can* we do?" a second masculine voice replied with a level of irritation.

"Once it is found out by the Ferrishyn Paladin that we knew, we could be killed... or worse," the first voice said with varied volumes as if he were pacing back and forth within a short distance.

Knew what? Crouching low, Daegan was able to view the two men through some branches of the bush he was behind. One of the men was leaning against a tree fidgeting nervously with something in his hand, but appearing to remain calm while the other man was, in fact, pacing. They each wore cloaks that covered them from head to toe. The darkness of night prohibited Daegan from distinguishing the different colors of the cloaks they wore. Their words came out in chilled fog, their breath visible as long green streaks that dissipated up. Daegan gasped. *These men were Elders!* Of which tribe he was unsure, but green had been used to signify the Elders in the past. Why he was suddenly able to see the power laced in their words, was beyond his current knowledge and present set of gifts. Elders had been very rare since the last battle. He didn't even know how to find one if he had wanted to. Realization also dawned on him that they were cloaked with a magic that would camouflage them with their surroundings and muffle their voices to an almost inaudible level. *How do I know that?* More intrigued by who they were, he focused his gift with all he had so not to miss anything. Sweat began to bead at his brow but he couldn't relax yet. He couldn't miss anything they said.

"Do the others know?" the first, and apparently more nervous, Elder asked as he continued pacing and wringing his hands.

"No, I do not believe so, but we need to be careful," replied the second Elder as he moved away from the tree. "We tell no one unless you forfeit your life!" he raised his voice slightly then thought better of it and peered around the dark burial site to ensure their privacy. "Our fate could be that of the Elf king and queen's son if we were found with the knowledge of the one that committed the crime and to whom it was committed upon." He moved closer to the other Elder now stopped and listening closely. With his voice lowered, he continued, "We must be wise with our information and await the proper time for justice. We do not want Alandria in an uproar—at least not yet." He looked to the Elder watching him with rapt attention, and gave him guidance. "For now we are safe, as he has not been seen or heard from in a very long time, but the *one* the prophecy foretold...is coming." The other Elder nodded in agreement as he removed his cloak from where it caught on a felled branch. Once he stopped tugging, the Elder speaking continued once more, his voice stern, "Remember your oath, brother."

They each secured the cloaks enshrouding their heads, and without another word turned in toward one another, bowed, then disappeared with a flash of light similar to lightning. Daegan was left staring at a suddenly empty clearing, trying to make sense of anything that he had just heard.

❉❉❉

Hal was the lighthearted one, playful, not taking most things too seriously. Daegan sometimes wondered how Hal had actually made it through training while being so nonchalant, but truth be told Hal was a fierce warrior and outperformed most in their division, which was why Daegan trusted him with his life. On more than one occasion, Hal had stood up for Daegan, physically and verbally when it appeared Daegan wasn't going to do it for himself. This happened both when they were children and then again when they trained as men becoming warriors. It didn't matter to Daegan that he would have dealt with it on his own out of the public eye, but the fact that Hal did it with possible reprimand from his mother spoke more to him than most things. Halister was also loyal to a fault and could be counted on for his perspective and positive outlook.

During breakfast, Daegan discreetly recounted to Halister what he had witnessed in secret the previous night. Afterwards, they went out to sleuth about the town to see if they could learn anything regarding the Sol-lumieth, their actual reason for being there, although now there seemed to be another.

"The mystery is growing," Hal whispered with intrigue. "I will continue searching for information regarding this new discovery as long as you can bear my presence." He smiled conspiratorially.

"Your service is most appreciated," Daegan graciously accepted and bowed, playing along, knowing that Hal was there for his own frivolity as well. He did, however, truly value Halister's presence though they played up the need for Maleina's sake.

They would head into the heart of Adettlyn, the center city, together as it was more dangerous, but only after they scoured the village of Anise if need be. Deciding to split up then meet back at The Drunken Boar by the inn for lunch, they went their separate ways. Hal headed toward the center of the village, but Daegan retraced his steps back toward the forest and the edge of Anise to see if he could find any more Elders.

Nothing. He walked for miles and all for nothing. *What a waste of time!* Grumbling his way back to The Drunken Boar, he caught sight of Hal across the street leaning close to a girl, too close. She was a Faerie, but there was something different about her, and they were definitely being friendly. Rolling his eyes, not feeling very hungry yet at this point, Daegan headed around the side of the old brick building that housed the tavern. Even with its old broken sign hanging above the door and shutters barely hanging on by their hinges, it was one of the better places to find beyond edible food. They had the best homemade soups served in bowls made out of bread. Maybe he was hungry after all, or at least take the opportunity to consume some fine ale, but not yet.

Around the back, he found refuge under the canopy of an enormous old tree. It was one of the NaNai—the ancient oaks—he judged by the amount of energy it was giving off. He positioned himself between some very large roots that had escaped their home in the earth. Hal was bound to be a little while longer with the girl he was currently in "conversation" with. Daegan started to doze off when he was startled awake by the sounds of very distant whispers. But when he opened his eyes he couldn't decipher from which direction they were coming. Subtly looking around so as not to draw attention, he saw no one. *Strange.* The only whisperings he could distinguish were from Hal and his "friend" and not who he was trying to hear. He could hear the breeze whistling through the leaves above him, the singing of birds in nearby trees, and the chattering of woodland creatures also not what he was trying to hear.

After a minute of nothing but the sounds of nature, he closed his eyes again and suddenly heard a faint buzzing. *There!* The whispering started again, but this time he kept his eyes closed, trying to sense where they were and if he could make something out of what was being said. Either he was becoming more adept at listening to the whispers or they were getting closer. Again, he opened his eyes but saw nothing... no one. Frustration caused him to close them once more and simply listen. He stiffened. Now he wasn't sure he wanted to listen.

The whispering, the voice... it was saying his name. A woman was saying *his* name and he was sure he had heard that voice before.

Daegan... Can you hear me?

Then another voice, familiar and rich with a deep masculine tone seemed to be arguing with her. *He can't hear you. Is there another way?*

A different woman, this one not familiar, with a gravelly and much older timbre spoke. *This is the only way. Give him more time.*

The first woman—her voice was so sweet, so soothing, almost like a lullaby that calmed his uncertainties, yet he could feel the power in her voice, in her words as she said his name, reaching into his very being.

Daegan... need... reach... power... coming... help.

Some type of static broke up her words, her voice fading in and out. Then she was gone. They were all gone, leaving Daegan with a feeling of loss in the pit of his stomach, for what, he didn't even know. Very alert now, he looked around, breathless and sweating. Almost whispering, his voice hoarse and strained, he called out, "Hello? I hear you. Are you there?"

"Daegan, I'm here. I yelled at you from across the street, trying to get your attention," Hal said as he trotted toward him. "You all right? You look like you've seen a ghost."

"Or heard one," Daegan mumbled to himself as he tiredly wiped his hands down his face. "All is well. I must have fallen asleep waiting for you. Strange dream." Only it wasn't a dream, it was real, but he wasn't ready to share that with Hal just yet. Not until he could figure out a few things: *What was going on, who was trying to reach him and why, right along with how and where they were speaking from?*

"Let's get something to eat," Hal said, constantly thinking about his stomach.

"I'm not hungry. I think I might just go for a walk," Daegan clasped Hal's outstretched hand and jumped up from the ground.

"Don't you want to know what I found out?" Hal said, batting his eyes innocently like a child holding a secret that he was dying to share.

"I think I know what you found," Daegan retorted sarcastically, nodding across the street as he punched Hal playfully in the arm.

"Well, it's not what you think. I just happen to be very persuasive at getting information," Hal said with his eyebrows raised.

"She had information? What kind?" Daegan questioned, suddenly interested.

"Well, not exactly *her*, but she knows someone who does." Halister rushed out the last part as he stepped in front of Daegan, trying to keep him engaged. "If he doesn't, I don't know who else would," he said, the sound of defeat laced throughout his words.

"Hmm, why do I get the feeling there is a catch?" Daegan growled with hands on his waist as he looked up into the sky, exasperated at another one of Hal's "situations."

"There IS a catch... but I think her source is legit." Hal waited to see if Daegan would let him continue. When he didn't say anything to stop him, Hal proceeded. "We have to be blindfolded while in his presence and never speak of this meeting to anyone. I guess if he is found out, he will be killed." Hal shrugged his shoulders like it was no biggie, but in his eyes Daegan could see Hal's realization that something serious was going on. Hal had his attention with that—well, that and the little voice inside that kept poking him to pay attention.

"Just who is this source? And why would he risk everything to talk to us?" Daegan asked suspiciously.

"He's an Elder," Hal whispered. "And I'm not sure why, because Ella—that's the girl, his granddaughter—wasn't letting anything on until I mentioned your name. It was weird. She said that her grandfather told her to contact him if she ever crossed paths with you, which she did last night when we walked in The Drunken Boar. She contacted him and that is when he told her the conditions." Hal looked a little upset that it had been Daegan's name and not his since he was, in fact, the son of the Paladin and Daegan was not. But he shrugged it off and the smile returned to his face in anticipation of an adventure.

Daegan took a moment and stared out into the forest behind the tavern, trying to understand what was going on. First the voices, and now an Elder actually wanted to talk to him. "This does not make any sense. There is much going on here, Hal, and somehow we are involved," in Daegan's voice a rare moment of vulnerability surfaced. He ran his fingers through the longer strands of hair on the top of his head trying to regain his composure.

"Should we go find out?" Hal said, placing his hand on Daegan's shoulder in a brotherly manner. Daegan found it oddly comforting, which he assumed was why Hal did it. Looking in Hal's eyes and seeing his agreement, Daegan nodded. Hal turned back toward Ella, who was waiting across from The Drunken Boar, leaning against a tree, arms crossed, examining her nails on one hand, like she had nothing better to do. Maybe she didn't. Hal gave her a quick nod and a wink.

Where other Faerie girls were thin as rails and otherworldly pale, Ella had slight curves. Although she possessed that "otherworldliness" which made her similar enough to belong, she had a hint of color in her face and a stunningly beautiful luminescence that made her different enough to be excluded. He wasn't sure what Faerie tribe she was from, but seeing as how he hadn't seen others like her, he assumed she must be either a mixed race trying to fit in—although she sure didn't try too hard at that—or something different altogether.

Ella sauntered toward them with the confidence of a woman about to claim her prize. Her clothing was similar to other Faeries representing nature, but hers fit... better. There was a fierceness about her, a fire in her eyes that would indicate warrior, but also a softness that spoke *woman*. She was entrancing.

Daegan glanced at Hal, and saw that Hal was looking at her, watching her every move, that is, until she stopped and looked at Daegan. He watched Hal briefly deflate, then pick himself up again like nothing had happened. Daegan felt irritated for him. This woman had just played Hal to get to him. This was not the first time this had happened, but Halister seemed to be attracted to the wrong girls. Although, if he didn't play games with them, he might actually find someone to belong with. So maybe the turnabout was fair. Nonetheless, Daegan did not trust this woman. Clearly she held many secrets in those steel-gray eyes that accentuated the short white hair that hung sharply below her ears.

"Ready, boys? Follow me," she said, swinging her hips as she headed straight into the forest. It was still daylight, but as soon as they reached the edge of the forest it grew strangely dark. She paused just inside the boundaries, as if waiting for something—no, listening for something. Confused, Daegan studied her, as he didn't hear anything which was odd, but he didn't want to let on. Her head cocked to the side, and in a flash of movement, she was pressed up against Hal, stroking his hair and kissing his neck, which put Daegan on edge.

Turning back toward Daegan, Ella grabbed his face between her hands and kissed him good and hard. As she kissed him, he heard her voice in his head. *Someone is watching, maybe even following. Play along.* Daegan kissed her back though it tasted stale and lifeless; an act for an audience. As quickly as it began, she broke apart from him and kept walking, resuming her mission as if nothing had happened.

"Whoa! What was that all about?" Hal stammered breathlessly as he pushed his hair back off his face, trying to regain his composure. He looked like he wasn't sure if he should be pissed or excited.

Still walking, Ella turned back with a sultry smile. "Keep up and stay quiet."

Hal looked at Daegan, totally confused. "Someone was following us. It was a diversion," Daegan explained to him as they walked after Ella, trying to catch up.

"Huh. Nice diversion!" was all Hal could say with a smile on his face. "But wouldn't that have drawn more attention?"

"Most people, of all species, are instantly embarrassed or shocked by seeing a scene such as that, and they look away for a second. That was all the time I needed to put a shield up to cloak our presence," Ella replied matter-of-factly.

"You can do that?" Hal's look at her was similar to Daegan's, although not so accusatory. Realizing she wasn't going to answer him, he tried something else. "Ella? I don't want to offend you, but you're not like the other Faerie girls. I mean, I like that you're not like them, but I'm curious. Which part of Alandria are you from?" As Hal spoke they stopped next to her in front of a moss-covered rock.

"No, I am not like the other Faerie girls," was all she said, but somehow it sounded sad.

She looked at Hal, studying his face, smiled a real smile, then looked from Daegan back to him and nodded. Not sure why she wanted Daegan to explain—or how he even knew all the information that suddenly flashed in his mind—he nevertheless answered for her.

"She is from a lost race that is from deep within the mountains. There are not many left of her kind... the Ehsmia. They have gifts beyond those of other Faeries, but I'm not sure all of what they can do. They keep to themselves, but she knew we were coming so she came out to meet us." He frowned. Turning to Ella, he asked, "Why us? I do not understand how you know *what* we are looking for, let alone that we are looking at all."

"In due time, all will be revealed to you," she said, looking deeply into his eyes, boring into his soul. It was personal and invasive, but before he could look away, she released him, leaving him with a sensation of warmth spreading throughout his body. "You are ready, Daegan of the Ferrishyn. Do not fear your destiny." She inclined her head slightly, but Daegan could only frown, feeling a sense of foreboding, as though everything was about to change. *What is she talking about?*

"The Ehsmia? I have heard stories... legends of your people. You are also called the Hidden People, are you not?" Hal asked in awe. When Ella only nodded, he continued. "I thought your people were no more, if they even had existed at all." He did not mean to be rude.

"That is how we prefer to be known... or not known at all. Otherwise, what purpose would our *hiding* be if we were known?" she said with a smirk on her face but said no more.

Ella turned to face the rock wall, which looked like a crumbling ruin of what was at one time a part of a great wall. It was built into the side of the Kandrian Mountains. Hal's look of confusion mirrored Daegan's own. Hal finally shrugged his shoulders, figuring they would understand "in due time." Oddly, his typical nonchalant response gave Daegan a sense of calm. Staring at the rocks that made up the wall for what seemed several minutes but in reality was probably much shorter, Ella laid her hand flat onto a rock that suddenly appeared smoother and duller than all the other old, jagged stones. There was a rumbling of the ground that stopped as suddenly as it started. She gave them a sneaky smile. Daegan still wasn't sure he trusted her, but at this point it seemed she might be the only one with answers of any kind.

"Are you ready to follow where not many have been before, a land within a land?" she asked. Without waiting for their answer, she turned around and walked straight into the rock wall, which had magically become an illusion. Daegan and Hal both knew there was magic in Alandria and that every species had their own type of magic. They had their own magic as well, but they had only heard of this kind of magic in their own legends. Halister and Daegan quickly followed Ella, not wanting to get shut out of what could be their only opportunity to see where the Hidden People were, well, hidden.

Chapter Five

I t was dark, yet they had no trouble following Ella through the murky tunnel of rock and stone that looked worn from centuries of use and natural erosion. Other than the thin layer of water trickling over some of the stones, it was silent and peaceful. They had been following a star, literally, for the past several minutes, but it wasn't above them. Ella's short, jagged snow-white hair allowed them to see the back of her neck, upon which was a horizontally stretched eight-point star from which a soft blue light emanated, marking her as *other*. Assuming she could see in the dark, they kept following and soon the tunnel began to lighten.

Green leafy vines began crawling up the sides of the tunnel as if coming to life as they walked through what was left of the tunnel, which ultimately broadened into a large opening full of white light. A light so bright Hal and Daegan both had to raise their arms to shield their eyes still sensitive from the dark tunnel. With eyes adjusted, they each turned in awe, trying to take in what they were seeing.

They were inside an enormous domed cavern, or perhaps it was a hollowed-out mountain. Everything so white. Everything so light. The two turned slowly in place, Hal with a reverent look of awe on his face and Daegan remaining still at the mouth of the tunnel. Surveying. Watching. Still, Daegan could not fight the slight twinkle of awe that entered his eyes. Ella remained to the side, not looking at what was before her but staring at Daegan. Impassive, but studious.

A small river with the clearest water Daegan had ever seen flowed toward the tunnel entrance but disappeared into a crack in the stone wall. The river stretched from where it was birthed by a waterfall tumbling in from an opening high above. Even though it was remarkably white, it was also full of color, as if the light creating the white was generated from the culmination of the energy from the color and the magic flowing within this place. Grassy knolls made of the greenest grass spread throughout. Several foot bridges connected both sides of the river, and on each side were large trees covering huge expanses and small trees learning to bud. Trees of all kinds bloomed and flourished; all so *alive*. It was a place of peace and tranquility.

Looking up, Daegan could barely see the boundaries of this sanctuary; the sky an atrium of lush foliage. It was unfathomable how all this could fit inside of a mountain, if that was truly where they were. Perhaps they had entered a different realm, but Ella had said a "land within a land." They must still be in Alandria. *Hidden*. There were hundreds of holes burrowed into the sides of this place, like caves.

"What are those?" Daegan asked Ella, pointing at the caves.

"Those are our dwellings. This is where we live," she replied with a sense of pride and honor. "Most have gone into their homes. They have been expecting you, but they still choose to remain hidden as they are not used to strangers."

"I understand. We are honored that you have allowed us here," Daegan said, suddenly feeling the need to be respectful.

"Come, let us go to my grandfather, he is waiting." She began to walk toward the waterfall. It took longer to get there than it seemed like it should, as if the land were stretching the deeper they got inside. Hal couldn't stop looking around. Daegan refused to let his guard down even here in this peaceful place. Especially in this peaceful place.

The most exotic species of butterflies, dragonflies, and other tiny creatures fluttered closely to the trees. One small butterfly flew around Daegan's head a couple of times before landing on his shoulder. It was shimmery white with larger than normal wings; the lower ones extended further than the tops and trailed behind her. She made a noise that sounded like she hummed a song. Daegan let her stay there, inclining his head toward her and accepting her invitation of friendship.

"You make friends with insects faster than you do with Faeries," Hal said sarcastically.

Ella stopped and turned to see what he was talking about. She stared for a second, confused, then raised one of her eyebrows and smiled. "Do not offend her and do not take for granted her size. She is very special. You are being honored with her presence." Ella inclined her head and closed her eyes for the briefest second. Daegan recognized that gesture as she listened. "She says she knew your parents and offers her services if ever you need them."

Completely confused, but not wanting to risk offense, Daegan quickly replied, "Thank you, I am honored. I do not mean any offense, but how does she know my parents? I barely remember them myself."

"They were good Faeries, and she is sorry for your loss, as are we. Some things are not easily forgotten. Many things were set into motion with their deaths." Ella bowed her head slightly in solemn reverence then continued with a small smile, "All the information you seek will be made clear to you when it is time." Ella then turned to find her grandfather.

"You must be seeking a lot of information. That is the second time she has said that to you," Hal said, slapping Daegan on the back and chuckling as he followed Ella.

"I guess I am," was all Daegan could mumble. He wasn't entirely sure what he was seeking. Oddly, things were both becoming clearer and yet more confusing at the same time. There was a slight pressure behind his eyes that caused him to falter and blink excessively. It had happened before, but had never lasted this long. He pinched the bridge of his nose and took deep breaths. Hal came back to him, noticing he hadn't followed.

"You all right?" Hal said lightly, his voice laced with concern. Daegan simply nodded as the pressure decreased, and they moved forward to keep up with the beautiful white-haired Faerie.

Ella had disappeared behind the waterfall through a narrow opening between the water and the rock behind it. Hal looked back at Daegan, who shrugged, and the two followed her. The fissure in the rock opened into a large room made of smooth tan stones. There was a homey warmth to it which was only added to by the large stoked fire built into the stone, a stark contrast to the bright whiteness on the other side of the water.

It was furnished most comfortably and with all-natural earth tones and textures. A large area rug, a couch made of various leathers that looked like you might sink in it, and several mismatched overstuffed chairs took up the middle of the room. There was a coffee table made of stone on which stood a tea service that appeared to be ready and waiting for them. Ella offered them a seat and some tea.

How do I know she's not just wasting my time? Daegan mused. *How credible can information be coming from Faeries who hide away in a rock?*

Ella looked sharply at him as if reading his mind; for all he knew maybe she could. Seeing her slight smirk, he thought perhaps he'd better watch his thoughts, just in case.

Hal sat at the far end of the couch and Daegan stood behind one of the chairs that faced both the way they came in and an additional opening off to the side in order see all points of entry. Ready for whatever came next.

It proved not to be necessary as Ella then held out two long pieces of material that were meant to cover their eyes as they had agreed to. Daegan stiffened, on edge. He did not like having his senses at a disadvantage. He could still fight without his sight, but preferred not to. Seeming to understand, Ella looked him directly in his eyes, giving him the assurance he needed.

"You will come to no harm here. You have my word," she said solemnly, and Daegan nodded stiffly. "I will go get my grandfather now." Ella exited through another small opening on the opposite side of the wall.

"I wonder which Elder he is. Not that I could pick one out, I have never met one of the Elders. Daegan, have you?" Hal chatted as was his nervous tendency while they both put on their blindfolds.

"No. Just the ones I heard last night. This should be interesting." He took a deep breath and rubbed his hand through his hair. "There is something very familiar about this place, or at least about the feeling I get being here," Daegan said, still trying to place what he was feeling.

"You have been here before, young Daegan." It was the voice of a very old man, sounding like he was already seated in front of them even though Daegan had heard no one walk into the room, which was a feat unto itself. He stiffened even more, really hating that he was blindfolded. He would have to depend on his other senses more strongly. Shocked, Daegan flinched when he heard the Elder's voice in his head like he had with Ella.

Open your eyes, Daegan. I'm allowing only you to see me through the blindfold. The blindfold will still be blocking your eyes and will not allow your brain to register what you are seeing in the event someone tries to steal it from your mind—as I fear has already been tried. Our wards are very strong here. Will this ease your mind and free you to hear what I have to say?

Daegan nodded. The old man smiled and went on talking aloud, as though he hadn't just invaded Daegan's mind. It was bizarre looking at him through the fabric. He couldn't see clearly—more like looking through particles or a veil.

"I don't remember being here, sir," Daegan replied to what the Elder had said, although as he said the words they did not ring true.

"You were very young indeed. You came with your parents. They didn't deserve what befell them," he said as Ella handed him a cup of tea. *I regret that they were unable to fully realize who they were, who you are to be, and what part they had to play. We all have a part to play. Now it has been left for you to fulfill. I know you do not yet understand, but it is part of your journey to discover the truth.*

Daegan just stared at him through the blindfold. Angered. Saddened. Confused. His emotions spiraled out of control. Frustrated. Frustrated that everyone around him seemed to have known his parents when he couldn't even remember them. Frustrated that everyone spoke to him in riddles about something they obviously knew about *him*, but weren't telling the one person it most concerned... *HIM*! While Daegan sat brooding in his own thoughts, the old man continued.

"Where are my manners? I do believe introductions on my part were passed over." He inclined his head and placed his hand on his chest. "You may call me Arileas, and you have, of course, met my granddaughter Ella." He gestured her direction. "And you, young warriors, are Daegan of the Ferrishyn and Halister, son of the Paladin of Feraánmar," he finished with a smile and a wink.

"How do you know who we are, sir?" Halister asked, clearly having not heard any of the other conversation going on in Daegan's head.

"I know much of the goings-on in and around Alandria. It is what I do. I am connected to her, you see"—her obviously referring to Alandria. "It is my responsibility not only as an Elder, but who and what I *am* that I feel what concerns *her*," Arileas continued, motioning his hands all about in an ethereal way. "Which brings me to why you have been brought here," he said as he looked directly at Daegan. "You are seeking the rumors of a Sol-lumieth, am I accurate?"

Daegan nodded rigidly with great suspicion, trying to figure out how Arileas knew their mission, when the Elder spoke into his head again. *The Orchids, or you may refer to them as the spirits beyond—although they haven't always been, spoke it to me. They have tried to get in touch with you without success. I think you have simply not known how to connect with them.*

Daegan's mind suddenly flashed to the voices he heard when he was sitting under the oak tree. *Spirits beyond? Contacting me, why?* Daegan asked back inside his own mind, not sure if the communication was two-way.

It is a warning that the mission you are on and who it is for will cause a great tragedy for Alandria. She is already weeping for what may be. When you find the Sol-lumieth—and you will—you must remove it from the hands of those you serve. As quickly as he was in Daegan's head speaking, he was answering Hal's question about what he knew about the Sol-lumieth that Daegan hadn't caught.

"There is an ancient prophecy stating that in the time of the desolation and transition after the great battle, when Alandria sheds tears for the fallen crowns, darkness will enshroud the skies, the moons will grow weary, and the time of color and life will be drained by the hands taken by force. It speaks of a new power that will come of age out of the hidden places and outcast of the land. An heir from the mountains and the ancient oaks will be born and reborn to restore the energy and bring forth a united Alandria. BUT should the power be squelched by the darkness, hope will fade, the mountains will collapse, and all that is hidden will be lost." Arileas spoke the prophecy first in the ancient tongue of the land and then again in the tongue of today so that they could understand.

Arileas seemed to have gone elsewhere as he recalled the prophecy. His eyes were staring ahead, but glossed over and unseeing. There was a great and heavy power when he spoke; it left Daegan with shivers racing up his spine. Daegan didn't know how to respond, but he was not about to give away any shock or confusion at what he just heard. Emotions were a weakness. He knew there was a lot of meaning behind the words, but wasn't sure how it involved him.

"What the..." Hal, on the other hand, had no problem showing emotion. He abruptly stopped what he was about to say when he remembered in whose presence they were. "I beg your pardon, sir, but what does it all mean?" he added with deference.

Arileas, back to the present, smiled then and even let out a chuckle. "I was once young and feisty like you, Master Halister. Do not lose who you are as you learn to temper it, for it is one of your virtues." Serious again, he looked at both of the warriors and said, "As for the prophecy, there is new power, or some would say new magic that brings new power about to be revealed. It has been called the Sol-lumieth because it will carry an illumination so bright it will drive out the darkness. From what or who it comes, we do not know for certain, though there is rumor whispered into the dreams of those who dare to listen of it being someone from the human realm." Arileas spoke with an odd expression as he slid a look of curiosity toward Daegan.

Daegan's eyes sharpened and his fists clenched as he began to feel like this could be a joke. At the same time, Hal gasped at the very idea of a human bringing power to Alandria. *How could they?* Daegan thought. *Humans have no power!* Daegan stood abruptly and slowly made his way, following the sounds, as he didn't fully trust his limited sight to the backside of the waterfall.

"I don't believe it!" Daegan ground out between his teeth, but once again he couldn't ignore the truth he felt in the words Arileas spoke. *Maybe Maleina hadn't heard the rumors right. She wouldn't concern herself with a human, would she?*

To his shock, it was Hal who refuted what Daegan said. "Daegan, brother, he is an Elder. He does not lie, and I feel truth in his words whether we agree with them or not. I think you do too. Plus he is old, he probably was there when the prophecy was written," he said with a smirk in the playful way he tried to lighten the atmosphere when he was nervous. Daegan first looked at Hal, still blindfolded and cocking his head as if to hear better. He then looked over at Arileas, who was clearly amused, but Hal must have realized what he said because he added, "No offense, sir." Arileas simply laughed heartily.

Daegan turned, seeing Hal through the veil, and then at the ancient wise man. "How does this involve us? What are you asking of us?" And in his mind he added, *of me?*

Looking directly at Daegan like he was searching his very soul, Arileas said both audibly and in Daegan's head at the same time, "You must find the human child. You must find the child and bring it to Alandria. Protect it, both of you. The child will have to discover the power within, but right now it is vulnerable and can still be brought into the darkness. There are those that want to use the power for their own." Suddenly, his voice, gone solo in Daegan's head, said, *You must keep her from them. You know what they would do, the power they wish to possess. Help her find her way as you find yours. Bring her back here to us. Everything depends on it.*

I don't know if I have what it takes to turn from them. *She cannot be my responsibility. I may not even have the ability,* Daegan responded almost sadly in his head.

It is your choice.

Arileas turned from Daegan, releasing him from the eye-lock that Daegan couldn't break out of as the Elder tried to anchor the importance of what the prophecy was asking of him into his soul. Hal spoke up while Daegan was regaining the breath he didn't realize he had been holding, surprising him when he simply and matter-of-factly asked, "How do we find this Sol-lumieth?" Hal shrugged when he must have felt Daegan frown over his direction even through the blindfold. Daegan had not agreed to this and it sounded like a waste of time. Hal knew this was something that they needed to discuss, which only frustrated him even more. Why did he feel so conflicted and on edge in his soul?

"Ah, Daegan will know the way. The Orchids will reveal the path to be taken."

Again with the Orchids? Daegan mused, but then remembered *her.* He wanted to hear that voice again. Maybe he could.

"They will begin to speak to you if you ask them," Arileas told him directly, as if he had just read his mind. He probably had. *You have been marked, have you not?* Arileas added in his mind. Daegan instantly touched his waist, thinking of the small marking that had showed up the same time his *srontas,* marking him as Ferrishyn, was revealed. But this he had kept hidden unsure what it meant—the marking of an *orchid.*

No, it could not be, he thought to himself, and Arileas nodded at him.

Then Arileas addressed Halister. "You, young Halister, your role will be extremely important should you awaken to realize who you are." Hal folded his arms, a question on his face, but did not say anything. Arileas continued, "Ella will now show you out. I have divulged as much as I am able at this time. Do not think on this too long, time is failing. You must return home for Rheina's debut, then make your decision swiftly. Until we meet again."

And with that he stood, inclined his head, and took his leave behind the back opening before Hal could finish asking, "How do you know about Rheina's—never mind." He shrugged.

Having almost forgotten Ella was still there, Daegan suddenly felt her behind him untying his blindfold. He had been pitched back into darkness as soon as Arileas left the room. After she untied Hal, she began to walk out from behind the waterfall where they had entered, but then she turned and said, "Remember when you agreed to come here you were bound by your oath of secrecy to the Ehsmia. Safe journey home."

They followed her out from behind the waterfall, but when they turned the corner she was suddenly nowhere to be seen and they were no longer in the land hidden within the mountain. Instead, they were suddenly and unexplainably in the middle of a crop of NaNai standing guard, creaking as they swayed in the wind. There was nothing behind them but forest and nothing outside of the NaNai but more forest. The magic of the Ehsmia is unremembered to most. Their horses stood there, looking at them with silent anticipation.

Looking at each other in surprise and confusion, Hal and Daegan were left with their silent thoughts of an ancient prophecy that now loomed over their heads with the promise of forever altering their lives, whether they chose to believe in it or not. Quietly, they headed home.

❊❊❊

It didn't take them long as they had been placed closer than they knew. Just north of their city, Elnye, back in the territory of the Faeries, Halister took a deep breath and turned to Daegan. "How do you want to proceed? *They* are going to want to know something," he said, very diplomatically referring to his mother and father. Hal most often put on the mask of the foolish and carefree son of the Paladin, but more often than not that is what it was: a mask to distract him from thinking of things he wished he wouldn't remember or things he wished he could change because then he would have to face himself. He was not yet ready to do that.

"They are your parents, I cannot dictate to you your course of action. I can only speak for myself and even then, I have not yet decided."

"Daegan, my brother, yes, they are my parents and I love them, but I do not agree with everything they do, and I have a bad feeling about what will be done with this information." He took a long look around them, sighing. "This goes way beyond them and our people." Then, in an unexpected show of fealty, Hal said, "I trust your instincts with this and am prepared to follow your lead."

Still conflicted, Daegan responded, "I appreciate that, but it is not I who should be leading this. You are the son of our Paladin and should decide for us what is the best course of action." Even though Daegan spoke humbly and honestly from his heart, when he looked into Hal's eyes, they both knew the truth in this case was for Daegan to take lead. So again, Daegan bowed his head, humbled by Hal's trust and easy acceptance.

"I do not understand all that happened back there in the mountain, but I do know that the old man had words for your ears alone." Daegan stiffened at Hal's perception. "I respect that and trust you to make the right decision for our futures and that of Alandria." Hal smirked, knowing that Daegan was uncomfortable being placed in such a position.

Daegan took a deep breath. "No pressure," he said, giving Hal a little smile to try to keep the mood light even though what Hal and the Elder were asking of him, what the Hidden People were asking of him, was going to change everything they knew for the good or the bad.

Shifting back and forth on his saddle, Daegan could tell he was agitating Mayfair and tried to stay still. He had never been comfortable with the way that Maleina ran things. Could this be his chance to possibly do something about it for himself and others? Could he really do what needed to be done? *Protect the Sol-lumieth—the girl—and help her along her journey to unleash her power for a better Alandria?*

That didn't sound too hard. He had played bodyguard before and if she was so powerful, she probably didn't even really need him. He could be more of a guide. Turning to Hal, he nodded. "Let's get home."

CHAPTER SIX

Hours later, after cleaning up and resting from their journey, they were summoned, as expected, to High Court. As he walked, Daegan remembered a time when, as young boys, they had all seemed more like a family. Hal, Daegan, and Rheina would run through the grounds, talk freely at meals, and be able to casually approach the adults. All that changed when they began training with the guard. Maleina had said that Halister and Daegan were now to become men and she expected them to behave as such. Every day thereafter, she grew more rigid and more suspicious of everyone, especially Daegan. He never could understand why. As the years went by, it became clear to him that his uses were becoming more important to Maleina than he himself would ever be.

He met Halister in the foyer, waiting to be granted entrance. A servant retrieved them and led them into the High Court chamber, where they were announced.

Wren and Maleina entered from a doorway off to the side of their thrones. Maleina was as close to perfection as always, dressed flamboyantly with expensive fabrics in rich colors. Her long flaming red hair was braided and draped down below her shoulders. But in a flash, Daegan saw instead of hair, six snakes entwined, heads raised above her shoulders. He was seeing beyond the glamour he realized she had so carefully constructed. It almost broke his composure. There were three more, one encircling each wrist and the last one wrapped loosely around her neck. He blinked and they were gone. He looked at Hal, who appeared to see nothing unusual.

After formally greeting them, Wren quickly sat down, seeming a bit wobbly on his feet, holding a glass of his favorite drink. As usual, he looked the part of a royal, dressed in a dark blue expensive velvet jacket with tails and a gray ruffled blouse.

"Welcome back, dear ones. What news might you have discovered on your journey?" Maleina asked, her words drenched in slippery sweetness.

Daegan cleared his throat, gave a slight bow of his head, and, re-focusing his mind from what he just saw, spoke. "We scoured the city looking for anything unusual and listening intently to all conversations and whisperings we could find. We heard firsthand the rumors of the Sol-lumieth. They say that it is coming from the mortal realm in the form of a human. It is rumored that the human may be vulnerable and unaware." Daegan snuck a quick look at Hal, who stood relaxed but focused with his hands behind his back. Hal's eyes spoke his agreement as to where Daegan was directing the conversation.

Hal looked back to Maleina. "If it is your wish, Mother, let us go to the mortal realm and find the human. If these whispers are true, we will bring this Sol-lumieth back to you."

Hal looked quickly to Wren. "What do you think, Father?" Hal knew this would irritate Maleina, but he really wanted to know. As the years passed, he had watched his father withdraw into himself.

Maleina turned her gaze out a window, as if aloof to the present conversation. Wren looked at Hal with eyes of love and remorse. "You know me, son, I have no use for the whispers of Elves and Shifters," he said softly with a smile as he took in the stature of these two young Ferrishyn warriors. "But you know your mother... she—" he started with a soft chuckle.

"It probably means nothing, especially if it IS *human*," Maleina said loudly, cutting off her husband as if she'd heard nothing. Then with a calm voice, "But for the sake of our people we should look into it. It would be the wise thing to do." Maleina rose, looking both in the eye, but folding her hands to her mouth as if thinking up a plan. "Halister, you will remain here," she stopped abruptly, seeing Hal's eyebrow raised in question. Irritated at his insubordination, she explained then continued, "Rheina's debut party is tomorrow evening. Daegan, you will go retrieve the *human*. It is to be unharmed and brought here to us as swiftly as possible. This will be your sole responsibility until you return." She turned and looked from one to the other. "This is my decision. Carry it out at first light."

With that, she walked toward them both. Stopping at Daegan, she looked briefly into his eyes with her right hand on his arm. He felt a shock, but refused to register the sting on his face. Then moving to her left, she grazed Hal's right cheek as she kissed his left. Without another word she left the chambers.

Wren rose from his seat. Approaching Daegan, he smiled. "Be safe." He paused, looking down for a moment, then continued. "You are the best of our kind, Daegan. I've never known your equal." Then leaning into Daegan's right ear, he whispered, "If any of this foolishness proves true, let caution guide you, my lad. It will likely mean the end of us all." Then smiling, he turned to Hal. "My son, your sister will be so happy you are here." Patting his shoulder, he turned and left the chamber.

Hal turned to Daegan once they got outside. "Are you all right? You flinched when Mother touched you."

Absently placing his hand on his shoulder, Daegan replied, "I'm fine. It was just a shock." He shrugged and Hal left it.

"Well, that wasn't exactly the outcome we were going for, was it? I was planning on going with you," he added, sounding frustrated.

"No, that wasn't what I thought she would say. It makes me wonder if she was suspicious of me for some reason. We will have to go with it, though, and come up with an alternative."

"If she was suspicious of you, then why not send me instead?"

"She has her reasons, I'm sure," Daegan practically growled as he turned to walk away. He was finished talking about it. Maleina knew he would never leave Halister; they were too close. She was using her own son as insurance that he would return. He was almost sure of it. When they were younger, some of the older Faeries would pick on Halister and beat him up. Daegan had been there but had been unable to help him, and she knew that he felt responsible. She preyed upon his guilt and made him swear an oath to always protect and serve Hal, unbeknownst to him. Hal himself would never have asked that of Daegan and Daegan knew Hal would be furious if he ever found out. Daegan had trained harder and given himself more to the guard than any other to make sure that he could keep his end of the oath. He had ever since and would continue to the best of his abilities. She knew that. Hal was like Daegan's brother, but if Hal knew that was a burden that he bore, he would not allow him to be who he was, his warrior.

"I am NOT staying here! I'm going with you. What if you need help? We are in this together." Hal's volume was getting louder as his short fuse was about to ignite.

"You need to stay here to make this work—at least for now," Daegan replied calmly but sternly. "I will send you word when you can find us, if you still want to." Hal was not happy and was ready to fight about it, but before he could speak Daegan added, "I need you to keep up appearances here, keep Maleina distracted, and give her messages from me when I send them. I'll send for you as soon as we re-enter Alandria and find shelter. Plus, it is important that at least one of us is here for Rheina and her party; she is your sister. The old man said as much," he said, referring to Arileas. Daegan was pacing now with his hands on top of his head as he did when he was lost in thought.

"I believe it is especially important for *you* to be the one here," Daegan said, "though I am not sure why. I'm sure Maleina knows nothing of that and we should keep it that way. Give Rheina my love." Daegan left abruptly, heading for his room to pack whatever essentials he might need for the journey. "Don't do anything foolish!" he yelled over his shoulder to Hal, who was still standing where he left him brooding. He'd get over it; he always did. Daegan knew it would break Rheina's heart if her brother missed her party and so did Hal; he wouldn't miss it. She had always been like a little sister to Daegan, and he regretted not being able to be there for her, but she would understand.

It was a few days' ride to the entrance to the mortal realm, and then however long it took him to locate this girl, which, by the way, he had no idea how to do. Daegan also couldn't help noticing that the Elder had only spoken of her as a *girl* in his mind. Arileas apparently didn't want that information widely known. So that helped eliminate a great number of the population in the mortal realm. *Right*. The Elder, Arileas, instructed him to ask The Orchids to show him the way. He unfortunately hadn't told him *how* to do that. Time to figure it out.

Chapter Seven

Present day. Missoula, MT.

The first several days at her new job went pretty smooth. She met some nice people, served a nice old couple that lived in her building, didn't break any dishes, didn't mess up too many orders, and even made some decent tips.

I think I'm getting the hang of this, I might even like being a waitress, she thought with an upbeat smile. It was her last hour of work for the night, and as she was putting in an order with the kitchen, one of her coworkers approached her. *I can't remember her name, what is her name?... Maybe she won't remember mine.* "Hi," Kaeleigh said.

"Hey. Kaeleigh, right?" she asked a bit hesitantly.

"Yep. I'm sorry, I don't remember yours," Kaeleigh stated sheepishly. *Crap!*

"It's Alex, but don't worry, you have a lot to remember your first week. I've been there myself," she said with an understanding smile. "Do you know the gorgeous guy at table thirteen?"

Which one is table thirteen? I should remember this... I think it's over by the... WOW, if that's table thirteen, he IS gorgeous! "Over by the fireplace? Is that table thirteen?" she asked shyly, looking to the other waitress. Alex just nodded. "No. I don't know who he is, but I wish I could say I do." Kaeleigh ducked her head and blushed, realizing she had said that out loud. *Oops!*

"You may get your chance," Alex said with an eyebrow raised. Kaeleigh looked at her, confused. "It's one of my tables, but he asked for *you*. By name. You should go meet him, he's been staring at you ever since he arrived." She sounded a bit put off that he didn't want her as his waitress. Kaeleigh was a bit surprised herself. Alex was early twenties, beautiful, tall, leggy, and blonde. The kind of girl you think is every guy's type, especially since she'd actually been hit on by almost every guy—single or otherwise—that she'd waited on tonight. It was pretty obvious that she knew it and played it to her benefit, at least judging by the tips she counted out at the end of each night.

"Okay." Kaeleigh drew the word out suspiciously. "It must be a mistake, though, I don't think I'd forget someone like *him*." Kaeleigh shrugged her shoulders, but curiously headed to table thirteen. She wasn't superstitious, but heading to that table gave her a shaky feeling.

How does he know my name? I'm sure I'd remember that raven-black hair and those eyes... those deep-set chocolate eyes that look like they're staring into my soul... eyes that are looking directly at me with a slight twinkle.

Just below those eyes was a set of full lips that caused her tongue to have a mind of its own, wetting her own like an excitable teenager. Those same lips lifted with a cocky, faint smirk that said he knew what she was thinking, and Kaeleigh quickly snapped out of her blatant ogling with a blush creeping up her neck. She took a deep breath, straightened her shoulders, and remembered she had a job to do.

"Welcome to Antonia's, my name is Kaeleigh. I see you already have your beverage. Are you ready to order?" she said, trying to remember all she was supposed to say. It didn't help that he stared openly at her with an amused look on his face.

"No, but thank you," he said, looking directly at her with intense dark eyes that caught her off guard. His gaze softened, then smiling, he said, "I've been observing you for the last few days, and it appears you are completely unaware of who you are."

She was so taken aback by his bluntness and so confused by his smile that she just stared at him for a minute, not sure how to respond. *What?! Is this guy for real?*

Lost in her inner monologue, she almost missed him walking past her as he got up abruptly and left the restaurant. Kaeleigh had just barely tuned back in to reality in time to see the back of his head and his... well, his back—and all that entailed—walking out the front doors.

What a nice back it was! *But why is it walking away?*

In her confusion, or maybe out of shock, her feet seemed to have forgotten how to move because she stood firmly planted by the table holding her order pad, not really sure what to do next.

"That was incredibly bizarre!" Kaeleigh thought not only to herself, but also out loud, causing the couple at the next table to stare at her. Her cheeks blushed again and she turned to go check on the tables in her own section. Passing Alex on her way back, she just shrugged.

"So did you know tall, dark, and handsome? I know… so cliché, right? But he definitely was tall, dark, and handsome. AND he had that totally mysterious, badass vibe too!" Alex said a little too excitedly. "What did he want?" she asked in a teasingly sultry voice and raised eyebrows.

"No, I didn't know him. He thought he knew me, but I think it was a mistake. He didn't make much sense and then he just… left." Kaeleigh shrugged as she kept heading to her tables. *He was tall, dark, and very handsome and he asked for me… even if he was a little crazy*, she thought as she held her head a bit higher. The rest of her shift went by quickly as she looked forward to meeting her friends for their movie night. Kaeleigh periodically thought about the strange guy at table thirteen and the odd sense she got from him that she couldn't quite shake. She also couldn't shake images of deep vats of chocolate in the form of his eyes, or of the blackest hair she had ever seen; shorn short on the sides of his head with a longer section on top. So soft looking it made her fingers twitch with desire to touch it and run them through it; his lightly tanned skin and broad, sculpted muscular shoulders. Not to mention how well his jeans fit as he walked out the door. She wondered if she would ever see him again.

As she arrived back at her apartment, her inside lights already on made her smile. Her friends Chel and Finn were there waiting for her even though it was Saturday, not Tuesday. They had a standing hangout night every Tuesday, so this was a bonus. She also didn't like coming home alone at night so this was one less night this week for that. *Maybe I should get a cat.* Since Finn had figured out her unfounded fear of being alone after Chel moved out, he made her check in every night via text or phone so she wasn't "alone," just until she got settled.

Finn had become like a big brother; she felt safe with him. He wasn't a big guy, but he carried himself strongly and was very protective. He could be intimidating with his usual scowl and almost always wore black. He had a light complexion and sharp angles, his hair a shaggy sandy-brown and his eyes, the best hazel. Lately, Kaeleigh would notice him looking at her when he thought she couldn't see him. He looked... conflicted was the only word she could come up with. Kaeleigh couldn't help wondering if maybe his feelings for her were more than hers were for him. Or perhaps it was something else altogether. But if he ever acted on *other* feelings, she didn't know what she would do. Sometimes, she pondered what it would be like to have those *other* feelings for him, but she just didn't, at least not right now. The last thing she wanted to do was hurt him or worse, lose his friendship. Rolling her shoulders and shaking out her arms, she shook off those thoughts and headed excitedly into her apartment to spend time with her friends for a belated birthday.

"Surprise!" Chel and Finn yelled as she walked in the door.

"Hooray! But I knew you were going to be here so it's not really a surprise," Kaeleigh said, somewhat confused, but grinning anyway.

"Yes, but did you know there would be a spider web of streamers AND balloons that Chel seemed to find in every color imaginable? AND that she would hang them from every available square inch of your apartment?" Finn sarcastically replied as Chel just rolled her eyes at him.

"I had *NO* idea you would decorate and I L-O-V-E them!!!" she shouted as she looked around in awe and giving Chel the biggest hug she could without smothering her.

"Hey, what about me? I might think they're silly but I did help," Finn said with a sheepish grin.

"Yes, he did. He even took a breath from complaining for all of five minutes at one point." Chel rolled her eyes.

Kaeleigh threw herself at Finn, almost knocking him over, and gave him a big hug too and a kiss on the cheek, which always embarrassed him even when it was just the three of them. "Thank you! THANK YOU, both of you! It means a lot to spend my birthday with you guys."

"Well, go get out of those black clothes. I'm sure you've been dying to put your own clothes on all day. Then we will have pizza, dessert, and movies!" Chel said as she ushered Kaeleigh toward her bedroom to change. Chel knew how much Kaeleigh needed color to relax. After all, they were best friends. She didn't understand it, but she didn't question it either. It was just a part of Kaeleigh. Accept it all or not at all. That was Chel's motto.

"That's so much better!" Kaeleigh said, sighing practically in euphoria as she came out of her room wearing her favorite faded blue jeans and fitted yellow T-shirt with a big orange and white star on the front. She had let her hair down from the tight ponytail it was trapped in all day, and had bare feet. "Pizza sounds so good, I'm starving! Ooooh! And look at the cupcakes with purple frosting... Yumm!! They match the new amaranthine strips in my hair, Chel—way to coordinate!" She winked as she squealed, bouncing up and down trying to swat at the balloons like a little kid. She loved fun, lighthearted celebrations like this. Even though she was eighteen now, she didn't see any reason to suddenly become adult-like, sophisticated, responsible, and serious, at least not completely.

"Chel, get the movies, I'll get the pizza and plates, Kae, you can get the purple cupcakes," Finn delegated as they headed toward the TV.

"Let's get this party started! What movies do we have?" asked Kaeleigh as she did a little happy dance, excited to be with her friends and let the events of the day roll off her.

"We have an eclectic mix, including the original *Footloose* with Kevin Bacon—an oldie but always a goodie," she began with a "Vanna" flourish of her hand highlighting the DVD box. "*Star Trek*—'to boldly go where no man has gone before,' but the Chris Pine version of course..." Chel held out the movie for Kaeleigh to see. "*27 Dresses*—kinda girly; and *The Royal Tenenbaums*—artsy fartsy picked by none other than our resident emo over there," Chel said looking over both movies then rolling her eyes toward Finn sitting on the couch. "We're practically a movie store, take your pick!" Chel said dramatically.

"Wow! That is quite the mix... um... any one is great, you guys pick," Kaeleigh said as she pointed to both Chel and Finn.

They both looked at each other, smiled, and simultaneously said, "*Star Trek*," then laughed. They knew that was one of Kaeleigh's favorites. She smiled. "Good choice! Let's eat and start the movie!" Somehow a purple cupcake ended up right in front of her on the table, so of course, she had to lick off the frosting. And of course, she had to stick out her newly dyed tongue, flaunting it to her friends.

✼✼✼

After the movie, Kaeleigh yawned and stretched, "Yeah, it'd be great to transport with the push of a button to another time, place or space, you know? See other races, beings, etc..." Kaeleigh trailed off as her face took on a far off expression as her imagination ran wild.

"It would be totally cool!" agreed Chel. "Although I don't think I would like to meet a cyborg. That would creep me out."

"It may not be all it's cracked up to be. What if the creatures are evil or what if there are interplanetary wars going on? How would you defend yourselves?" Finn asked in an oddly serious way.

"Interplanetary war, huh?" Chel said with her eyebrows raised and hands on her hips. "I'm sure we could figure something out," she said with an intriguing expression on her face. "Perhaps Chris Pine would come to our rescue as Captain Kirk!" she retorted with a "so there!" look.

"He would totally come to our rescue! Right? I mean why wouldn't he! Oh! Maybe we would get super powers too, then we could defend ourselves and kick some bad-guy ass!" Kaeleigh shouted as she jumped up and took things to the kitchen to clean up... even though it would probably just sit until tomorrow. At least she took them in there, right? It was the little things that counted in her mind.

"Thanks for the fun, guys! I'm exhausted from work today and I work the lunch shift tomorrow. Is this a sleepover or should we continue this in the morning over coffee and scones at The Station?" Kaeleigh asked with a quirky little grin.

"Ooooo! Scones sound sooo good! Count me in for breakfast, but I got to get home. Sam should be home now," Chel said with a mischievous smile, turning dramatically toward the door with her hand on her heart. Kaeleigh still couldn't believe that Chel was living with a *boy*. It just seemed too grown up for them. She just hoped Chel was happy.

"I'm going to go too, but scones sound great, I'll see you there. Happy late birthday, Kae!" Finn said as he gave Kaeleigh a hug and a kiss on the cheek and headed for the door. It always warmed her heart that he used a nickname for her, even if was just the first syllable of her name. Not to have her exit overshadowed, Chel turned and ran at Kaeleigh with arms open for a bear hug and a noisy kiss on the opposite cheek. "Happy birthday!!" Chel shouted then ran toward the door.

Laughing, Kaeleigh locked the door behind them. Looking at Chel, no one would assume she was a lighthearted, affectionate person. She tended to give off her other more artistic side to people who didn't know her. She had mostly blonde hair, but black and caramel colors coated the underside along with a few black peek-a-boos throughout the rest. She tended to use her body as her "personal canvas," as she liked to call it. Unfortunately, she got judged a lot because of her dimple piercing, eyebrow piercing, and partial sleeve along with other miscellaneous tattoos. She wore her heart and her art on her sleeve—literally—but she was one of the most loving and fiercely loyal people Kaeleigh knew. She was proud to be her friend.

As Kaeleigh got ready for bed, she couldn't help her mind wandering back to that gorgeous stranger at Antonia's tonight. She still wondered who he was and what his deal was. He couldn't have been looking for *her*. It had to be a different Kaeleigh. *Well, of course he had the wrong person. He was nuts! And he didn't make any sense.* But the way he looked at her, studied her, gave her chills even now thinking back on it—and not necessarily the bad kind. Still, something nagged at the back of her mind, telling her maybe it *was* her he was looking for... but why?

CHAPTER EIGHT

The buzzing and dizziness hit her harder this time. At least Kaeleigh had just gotten into bed as she was practically thrown into the current images and feelings that came to life, much more like a movie this time. She clutched her sheets as the bright light once again blinded her.

The air shockingly cold; an eerie feeling that something dark was near sent chills up her spine. As a slight breeze began to blow in her face, there were very faint, high-pitched noises. Kaeleigh listened intently, trying to make out the sounds she was hearing. The wind was picking up, throwing the noises louder into her face. She froze... people were screaming... LOTS of screaming. Something else mixed with the screams that she couldn't make out: crackling like a giant sparkler on the Fourth of July.

A hand holding hers tightly. Everything in her was screaming at her to RUN! The hand, sensing her anxious feelings, began to rub small circles into her palm, sending calm, peaceful feelings through her whole body. Looking down at the hand she was holding, she noticed something... a ring. It was his.

She didn't know him, but she took comfort in the mysterious man in her vision. She couldn't run if she wanted to. At the mercy of the vision, trapped within her own dream, she watched it unfold.

As she headed uphill, the screaming and the loud noises receded, allowing her to breathe a little steadier; however, she could still hear their terror and they deeply unsettled her. The pain and sorrow she felt escaped description. She squinted, trying to see better, trying to see anything, but everything seemed obscured by an all-consuming fog.

She was still holding his hand...still receiving deep comfort from his strength. Just under the surface of her skin, where their hands met, a spark of electricity hovered between the two of them. Kaeleigh looked straight ahead and saw the backs of several people standing on what seemed to be the edge of a cliff. Not sure who or what these people were doing or if they could even see her, she quietly took a couple of steps forward to try to see what they saw. The people, mostly men, wore what looked like ceremonial robes or cloaks like nothing she'd ever seen before, and looked quite official even from the back. The vision brought Kaeleigh's sight forward. Although they didn't seem to notice she was there, she was afraid of what she might see. That same creepy, eerie feeling that sent chills up her spine when she first entered the dream was back. Something was really wrong here, her brain kept telling her. Suddenly, she could see out over the edge of the cliff. Not actually a cliff as she first thought; she was high up on what looked like some kind of a rock overhang on this hillside. She actually wasn't even as high up as she originally thought; still high enough not to want to fall off. Peering out over the edge, she gasped, falling to her knees at the sight before her.

A battle. She was witnessing a real battle... people fighting... swords... screaming and blood... both men and women... sparks flying through the air... and oh the gods, are those children? or small people?... and... and... some kind of creatures—*NOT HUMAN!*

Kaeleigh's head was spinning. Her heart hurt; she was breathing too hard, too fast. Her vision was getting spotty and she was starting to panic. Suddenly, a presence next to her knelt down beside her and then a warm, gentle, yet firm hand gripped her shoulder. His hand. Her breathing slowed, and she began to relax as calming waves rolled through her body. Grateful for the relief, she looked up at him then was instantly angered that she was brought here to this tragic scene.

Did he *bring me here?*

"Why the HELL did you show me this? What is this?" she yelled into the vision, not knowing if anyone could hear her.

The man responded, "You need understanding..."

"You mean this isn't real, there aren't really hundreds—thousands—of people dying down there?" she asked, confused.

"No, you misunderstand. This was very real. Many were hurt and many died, but that is for another time. Please, look once more and learn."

Kaeleigh's fear had forced her eyes shut and a sharp tension seized her body. She didn't want to watch people fighting and dying. Beads of sweat *formed more quickly, faster, dripping down her face. Her mind caught in a fight between what she knew was true now and what she was being shown was true of the past. His hand gently grabbed hers once again, let the calm wash over her, and her vision directed her sight over the edge once more.*

In that same instant, Kaeleigh felt a tug in her mind and heard someone calling her name from far off in the distance. She stopped and looked around her, but it hadn't come from within the vision. Shrugging it off, she looked out over the edge, waiting to be shown what was there. Kaeleigh heard her name being called again.

"Do you hear that? Someone is calling my name," she said out loud. The friendly hand that was holding hers suddenly gripped harder, while the melodic voice that had spoken to her before spoke again.

"I am not finished showing you what you must see to understand. He is interfering," his voice took on an edge as he spoke aloud. "If he succeeds, he will pull you to his side of the veil. Quickly look out over the edge so that I may reveal truth to you." She looked, but it was getting foggy again.

"Kaeleigh... Kaeleigh..." the voice persisted, louder each time.

"It's Finn's voice," she suddenly realized and looked around for him distractedly, knowing she wouldn't find him in this place. As she recognized Finn's voice, she began to feel fuzzy and the mist began to roll in from the peripherals. He grabbed her wrist firmly to get her attention and demanded she look out over the edge. Everything was getting hazier, her mind started spinning with a dizziness that made her want to be sick. There were flashes of light—flashes of images that were thrown before her eyes, although she couldn't make sense of anything she saw. There was a glimmer.

"We need you!" she heard shouted from the man as it all started to fade away. Panic started to come upon her as did the darkness. She longed for that calming sensation that came from his hand. Then suddenly, she heard a familiar voice piercing through that veil, trying to bring her out.

"Kaeleigh... Kaeleigh!" Finn's voice was full of panic. Even his hands as he shook her awake felt panic-stricken.

Kaeleigh stirred with a jolt, gasping for air as she took in her surroundings, like someone having been under water a little too long. She saw Finn, not quite comprehending that he was there with her in her bedroom—with an extremely worried look on his face. Then she saw him again with recognition.

"Finn! You scared the hell out of me, what are you doing here?"

"Me! I scared you?" Finn practically shouted, furious with worry as he paced back and forth in her small bedroom. "I had my window open," he sucked in a much needed breath, "I thought I heard you scream. I tried calling, but you didn't answer." His hands alternated between clenching into fists and running through his hair. "I decided to come by and check on you. I knocked at the door, but thought I heard a crash—apparently you knocked your lamp over," he reached for the lamp setting it right as he continued, "so I used the spare key." Again he began to pace. "I come in here to find you in a coma-like sleep that I can't wake you up from." He finally stopped moving and stared directly at her, his hands resting atop his head and sighed with exasperation. "I've been trying to get through to you forever, and you think I scared *you*! What is going on?"

Kaeleigh's eyes instantly filled with tears, a dam ready to burst, her lower lip quivering on the edge of control. "Bad...bad dream..." Kaeleigh struggled to even get the words out, interrupted by tears and choked sobs. "It seemed...so real." Tears flowed, a raging river, heaving sobs wracked her body. Dropping his hands, Finn deflated, letting all the air out of his chest and sat on the bed beside her. Finn wrapped an arm around her shoulders comfortingly and brought her close to him. He let her cry on his shoulder until her breathing calmed and she regained control.

"Thank you for checking on me," she said as she wiped her eyes. He handed her a tissue just before she was about to wipe her nose on the material of her shirt. She took it with a slightly embarrassed laugh. Then taking a moment to collect herself, she breathed slowly in and out. "I'm glad you live so close." Kaeleigh smiled, but still felt a little wobbly.

"What was it about—the dream?" he clarified at her odd expression, unconvinced that she was okay.

"Ummm... actually, I don't really remember the details now that I'm awake. There was fighting and screaming and blood, like a war but smaller, I think; I saw part of it," she said, vaguely able to recall what it was she was supposed to remember from this dream. One thing was for sure, it wasn't exactly a dream, but she wasn't ready to tell Finn that yet. He noticed her hands were shaking as she tried not to relive the images that were coming back to her in rapid succession. "It must have been from the movie we watched and all that talk of interplanetary wars," Kaeleigh said, smiling, trying to make light of what she had just witnessed to put off dealing with it.

"It's all right, don't think about it anymore tonight. If it's important it will come back to you when you need it to," Finn said with a sigh, trying to comfort her as he rested a hand on top of hers to try to stop her shaking. Kaeleigh looked down at Finn's hand on hers then back up at him, not even realizing she was shaking. An odd expression flash across his face, but it was gone before she could define it. *Strange.*

Kaeleigh nodded at Finn and took a deep breath, trying to relax, wishing his hands had the same calming effect as the imaginary guy that was in her flashes. *Yeah, because that's not crazy.* She looked up at Finn to find that he was still looking at her with a concerned, yet softer look on his face until her eyes met his, and then she realized that his hand was still on top of hers. Kaeleigh suddenly felt awkward at their close proximity on the bed—*her* bed. She pulled her hands out from under his to pull the hair out of her face and tuck it behind her ears, hoping for a smooth transition, trying not to make him feel bad; after all, he had come to check on her. Finn suddenly got up from the bed and walked out the door without another word.

Crap! I made him feel bad. I can't believe he would leave without saying goodbye. What's his deal? Twice now a guy has just walked away from me. Kaeleigh made to move from the bed, not remembering what she went to bed wearing (or not wearing). She looked under the covers to make sure that she was decent in her tank top and pajama pants.

"Finn?" Kaeleigh shouted as she walked toward her bedroom door. "Are you leaving?" she asked out the door just as he walked back in. Finn handed her a glass of water he got from the kitchen. "Oh, thank you," she said, inclining her head. Kaeleigh pulled back and frowned at her awkward reaction. *Why am I so strange?* Shaking off her faux pas, she took several drinks, hoping to wash down whatever awkwardness that was suddenly between them. Finn was one of her best friends, but their relationship felt strained and different in a way she wasn't yet sure she wanted to explore. Not about to let the strain and awkwardness dominate their friendship, she rolled her shoulders to shake it off.

"You want to go back to sleep or would you like to play cards or something to distract you?" Finn asked, obviously picking up on the very tangible discomfort. With his hands now in his front pockets, standing just outside her bedroom door, he looked like a young boy not sure how to talk to a girl. Endeared by his gesture, her face lit up with a smile.

"Sure, let's play a card game, we haven't done that in a while. I'll get the cards." Kaeleigh ran into the living room and pulled a deck of cards out of the basket by the television.

They played a few different games—things like: Speed, Gin, Go Fish—the last was particularly funny as it didn't work well between two people, but it didn't matter. The laughter accompanied with casual conversation, enabled her to relax in the ease of their friendship. Kaeleigh gathered the cards to be put away and yawned as the need for sleep hit her once again. Getting up from the couch, Finn grabbed an extra blanket out of the closet.

"I guess I'll take one of these toss pillows," Finn joked and promptly tossed it to the couch.

"Throw pillows," Kaeleigh corrected, "Decorative throw pillows to be exact."

"Oh, excuse me then," Finn rolled his eyes. "You won't mind if I throw them then will you?" And with that, he threw two more much like you'd throw a baseball, if a baseball were several times more square and tasseled.

Kaeleigh watched in mock horror as he threw her pretty pillows so rough... so... so like a boy! "What are you doing, Finn?"

"Go to bed, Kae, I'll sleep on the couch to keep you company in case you have another bad dream or need anything," Finn said and headed back to the couch to his makeshift bed.

Kaeleigh got into her bed, feeling slightly guilty that one of her best friends, who had been so great to her tonight when she needed a friend, was going to sleep on her springy and not-so-comfortable-for-sleeping couch. After all, things seemed back to normal and Finn had spent the night before and it was no big deal, although Chel was usually there too. *He'll be fine out there on the couch.* The couch squeaked as Finn plopped himself down and made himself comfortable, or at least tried. Every time he turned over or adjusted his position on the couch, it squeaked. *Ughh! I'll never get any sleep with all that racket out there.*

"Finn, you don't have to stay out there." Kaeleigh's shout sounded muffled from under her comforter.

"I'm fine, I'm not leaving you tonight. You're still a bit shaken up, I'll stay the night... or what's left of it," Finn replied in a tired voice.

"No, I mean you don't have to sleep out there on the couch, there's plenty of room in here," Kaeleigh said, looking at her king-sized bed.

"I'm good, Kae. Go to sleep." Finn yawned.

"Please, Finn?" A slight tremor in her voice revealed the depth of her fear at returning to sleep.

"Well," Finn began as he rose from the couch, "Your bed *is* more comfortable, but only if you're fine with it." He leaned against the doorframe into her bedroom. "You can't tell Chel we had a slumber party without her though, she'll never forgive us for that," he said with a playful grin as he walked in her room.

"Tell me about it! She hates to feel like she's missed anything. The other day when we had lunch without her she went on and on about it that whole day," Kaeleigh rambled dramatically. "It's our secret," she said, scooting over to the far side of the bed to give Finn space. Her room wasn't that big, but when Chel had lived there they had decided to share so they made the king bed fit. It always made them laugh when they reminisced about their acrobatic maneuvers attempting to get it in the door and turned properly inside the room. Smiling, she thought, *See, totally normal, no big deal.* Then she heard his belt buckle as he was taking it off. Kaeleigh quickly flipped over and froze. Her gaze fixated at the opposite wall, blushing like a little girl at the thought of a boy in her room taking his clothes off. Nervously, she smoothed the hair away from her eyes and clutched her pillow within her talon-like grip. *Why am I freaking out?* Realizing Finn was laughing, she rolled slightly back toward him.

"What's so funny?"

"You." He looked in her eyes and took in her face with a humorous twinkle in his eyes, but there was also a hint of something else—something resembling desire. "Don't worry, I'm just taking off my belt." He held it up for her to inspect. "It's uncomfortable, but everything else is staying on unless..." Finn waggled his eyebrows suggestively at her, "*you* want it to come off, Kaeleigh," he said teasing her but equally making fun of her. Kaeleigh's mouth fell open in mocked shock.

"Shut up and go to sleep." She threw a pillow at him and rolled back over. Of course he'd be the perfect gentleman. At least she was pretty sure he would be. "Good night, Finn, thanks for being here."

"That's what I'm here for." Finn lay down on his side of the bed and got comfortable. "Maybe my being here will keep the bad guy in your dreams away." He paused. "Good night, Kae." Finn rolled the opposite direction, but did not fall right to sleep. His eyes wide, realization hit Finn that he had slipped. Hopefully Kaeleigh had too much to think about that she would not catch what he had said, but he knew her better than that. Something was changing and it killed him that he couldn't talk to her about it. If he could only get her to talk to him about it.

Kaeleigh smiled, fully satisfied from the middle of the night fun. As she drifted asleep his last words about the bad guy kept rolling through her mind.

I don't remember saying there was a bad guy...

Chapter Nine

Exhile. The Realm of the Unforgiven Dead.

While Daegan was scouting the mortal realm, evil was restless in another realm. Hidden away in the obscurity of a jagged mountain range of the desolate dark realm, also known as Exhile, was a labyrinth of caves. In the tallest, darkest mountain peak, there was one particular cave hollowed out of the rock through time and death. This was of the oldest of all the realms. It was where the lost souls and the souls of the unforgiven dead—the ones that became the Droch-Shúil—were sent to live out their afterlife. The souls were escorted by the Ferriers, a race of Elves who traditionally remained neutral on all concerns other than their purpose, which was to ferry the souls. Recently, that had changed and some had begun to choose sides, in particular, the dark side. Those who chose to side with darkness... with *her*... became dark themselves and thus created the Ónarach. They chose to be counted among Alandria's enemies when they went against nature, against their purpose, by enslaving stolen souls... specifically, the souls of the passing Orchids.

A primitive, ancient evil dwelled there, carried through the centuries, attracted by the torment of this realm. It was cold. It was dark. It was lifeless. Except for the faint, struggling hidden heartbeat that for centuries had fought for its survival against its keeper—*her*—this was a place of death.

Until now.

The tides had turned. It was about to become more. *She* was about to become more.

The Council of the Kings had been destroyed long ago. The Orchids had been silenced; their last had been marked. The Elders were almost extinct. It was all coming together. The time of the prophecy to be fulfilled was approaching, but it would not come to pass; of that *she* was confident.

The Droch-Shúil had been given free rein in Alandria, as long as they still made contact with her. *She* was their master, and it was almost time for her to reign.

CHAPTER TEN

PRESENT DAY. MISSOULA, MT

Kaeleigh woke up on the far left side of the bed, facing her closet. Stretching her arms above her head and pointing her toes as if she were a ballerina, she rolled to her back and relaxed back into her warm mattress, luxuriating in the feel of her soft blankets...then she froze. Finn was in her bed. Kaeleigh shut her eyes, but it was too late to pretend sleep. She licked her lips, bringing some moisture back to her mouth then checked to make sure all of her night apparel was in its proper place. With hesitation, she brought her arms back to her sides and slowly turned her head toward the other side of her room...toward the boy that had slept in her bed to protect her from her "dreams," and possibly from herself.

He wasn't there. *Whew!* Kaeleigh felt all the muscles in her body relax and let out the breath she didn't realize she had been holding. Where Finn had been lying, there was little evidence that he had actually been there. *He must have gotten up early and gone home before breakfast. He's such a good friend.* But why the awkward feelings?

Maybe because I'm afraid he wants more out of this friendship than I'm willing to give and I don't want him hurt... "Ugh, who knows!" she breathed loudly and threw off the covers.

Quickly Kaeleigh changed her clothes and got ready for the day, twisting her long hair into a crazy bun high on the top of her head. Pulling on her shoes, she half hopped as she headed to the kitchen for breakfast and much-needed coffee, but her progress was halted in the entry. In her kitchen, reading the newspaper as if he lived there, sat Finn. His hair was wet as if he had taken a shower, but was still wearing his clothes from yesterday. Hearing her enter the room, he looked up from his paper and smiled.

"Morning, Kae, did you sleep well?" he said.

"Morning. Um, yeah. You?" she half-grunted, half-grumbled.

"Good enough," he shrugged. "Took me a few minutes to get used to your bed—it's a bit softer than mine."

Well, don't get used to it. That was the last time you will ever be in it. Instead, she heard herself go a completely different route. "I'm surprised you're still here really, I thought you might need to go home and get ready for work or something." *Yeah, subtle, Kaeleigh. Wow, somebody is IRRITATED this morning! Why am I so irritated?*

"Nope, no work today," he said, putting his paper down. Standing up, he folded his arms and leaned casually up against the counter, but she thought she saw a twitch of his lips indicating she wasn't hiding her mood very well. "We made plans to have coffee with Chel at The Station this morning, remember? I thought we could just go together." He got out her favorite purple mug with the brown polka dots and poured a cup of the steaming, freshly brewed, dark roast from the coffee pot. "Wanna pre-cup," he chuckled, laughing at his own joke, "you know, to get you ready for the real thing?" He held out the mug, offering it to her.

Not wanting to leave him hanging with her favorite mug, Kaeleigh grabbed the mug. Eyeing him, she held it between both hands and began to drink the hot, smooth liquid life. She closed her eyes and took deep, soothing breaths, willing her irritation away, and awaited the fresh energy that would soon be buzzing through her veins. Although what she suddenly felt was not just caffeine but a subtle hum of light-blue energy she could see and feel flow through her. She opened her eyes with a smile.

"Better?" he asked, just as oblivious as Kaeleigh to the magic at work.

"Better," Kaeleigh said with a rush of guilt, realizing that he had sensed her irritation. "I'm sorry I was irritated," she stopped, staring at her coffee mug. "It's just...for some reason I feel awkward about last night. I mean, I don't want that between us." *There. Always better to just talk about it.*

"Oh come on. Lighten up a bit, Kae. I think that dream threw you for a loop last night," Finn said, his tone suspiciously light as he grabbed his own mug and took a sip, "but no worries, everyone gets thrown for a loop now and again, you know?" Finn turned away from her and went back to his paper at the table. Something about the absentminded way he trailed off at the end was a bit forced, almost like a father trying to refocus a child's attention.

Kaeleigh watched him retreat with a careful eye. *What is going on in this guy's head?* Too annoyed to dig deeper, she sighed and flipped her hair behind her. Kaeleigh took a sip of her coffee and cradled the mug close to her chest. "Yeah, maybe you're right," Kaeleigh said quietly, her gaze lost in the depths of her mug and her memory, her hands clenching the mug so tight that it didn't shatter was a victory. She took a deep breath. "It *was* an intense dream... or whatever it was," she said absent-mindedly, setting her mug down and stretching her fingers out from her intense grip. She realized she probably looked stressed or disturbed or something by what she was doing, so she straightened her posture, pasted a smile on her face, and took another carefree sip of her coffee. Kaeleigh saw Finn watching her from behind the paper, pretending—not to well—to read so she turned to leave.

"Wait," Finn said abruptly as he lowered his paper. "What do you mean 'or whatever it was?'" He frowned with sudden confusion. "Wasn't it a dream, Kaeleigh?" Finn questioned her, but a spark of panic lit into his eyes.

Kaeleigh leaned against the doorframe, caught between leaving and staying. She took another sip of her coffee to stall and looked away. "What else could it be?" she said with a forced laugh. Her eyes found his and she sighed in resignation. "I don't know why I said that. Still tweaked, I guess." She shrugged her shoulders.

"Kaeleigh?" Finn prodded. "Is there something you want to talk about?"

Kaeleigh walked over to the window framed in simple turquoise curtain panels. She looked down at the street below, littered with the colors of fall.

Do I want to talk about it? Her hesitant silence, telling. She did want to talk, but something about last night nagged her subconscious more. Finn started to read his paper, giving her time to decide.

"Why did you think there was a 'bad guy' in it?" Kaeleigh turned to face him. "I don't remember telling you about anyone involved." Staring intently at him, she gauged his reaction.

Finn continued to read his newspaper, taking his time to respond. He looked up at her confidently. "Oh, I guess you didn't." He shrugged it off, "Aren't there always bad guys in dreams like that though? I just assumed." He paused and took a drink of coffee. "So I was right then?" he asked then looked back down at his paper. He continued to avoid eye contact with her.

Odd response, and very unlike the typical disinterested Finn. *But why? And why is he refusing to look at me? What could he know?*

"Yeah you were right," she answered giving him something. "You're acting kind of strange, ya know? And what is so important in that stupid newspaper?" she threw out just to see if she could make him squirm. *This would be kinda fun if it didn't also freak me out.* Finn lowered the newspaper and folded it, giving her his attention. Sighing, she rolled her eyes. Kaeleigh added, "I do have something I want to talk about, but let's wait until we're at The Station so I can clue Chel in too. She'll want to know." Kaeleigh paused as Finn finally looked up at her with concern and also relief. "There's something that I haven't told you guys."

Chapter Eleven

Finn and Kaeleigh waited for Chel in their favorite booth in the corner between the side wall and the front windows of The Station. The Station was a unique combination coffee, bakery, and fresh flower shop. Kaeleigh reveled in the warm atmosphere, relaxing in the natural energy given off from the worn leather seats, exposed wood beams and restored barn wood floors. Accents of raw branches came out from the walls wrapped with growing green ivy. Set in moss covered pots, other levels of greenery were strategically placed through the room. Shades of brown and gray, united the décor with placements of iron fixtures, sprockets from early steam engines, and black and white train art. Fresh, fragrant scents permeated from the back of The Station where a permanently open sliding glass door separated The Flower Depot from the rest of the café. Unlike no other café in the area, The Station had grown in popularity since its opening several years ago.

The sun, low in the daytime sky, blanketed the booth they sat in with warmth as it flooded through the window. The glass served as a barrier, creating a haven safe from the threat of the cold winter on the inside as it lurked outside, the approaching season just around the corner.

Kaeleigh sat under the sunlight, letting it saturate her body. Energy from the sunlight soaked into her pores in a myriad of colors, tingling her skin the deeper it sunk. Renewed and rejuvenated, Kaeleigh's soul rejoiced at the infusion of light.

Finn subtly cleared his throat. Kaeleigh opened her eyes, a hint of pink creeping up into her cheeks. She hadn't meant to have gotten so lost in the moment. Looking at Finn, Kaeleigh was taken aback at the clearly shocked expression he wore. Finn's mouth opened to say something, but was interrupted by Chel as she flung herself through the front door, a piece of debris thrown from a twister on the move.

Chel, in her brown peacoat and olive stocking hat, started unwinding her scarves. She had an obsession with scarves, so much so that literally unwinding herself from three separate scarves was no surprise to Kaeleigh. Kaeleigh laughed as her friend got tangled in variegated yarns of yellow, purple and olive green, and brown the more she unwrapped herself. The rest of Chel was quite put together, wearing skinny jeans in a dirty wash, and purple ballet flats. She was quite the sight, but her presence and light made Kaeleigh smile. Kaeleigh looked down at her own ensemble of a green long-sleeved-T accentuated with her uniquely handmade-by-Chel purple scarf, and short dark jean skirt. Her thick, multicolored striped tights and purple dragon-printed Cons tied with pink laces made their own statement.

Finn was pretty much the man in black: black shirt, black jeans, black jacket. When he didn't wear black, he was clothed in another dark color. He was the backdrop needed for them to shine, he would explain. The girls often harassed him, but concluded he would get lost in their craziness if he wore anything else.

"Good morning! Sorry I'm late," Chel said out of breath as she dropped her pile of scarves between herself and Finn. Finn, rebuffed, scooted over. "Hey! Why don't you go sit by Kaeleigh?" Finn grumbled with annoyance at Chel.

"I can't sit by her, silly! Look at us! We totally clash. My flats, her... Anyway, don't you want to sit by me?" She batted her eyes in her coy way. Finn grunted and scooted over to give himself as much room as he could. Chel laughed and looked at Kaeleigh curiously. "So, I got your text... spill."

Kaeleigh opened her mouth to start explaining things she had already waited too long to share, but the expression on Chel's face—similar to the one Finn wore earlier—brought Kaeleigh up short.

Chel cocked her head and looked at Kaeleigh curiously, leaning in close to her face. Chel's eyes opened wide as she examined Kaeleigh. "Are you wearing colored contacts these days?"

"What?" Kaeleigh asked, surprised. "No."

"Yeah your eyes were super vivid green, then suddenly faded back to normal... must have been the sun reflecting in them, or I'm seeing things. Strange." She kept staring at Kaeleigh.

"Quit staring at me! You're weirding me out. It must have been the sun or your imagination," she replied self-consciously.

"Get on with the deep dark secret already." Chel shook off her stare and leaned forward with intense focus.

"Okay, well," she looked down at her fingernails, "Yesterday at Antonia's this guy came in—a really hot guy I might add—and asked for me specifically... by name!" Kaeleigh glanced up with a slight blush. Then, in stark contrast, her face paled. She picked at her scarf, removing the invisible lint. "He said something weird about watching me and how I was unaware of who *I* was." She looked up at Finn then over to Chel. "Then while I was trying to figure out what he was talking about, he got up and left. Just like that—he was out the door." Her face shot to the window, her line of sight following the ghost of her memory as he escaped her sight. Kaeleigh, returning her state of mind to the present questioned her friends, "How weird is that? He must have been confu sed..." She scrunched her brow. "Or he simply got the wrong Kaeleigh... I don't know," Kaeleigh sighed. Raising her hand to swipe a piece of hair from her face, she noticed her hand had a slight shake, and as she lowered it, she realized she was not the only one to notice. She cleared her throat. "What do you guys think?" When she finished, she looked from Chel to Finn then back again, awaiting their responses.

Chel gave Finn an odd sidelong glance but just as quickly returned to her nonchalant self. "That *is* really weird, but I don't think it's anything to get worked up over." *That wasn't what I expected.* Then, much more characteristic of her, Chel leaned forward, elbows on the table. "So this guy was really hot, huh?" She winked at Kaeleigh who tried to hide from Chel that she realized she was trying to change the subject.

Finn's turn. Throw in more strange. Kaeleigh raised a questioning eyebrow at him, and was also surprised at him. He was texting someone! Distracted but a little concerned (and probably not a feigned concern either) he looked up from his phone. "It was probably a mistake, but keep an eye out just in case he comes back."

"Who on earth could you be texting? Aren't we your only friends?" Kaeleigh asked annoyed, motioning to the three of them.

Finn looked up and smirked as he waved the phone in front of her. "Work. Scheduling conflict."

Kaeleigh sighed and rolled her eyes. "That's not the only thing that I haven't told you guys." The strange guy and the more intense visions had to be related. She hoped her friends would be a little more attentive to this one. Then Kaeleigh with a slight wringing of hands began, "I've wanted to tell you so many times. And I almost did on several occasions, but..." Kaeleigh bit her lip, "but I didn't want you to look at me different. I didn't want you to think I was crazy. Heck, I think I'm crazy sometimes." She played nervously with the locket resting against her chest. Kaeleigh took a deep breath.

"What else happened?" Finn questioned, now with an edge in his tone. Kaeleigh looked at him sharply. *This wasn't exactly what I expected.*

"Okay, okay..." Kaeleigh began. Subconsciously, all three of them hunched in, lowering their voices. "So this is all going to sound silly"—*might as well rip the Band-Aid off, right?*—"but I've been having these weird um... flashes, visions really, of places and things I've never seen before," she paused, watching their faces as they comprehended what she was saying. "These places and situations I see are so real in the moment; I feel like I'm actually there... or should be there." Kaeleigh noticed Finn's paling face even behind its concerned scowl. Chel was biting the inside of her cheek. Both were quiet, maybe deep in thoughtful skepticism? Kaeleigh continued, "I can't figure out what they are trying to tell me—if anything—and I can't always remember them after the fact. They aren't regular dreams, that much I'm sure. I mean, sometimes they happen in the middle of the day." Kaeleigh started biting her nails, unsure of their reactions, but pretty sure based on what she was seeing in their expressions it wasn't something they were going to laugh away.

"How many of these dream slash flashes have you had? And why is this is the first time you've said anything?" Finn lashed out.

Why the anger? Whatever, he's a guy.

"I've had them since I was little actually. Why would I tell you when it just makes me sound crazy? I knew well enough back then not to draw attention that way—I would have ended up in the psych ward on more than one occasion." She laughed at herself. "I learned to live with them. It's not like they mean anything," Kaeleigh paused, grounding herself in the view out the window. "At least, I didn't think they did, but I'm not sure now—they're getting stronger... more deliberate... more real." Kaeleigh's thoughts transferred from her own mind out into the open before she realized they were both staring at her. "That's why I'm telling you now."

Finn looked pale. *Seriously, what is going on with him?*

"All right," Chel spoke calmly and quietly. "So what are these 'flashes' about?" asked Chel, her eyes shifted back and forth between Kaeleigh and Finn.

"Once," Kaeleigh hesitated; she had never shared a vision with anyone before. "I saw images of a wedding in a forest with a crowd of people and creatures I didn't know or had never seen before. This last one," Kaeleigh looked over at Finn silently asking if she could tell Chel about last night, but before she could even say anything, he looked at her and nodded as if he knew what she was going to ask. "This last one was filled with a horrific battle from the past that I was privy to watch." Kaeleigh shuddered at the sights her memory was recalling. "I already told Finn about it because he had some kind of premonition or something that I was in trouble and came over to check on me. Or maybe I screamed and he heard me, but whatever," she said with an embarrassed shrug. "Apparently, my vision had me in some kind of comatose state that he had a hard time waking me out of." She inhaled deeply and exhaled slowly. "I was pretty shaken up so he stayed the night." Kaeleigh quickly glanced at Chel from under her lashes to see how she was going to react to that last part.

"Uh yeah! That's intense. I'd have hit him if he had left you like that." Then in afterthought, she stopped. "Wait!... Oh man, that means you guys had a slumber party without me. Sad," she said with a pouty face. "It's okay, I had a slumber party of my own, if you know what I mean," winking unabashedly at Kaeleigh AGAIN. Kaeleigh blushed, which she was sure was Chel's intent, and hit her hand against her forehead. Only Chel would change the subject in such a way. Kaeleigh just shook her head.

"What's with all the winking today, or does your eye just have a twitch?" Kaeleigh bit out, slightly irritated as she exaggerated a wink back at her.

"If he comes back, let me know RIGHT AWAY, and for god's sake stop dreaming or flashing—or whatever it is!" Finn got up and stormed out of The Station. Chel and Kaeleigh both looked at each other, dumb-founded. *Again with the walking away?*

"What the F was that about? What is going on with him?" Kaeleigh asked Chel, but didn't expect her to have an answer.

Chel stared out the window for a minute, deep in thought, then shrugged and kept drinking her coffee. "He's just moody, maybe it's his time of the month," she said, laughing into her cup. "And did you just say 'what the F?'" Chel laughed out.

"What can I say, I didn't want to dirty the loveliness of this space." She shrugged.

"Well then, I guess you'd better stop flashing too," Chel laughed fully again clearly amused at herself, causing Kaeleigh to laugh too which was, of course, her point. Taking a deep breath and a more serious tone she added, "He is right, though, you should let us know if he comes back." Chel paused with a vacant expression on her face then snapped out of it, adding, "Well, at least me because I want a good look at him." She purposefully winked yet again.

Ugh! She really shouldn't be allowed to have her own 'slumber parties'—she's much too chipper, Kaeleigh thought.

Chel, then serious suddenly, asked, "Do you think the flashes really might mean something? You think they are some kind of self-imposed coping mechanism that your imagination created to deal with stress?"

"Wow. Well, *doctor,* I hadn't even thought of that until you so subtly pointed it out," Kaeleigh said sarcastically, yet sobered at the thought of its possibilities.

"Don't shut us out, okay, Kaeleigh?" Chel said softly, pleading with her eyes. "Please tell us—or me at least—if you have any more visions." Kaeleigh nodded.

"That is weird though, I mean with Finn." More Chel-like, she added, "It's not like you can just 'stop flashing.' What *is* the matter with him?" Chel said with a smirk, trying not to laugh while she gathered her things to leave. "You know, maybe it was the way the sun was shining on your face—earlier, I mean with what I said about your eyes. Your eyes seem their normal green now by the way." Shrugging it all off, she added, "Hey, don't you have to get to work?"

"Yep, sure do. Big second week on the job!" Kaeleigh fist pumped sarcastically, returned Chel's exaggerated wink, then took off for Antonia's.

Chapter Twelve

Daegan was sitting high up in an oak tree—though to his knowledge not one of the NaNai. There were very few of them in the mortal realm, but they did exist and contained some of the old magic. An Elder had the ability to draw from that magic, from that energy if he was in need.

Daegan was frustratingly trying once again to communicate with The Orchids, whoever they were. He was about to give up when a flash of white light threatened to blind him, bringing before him the bedtime stories—the legends—his grandmother used to tell him when he was very young. Stories of another realm filled with beauty and ancient magic ruled by the Council of the Kings. Her stories were of course filled with intrigue and good versus evil and dark versus light. Races of magical beings he had only thought to dwell in myth lived freely, until the darkness destroyed everything.

With the Council of the Kings eliminated, a group of beings comprised of all the races banded together to do what they could to save the realm. They united their individual magic along with the magic of the realm—magic the likes of which no one had seen before or since. Releasing the ancient magic to the extent they did required sacrifice, but death did not come to them all. No, the magic had had a mind of its own, the results of which still had yet to be seen. An escape portal to an unseen realm opened. As many went through as possible, but a small group took their stand, pouring everything they had into the portal to keep it open. They tried to send all the life and earth magic that they could through the opening to start again. The Elves of the forest took with them saplings from their great NaNai in order to preserve the ancient magic, but something went very wrong.

The opening threatened to collapse as the darkness searched for a weakness within their protective shield. Those keeping the portal open were failing in life and magic. They knew what they had to do. The sacrifice made. The opening closed, but not before a shower of orchids fell from the sky, slipping through. The darkness had been contained... for now.

Daegan jerked out of his flash, gripping the tree he was sitting in so that he wouldn't fall to the ground. Breathless, he looked around, making sure nothing had slipped past his defenses for however long he was trapped in the memory not his own. He had had flashes before, but never quite like that. Looking at the tree he sat in, he wondered if perhaps the mighty oak was one of the NaNai after all. The ancient oaks were harder to distinguish in the mortal realm. He knew now that his flashes were real. Somehow, the spirits of The Orchids were alive and they were trying to speak to him. Why though, he did not know.

❋❋❋

He jumped out of the tree and leaned against his well-kept black Ford Bronco. In the parking lot of Antonia's, where the girl, the Sol-lu-mieth, worked, he thought of how easy it had actually been to find her.

The gateway from Alandria into the mortal realm opened into the mountains of Montana. He had been on scouting missions into the mortal realm on several occasions, and part of blending in was learning how to adapt with twenty-first-century mortals. Daegan spent time educating himself on their history, their technologies, their behaviors, and their customs. He looked at his truck that was kept at the Faerie safe-house in the mountains for this very purpose. He definitely appreciated this particular modern form of transportation, although he could never replace the power and the feel of true horsepower.

Hours after entering the snowy forested mountain and trying to make contact with The Orchids, he was greeted by a wisp. They were rare, especially here in this realm, but magic did exist here, mainly in concentrated areas throughout this world, though hidden usually in plain sight as the mortals refused to see it, to believe in it. In the form of a glowing ball of blue light, the wisp stopped right in front of him. Playing images like a movie before him, the wisp showed him what he needed to see. It showed him a map of Montana (which coincidentally he was already in) highlighting Highway 93 from Whitefish, ending in Missoula. Suddenly, the image changed to one of three friends—two females and one male—in a café. Two of them had magical energies pulsing from them signifying *other*, although purposefully suppressed by a glamour. But the other girl offered no energy of any kind, which was odd. Even humans gave off subtle vibrations of life energy. The scene transitioned to the one girl—the one offering no energy—walking into a restaurant called Antonia's. With that, the wisp vanished, leaving Daegan to find his way and the Sol-lumieth.

The closer he had gotten, the more he could feel his energy being pulled by the girl's two companions. After that, locating her was quite simple. He had followed her, watched her, learned her name—*Kaeleigh*. Daegan couldn't understand this girl and why she had been chosen. She was nothing like what he expected. What could *she* possibly do to alter the state of his realm? An air of mystery surrounded her; that he couldn't even pick up base-level energy from her was extremely unusual.

Why can't I read her? Is she hiding something? Or is something hiding her?

❊❊❊

Leaning against the tree at the edge of the parking lot in front of Antonia's restaurant, he waited for her. The truck was not the only thing he had picked up to blend in; he also used glamour—an elemental magic that most Faeries and Elves alike learned how to use—to hide his true appearance. Not a lot changed, but he did change his hair; not that he really needed to in this century, but he could so he did, from blackish-blue to simply black, and also shorter, especially on the sides. Being a Faerie, his ears weren't as pointed as the Elves, but what little point he did have rounded out. Clothing became more modern, with T-shirts and jeans that were not as flexible and comfortable as the soft materials he was used to that allowed for hunting and riding. Nevertheless, he liked the clothes, even though he could care less if he actually fit in; he just didn't want to stand out.

Noticing Kaeleigh as she came walking around the corner headed for her shift at the restaurant, he felt drawn and compelled to watch her. He watched as she ran across the street just as a car sped around the corner. Instinctively, he jumped up and away from where he was leaning against his Bronco. To what? To stop the car? To run over and save her? Not sure what to do, he stopped to quickly assess the situation. His heart was racing. Thankfully, the car missed her and kept driving as she kept walking toward the restaurant. Shocked at his own reaction, he took a step back, trying to gauge his own body's betrayal to years of training.

As if sensing he was there, Kaeleigh looked up sharply over to where he was. Stopping in place, she tilted her head a bit and scowled at him, as though she were trying to solve a puzzle. Daegan stood still, watching, waiting for her to make her next move.

The next thing he knew, Kaeleigh was marching up the hill of the parking lot and straight toward him. Daegan stood there with his arms casually folded over his chest, waiting for her to come all the way up to the tree. *Stupid move, girl. You don't even know who I am or what I could do to you.* When she reached him, she stood there with her hands on her hips and an expectant expression on her face. They stood there staring at each other, daring the other to speak first, for what seemed like several minutes. *Stubborn. Fine!* Just as he was going to say something she interrupted his thoughts.

"You came to Antonia's last night. What's the meaning of you showing up twice in as many days? Are you following me? Do I need to call the police? Who are you and what do you want?" Kaeleigh fired at him, a slight tremor growing in her voice question after question.

So maybe not as confident as you appear. Good girl. You should be afraid.

He stared at her. He saw a sorrow behind her eyes and he felt challenged. *What can I say to this girl to convince her of who she is and to come with me?*

Lowering his voice, he said, "Where I come from, you are very important." He paused, looking for the right words. "I've been sent here to find you."

"What? I have no idea what you are talking about. You must have the wrong person. You may be gorgeous, but you are strange and you're making no sense." She mumbled that last part more to herself. Taking a breath, she looked him straight in the eyes. "My friends told me to stay away from you," she said as she started to back away toward the restaurant. "I should have listened. I have to get to work now." Eyes still on his, she continued to back away.

He wasn't trying to scare her, and the awkwardness of the moment caused him to try and stop her. "Not sure I've ever been called gorgeous before," he forced out, his attempt to lighten the moment. "At least not by a human," he amended. Then he closed his eyes in frustration at what just came out of his mouth.

"Ooookay," Kaeleigh's eye darted around the parking lot. Not seeing anyone nearby, she pulled out her cell phone, clutching it tightly in one hand. "I gotta go," Kaeleigh said, quickly turning and speed-walking into Antonia's.

❋❋❋

After some time had passed and Daegan had watched a number of people going in and coming out of the restaurant, he walked in and requested one of Kaeleigh's tables.

Not only was she surprised and a bit annoyed that he was back, but she was also excited in a strange way. Something in her fluttered at the sight of him. Something about him drew her in and called to her. Like a green meadow bathed in warm sunlight drew a butterfly; his very presence intrigued her. But that, of course, was unacceptable.

"What are you doing in here?" she snapped with a whisper, making sure no one was paying attention to her confrontation.

He spoke, this time more direct, looking intensely at her. "I'm not here to frighten you." He paused, never taking his eyes away from hers. "I have things to show you. We must be able to—"

"You have to leave now!" she interrupted with a shout-whisper. "I am not spending any time with you. I am not going anywhere with you." Taking a deep breath, she continued her tirade. "I will put your mind at ease right now. I am NOT the one you are looking for. This table is for paying customers." She pointed her index finger in his face. "Now leave before the manager comes over and you get me in trouble."

Daegan, unaffected by her outrage, noticed something blue on the underside of her right wrist as she was pointing in his face. The blue coloring was mostly covered by a wide strappy piece of material trying to look like an accessory of some kind, probably a bracelet. Grabbing her wrist, none too gently, he turned it over in the blink of an eye. He pushed up her bracelet to get a better look at what appeared to be a tattoo, but he knew all too well what the strange bluish-green marking most likely was.

"Hey!" she shouted as she whipped her wrist around and tried to jerk her hand back without success. He was strong, really strong. Her heart rate accelerated with panic at being touched, especially by a stranger. "Let me go!" she growled. Her mind raced with the different maneuvers she had received from Chel's dad in their many self-defense lessons. Kaeleigh placed her foot in the exact spot she needed it to be in for her escape if the threat to her escalated.

"Stop struggling," he whispered through clenched teeth. "I am not going to hurt you." His demeanor was calm and sober, willing Kaeleigh's reaction to be the same. He breathed deeply and relaxed his shoulders. "What is this mark? How did you get it? *When* did you get it?"

Kaeleigh's eyes widened with not only fear, but with shock at his confrontation. She hadn't even shown her friends, especially Chel, her newly acquired mark. Feeling his grip loosen, she took advantage and quickly though calmly pulled her arm from his grasp to recover her wrist. He'd released her arm just as her manager stepped up behind her. "Is there a problem here, Kaeleigh?" he asked, staring fiercely at Daegan.

"Uh... um, no sir, I believe this customer was just leaving," she replied with stern yet pleading eyes trained directly at Daegan.

Daegan stood to leave. He looked at Kaeleigh, then at the manager, nodded his agreement, and left Antonia's with more questions than he had when he'd arrived.

Chapter Thirteen

T he manager studied Kaeleigh for a minute and then asked, "Are you all right? Who was that? An ex-boyfriend?"

"Yes, I'm all right, thank you, and no, I don't even know who he is except that he has tried to talk to me a couple times before."

"Well, take a break and call a friend to pick you up so you don't have to walk home alone after your shift."

"Thanks," she replied, shaking off the weirdness of what just happened as she went to call Finn.

Finn worked the day shift at the stockyards of the Montana Rail Link not far from where he lived, so he rode the local Mountain Line transit system when he could, but some days he could get there faster—minus all the stops—if he bicycled on his own. Finn wasn't a big guy naturally. He was fit, but more lithe than bulky. However, working at the train yard had added a little defined bulk to his muscles. Finn liked the mind-numbing manual labor of his job; it kept him physically engaged and in shape.

Today though at work, Finn was approaching his tasks with almost no focus. Frustrated, angry, almost helpless, he kept letting Kaeleigh's words about the stranger roll over and over again in his head. As if on cue, his cell phone rang. His hands, sweaty with fear, slid the thing open. Kaeleigh Johnson. He knew it was her, hence the anxiety. He always knew when it was her. He didn't even need to hear her pre-programmed *Star Trek* theme song play to know she was on the other line.

"What's wrong?" Finn answered quickly, more sharply than was usual for him. This situation had him on edge, uncertain what to do and helpless when it came to Kaeleigh's future.

"Why would you assume something is wrong because I called you?" Kaeleigh's voice sounded shaky on the other end.

"I assume that every time you call. Now did you just call to chat while we are both at work then?" he replied sarcastically. Kaeleigh just sighed, both hating and loving when he was overprotective. It irritated her even more, though, when he was not only sarcastic, but right. "No? So what's wrong?"

"That guy I told you about came back to the restaurant today, but don't worry, the manager made sure that he left," she rushed out. "I was just calling to see if you would walk home with me after work."

"Are you all right?" Finn started interrogating. "What did he want? Who was he?"

"Calm down. I'm fine. I gotta go, I'll give you details on the way home. You'll walk with me, won't you?"

"Of course I'll be there. And we *will* talk then," Finn said, grumbling with impatience.

He had feared this day might come. It must have had something to do with her eighteenth birthday. Coming of age. Finn had been warned that they would come looking for her. He swore he would protect her to the best of his abilities and he damn well planned on doing just that even if it cost him his life. She deserved no less and he deserved no more than death. Losing his life protecting her could be his redemption.

But who had come? What did they want with her? To take her back, no doubt, but why didn't he just take her? Finn thought not for the first time.

Finn worked distractedly for the rest of the day until the time came for Kaeleigh to get off work. He wasn't supposed to be off for another couple hours, but he left anyway. He had to make sure he was there before she got off; otherwise, he knew she would just leave on her own. Stubborn girl! She didn't like to ask for help, so the fact that she had made him feel all the more protective of her. For causing her fear, that guy would be sorry.

❦❦❦

Relieved to be off work, Kaeleigh rolled her shoulders and her neck, taking in a deep breath then letting it out nice and slow. She was grateful there were no other incidents, although she could have sworn there were some odd customers watching her very... closely. She took off her apron, grabbed her bag, and headed for the side door, hoping Finn would be waiting for her.

Leaning up against the building, his scowl in place, arms crossed, standing with one leg propped behind him, he was a sight of fierce intimidation. His watchful eyes scanned the nearby area for anything suspicious. She had thought, not for the first time, he would be ideal for a good James Dean remake. She was glad to be on his good side. He pushed off the building, coming up beside her.

"You okay? No other problems?" Gripping her shoulders gently, causing her to face him head on, he searched her eyes to ensure her truth.

"Yes, I'm good and no, there were no other problems," Kaeleigh replied with an exaggerated eye roll. "Thanks for walking me home," she added seriously. He nodded.

"I called in some backup too," he said as he looked behind her. Chel jumped up beside her from the shadows with a big smile and a hug.

"So the hottie's a stalker, huh?" she said as she looped her arm through Kaeleigh's, an endearing gesture that made Kaeleigh smile. Her friends cared about her.

Kaeleigh grabbed Finn's arm and held onto him just above the elbow. She told them of both her encounters with her nameless stalker as they walked home. For some reason, she wasn't ready to tell them the part about the mark on her wrist that he had discovered. She would definitely tell them, but she wanted to have a better idea what the marking could be first so they didn't think she was... what, crazy? *Too late.* She chuckled to herself. Her stalker seemed to recognize it, though, so maybe she could find some picture of it online—or perhaps he was the insane one. But his reaction didn't fit with someone that might be crazy. Instead, he was... intense.

When they got to the apartment, Finn and Chel walked her in and did a once-over in the apartment just to make sure she felt safe.

"We can stay the night if you want us to," Chel offered.

"No, really you guys, I'm fine. Thank you for walking me home and checking everything out though."

"It just doesn't make sense," Finn said under his breath as though talking to himself as he walked through the apartment for a second time, seeking something apparently invisible to the naked eye. "Why the weird questions? Why not take you?" He stopped searching the apartment and paced in front of the TV. "Of course I wouldn't let that happen, but something seems off." Finn suddenly stopped in his tracks. "Unless... *they* don't know."

Chel and Kaeleigh looked at each other then back at Finn, totally confused. "What are you talking about?" Kaeleigh asked, no longer concerned that she might be the one who sounded crazy.

"Never mind," he huffed. "You sure you're okay? I gotta go check something out." He pecked Kaeleigh on the cheek. He stopped in front of Chel. "Stay here with her. Do not leave her alone. I will be back soon." Without more than that, he headed out the door.

Kaeleigh and Chel looked at each other again, and then Kaeleigh said, "Okay, now I'm actually a little more weirded out by Finn than the freak stalking me."

"I know, right?" Chel nodded, putting her hands on her hips and looking out the window. She paused, took a slow look once again around the apartment, and even stuck her nose in the air like she was smelling something.

Well, that was odd. What the heck is going on with my friends?

"All right, you're being a little strange too," Kaeleigh said out loud. "What are you doing? Do you smell something? You guys are kinda starting to freak me out." Kaeleigh looked over the apartment too but didn't see anything out of the ordinary.

Chel stopped what she was doing and sheepishly looked back at Kaeleigh and shrugged her shoulders. "I thought maybe I smelled something, but now I'm not sure."

Kaeleigh frowned. She knew Chel had always had a keen sense of smell, but she'd never really made a show of it, until now.

Before she could say anything about it, Chel perked up as though nothing had happened and sauntered over to the couch. She flopped down, sprawling herself across the smaller of the couches. "What should we do?" Chel looked up at Kaeleigh who was sitting down on the other couch.

Kaeleigh grabbed a nature magazine she had sitting on the coffee table. "I don't care. I miss having you here, Chel. We never hang like this anymore."

"I know," Chel said biting her lip awkwardly. "We need some time soon." There was a pause pregnant with words unsaid. Kaeleigh watched her friend, uncomfortable with the nagging sense that something was going on with Chel.

"Is everything ok with you and Samuel? Do you still like living with him?" Kaeleigh pried.

Chel's response was carefree, "Oh you know, it's a bit of an adjustment living with a boy, but I think we're figuring it out," but her fidgeting fingers belied what her words had not.

"Well, you know the door is always open to you here if things don't work out," Kaeleigh left open.

"Thank you, but I'm happy where I am...at least for now." Chel winked and sat up, finished with the conversation. "I told my parents I would come by for a visit tonight. I wonder when Finn will be back," Chel trailed off as she looked at her watch.

"Oh, oh, yes, of course!" Kaeleigh got out, her thoughts flooded with warm feelings for her parents who'd been her parents too for so long. "You should go see your parents. I'm fine," Kaeleigh was upbeat as she gestured around her apartment. "You and Finn both checked my place. I'll lock the door, plus I'm tired from work so I'll probably crash early."

Chel looked at Kaeleigh skeptically, her mouth twitched with indecision. "Okay, only if you're sure though. Finn is going to kill me," she groaned to herself as she stood. "But promise me you'll call me if you need anything, and let's talk in the morning." She grabbed her bag off the couch and headed for the door.

"Thanks, I promise, but I'll be fine. Tell your parents I said hello. I miss them," Kaeleigh said as she waved then shut the door to lock it, leaning her forehead against the cool door as she did. Heading into her little kitchen to get something to drink, Kaeleigh opened the fridge. Unfortunately, not much was in there and definitely not anything she wanted right now. With a disappointed sigh, she settled on boring water from the sink, thinking about which show she should watch before bed.

As Kaeleigh walked out of the kitchen she looked up, and with a sharp intake of breath, dropped her glass of water. In a panic she started to run to the front door when she remembered she actually knew some fighting moves. Chel's dad had told her, "Brace your feet. Stare your opponent down, they are in your territory. Don't let them chase you and don't let them see your fear." *Oops, too late for that one.* Kaeleigh quickly did an about-face in order to face her stalker, who was now sitting, very casually, she noticed, on her couch. She was suddenly angry that he dared to violate her space, her safe home, her territory.

"What are YOU doing here and how the hell did you get in MY house?" Kaeleigh shouted. She pointed her finger in his face, then lowered it again when she saw how bad she was shaking. *Don't show fear, Kaeleigh! Find my phone. Where's my phone?* Panic was starting to well up in her chest. *Breathe.*

"I'm not going to hurt you, I promise," he said in a quiet, nonthreatening tone with his palms up in surrender. He seemed a little surprised by her reaction. "I can see that I have upset you greatly and would like to explain, if you would give me the chance."

"You break into my house and you're *surprised* that I'm upset? I'm calling the cops," she said as she patted her pockets looking for her cell phone, only to remember she left it on the coffee table right in front of the stalker sitting on the couch. *Nice.*

"I would not advise that," he said just as quietly and calmly as before as he nodded at her phone.

Kaeleigh, remembering that she still had her land line, bolted over to the phone next to the wall in the opposite direction of her couch. Quickly, she dialed 911. Nothing happened. She hung up and started over again, her fingers shaking. Dead air, no dial tone, nothing. "You cut my phone lines? You bastard!" She looked at him fiercely in the eyes and the stare-down began. "Who the hell are you? What did you do to my phone?" she asked, gritting her teeth but not breaking the eye contact. Chel's dad, Ray, had explained how important once you were in a stare-down with an opponent it was that you not be the first to look away and that you never did anything to show submission to the other party. Kaeleigh inhaled slowly. *All right, I can do that.*

Laughing and now a little cocky, the stalker stood up from the couch, also not breaking eye contact. "Don't play that game with me, foolish girl, you will lose."

Kaeleigh gasped as she saw flames jump in his eyes, and she looked away out of sheer terror. She found her resolve once more—barely—but decided to be a little more cautious, as she had no idea who or *what* she was dealing with. Hands on her hips in a show of false bravado, she asked, "What do you want from me?"

With a sigh, he dropped his cockiness and sat back down on the couch. "My name is Daegan. Like I said before, I was sent here to find someone and I was led to you. I'm certain you are the one that needs to come back with me. Honestly, I have probably just as many questions as you do but—"

"I don't have answers to anyone's questions," she interrupted loudly. She began to break down. "Where are you from? Who sent you? This is ridiculous! You have to be insane." Then her front to stay strong failed her. She began to cry. She felt helpless. "Please leave. Please," she begged softly through her tears.

Daegan leaned forward on the couch, looking directly into Kaeleigh's tear-filled eyes. "I will tell you what you ask and then I will leave," he said matter-of-factly. "I am from a realm called Alandria. I was sent here to find you by the Paladin, who are the rulers of Feraánmar, which is my home. It is believed that you are of critical importance to Alandria. I confess that I was looking for someone a little more... well, a little more," Daegan said thoughtfully, studying her as he spoke. "Like I said before, I have many questions about these things as well. I'm certain there are answers"—he paused—"for both of us. Perhaps beginning with your wrist. Please, may I examine it?" he asked, reaching out, surprised at how compelled he felt to see it.

"Absolutely not!" Kaeleigh said firmly as she cradled her wrist protectively against her chest. "You need to leave right now!" she growled.

Daegan stood up. "I said I will not hurt you," he said as he suddenly like a flash was far too close for her comfort. He grabbed her wrist, twisted it, and shoved up her bracelet in one quick move as she was disarmed by his swift appearance. She gasped but held utterly still, remembering his unrelenting grip from the restaurant. Kaeleigh watched him as he studied her new marking intently, his brow furrowed, his expression perplexed. Her chest rising and falling rapidly, her breathing almost out of control. Strangely, his mere examination brought an irrational fascination out of her, calming her fear.

"Do you know what it means?" Kaeleigh asked, trying to keep her voice steady. "I don't know how I got it."

He looked into her eyes as though searching for something but not finding it. "There's only one place you can get a marking like this. It is definitely familiar," he said, frustrated, "but it is not quite right." Then he rubbed his thumb across her mark and everything changed. A jolt of electricity skimmed her skin, making them both jump apart. Each, breathing hard, looking at the other, stunned.

"What the... what *was* that?" Kaeleigh jumped back even further, shaking out her hand then looking at her wrist to ensure it remained intact.

"I don't know," Daegan examined his own hand. "I have never experienced that before." He turned and headed for the front door. "I need to find out," he said as he walked briskly out the door.

"What? Wait!" Kaeleigh said, running after him down the stairs. "You break into *my* apartment 'looking for answers,' make me think I'm some kind of freak because of this mark, shock the hell out of me, then take off?" Out of breath, she stopped at the bottom of the stairs then lowered her voice. "I want some answers too, you know!" Despite him being a stranger, *stalker*, despite him breaking into her home and scaring the crap out of her, and despite her better judgment, a spark of hope stirred to life within her. This man before her might actually be the key to unlocking the information she had been searching for all her life.

"I will give you some when I have them." A cunning smile appeared on Daegan's face. "You could come with me right now, you know. Save me the effort of persuading you to accompany me at a later time."

He was leaving, Kaeleigh, why'd you give him a reason to come back! she chastised herself.

Still shaking, she turned and ran back up the stairs. She turned to make sure he hadn't followed her, but he was gone nowhere to be seen; she closed and locked her door. Kaeleigh looked around her lonely, empty apartment. *How did he get in?* she wondered then collapsed to the ground. Alone and scared, she looked at her wrist; her hands were shaking. She cried, wishing so bad that she could run to her family for comfort, only to be reminded she didn't have one. Of course, she could go to Chel's or even to Finn's, but Chel was with her parents so she grabbed her cell and dialed Finn. Several unanswered rings later, she gave up. Pulling herself together, she walked dejectedly to her room, curled in on herself under her covers, and cried herself to sleep.

Chapter Fourteen

C hel had decided to stay the night at her parents' house since she had been there late talking. Staying in her old room, the one she used to share with Kaeleigh before they both had moved out to be on their own, brought back a lot of memories. She was so agitated that her parents had kept secrets not only from Kaeleigh, but also from her. She'd tossed and turned in the bed of her youth. In her mind, Chel replayed the conversation she had earlier that night with her parents, staring at an old, worn leather journal on her nightstand that stared back at her, taunting her to embrace what lay hidden within its pages.

Kaeleigh had come to live with them when she was twelve after she had run away from her last foster home. Things had not been good at the home, and Kaeleigh had felt she could do better on her own. It had taken some time for Chel's parents to track her down. All Chel had known was that Kaeleigh, her best friend, had a lot of trouble at home and she had come to stay with them. Before this though, Chel's parents had been watching Kaeleigh from a distance via Chel, unbeknownst to her, as they went to school together. They didn't expect that Chel and Kaeleigh would actually become best friends. Her parents had had no idea that her living situation had become such a troubling and negative foster home environment. That was a regret that they had lived with and always would. As soon as they found her, they brought her home to live with them.

Chel and Kaeleigh had become even closer over the years, so close that Kaeleigh had confided in Chel about some of her "dark times" that had happened at some of the foster homes. Chel had become very protective of her friend and always watched out for her, even though she knew Kaeleigh was a strong, self-reliant person. It bothered her to no end—truthfully it hurt—that Kaeleigh hadn't trusted her with her secret visions. But then again Chel hadn't been exactly honest with Kaeleigh about her feelings when it came to her current living situation. Living with a boy, or maybe just Samuel, wasn't quite what she had envisioned. She missed living with Kaeleigh and likely had made a mistake, but admitting that just yet was a blow to her pride she wasn't ready to take.

Chel's natural inclination to protect those she was close to was strong, but she had a special connection with Kaeleigh; she was like a sister. So when this strange guy first came lurking around, she went to her parents for some advice. Chel was shocked at how strong her parents' reaction was; she knew they loved Kaeleigh like their own daughter, but she would have called this overkill.

"Do not let Kaeleigh out of yours and Finn's sight," they had practically commanded her. They insisted she and Finn be glued to Kaeleigh's side until they could find more out about this guy: what he looked like, if he gave his name, what he wanted, how long he hung around, etc.

Okay, whatever! Chill, parentals, I'll keep an eye on her like I always do, she had thought to herself when they jumped all over her. But she hadn't taken the threat seriously. The girls weren't, nor had they ever been, unsafe or made irresponsible choices. They knew how to defend themselves thanks to her dad, Ray.

Then they took the conversation to a new level, and her parents started hounding her: How was she feeling? Was she feeling stressed by all this? Anything she wanted to talk about regarding her body?

What the hell, Mom and Dad? I'm feeling stressed by this inquisition now, thanks to you! Chel shuddered, weirded out by her parents' strange questions and feeling irritated all over again. She had come looking for advice, but WHOA!

Despite her irritation at her parents, when "stalker guy" came around again, she decided her parents needed to be brought in the loop. Clearly something weird was up. She could *feel* it. Looking back on their first conversation, Chel realized that her parents knew something they weren't telling her. She had thought that maybe he was somebody from Kaeleigh's past in the foster system that was looking for her, for what, who knew? *That could happen, right?* Chel remembered hearing a story about some boys at school that were harassing Kaeleigh, and she had put them in their place... by kneeing them in *their* "places." So maybe

Kaeleigh had taught some boys a lesson. What she learned from her parents last night though was quite a different tale of Kaeleigh's past that involved much more than just Kaeleigh.

The tall tale was unfathomable, so far-fetched she couldn't even believe it; she *wouldn't* believe it. Chel was outraged that her parents would make something up like that, especially now when she had come to them for answers. They had started to tell her a story about coming from another realm called Alandria. *A different REALM? Seriously? I know I'm out there sometimes, but COME ON!* Her dad had pulled out a dusty old book, barely held together by the leather stitching binding it. Ray blew the dust off and cradled the book close to his chest as if it had personal value to him. Calmly and slowly, he opened the leather tome, ancient secrets written by hand revealed from the pages within stained with personal memories and histories. Her father's eyes trained on the pages as he sought something specific, his expression reverent, even longing what he beheld. Chel's mother sat beside him, looking over his arm. She beckoned Chel to his other side. Baffled by her parents' actions, Chel sat purely curious.

Ray unfolded several times over a delicate piece of parchment. Chel watched as a map aged, tattered with the exposure of time, was laid bare before her eyes. On it, in a beautiful script, was the word Alandria.

"This is my family's journal...your family's journal filled with our history," her father started. "This is where we are from," he said solemnly. "This is where Kaeleigh is from." He paused, waiting for Chel to react. When she didn't, he continued slowly. "We are from a unique race of beings called Shifters; protectors and guardians of all we hold sacred."

"We were close to Kaeleigh's parents once, long ago..." her mother added, trailing off at the end, emotion shining in her eyes.

Stunned into silence, Chel listened numbingly to her parents as they talked about how they had made an agreement to come to this realm—the mortal realm as they called Earth—to watch over Kaeleigh and to intervene only if necessary. They had gone on to talk about different kingdoms, territories, and races of beings such as Faeries and Elves even pointing out on the map where they called home. Chel had pretty much started to tune them out when they began trying to tell her more of the race they belonged to... that she was supposed to belong to.

She didn't believe them...she couldn't. At least, she hadn't believed their story until her dad did something that shook her to her very core. Chel had run out of the house. She had to get out. Had to breathe fresh air. Her heart was racing so fast, she thought it might explode. Where she was going, she didn't even realize until she reached the riverbank. Chel subconsciously found the grassy spot under a big tree where she liked to go to think. Her body instinctively slumped to the ground. She replayed everything her parents had told her. Chel hadn't believed any of it, not even when he pulled out the journal and showed her the map, not until... he changed.

Her dad, had changed into something else... an animal.

❊❊❊

Finn went to the spot he was told to go to if he ever needed help. He shouldn't have left Kaeleigh, knowing that she was being watched, that she had even been approached, but he had to make contact, and besides, Chel was with her. Finn hadn't been there in years and didn't even know if it would still work; if they would still come. A sudden downpour of rain had begun as soon as he had passed the boundary of the woods. After an hour of waiting under a short tree that kept dripping water on him, he got up and began pacing. It had happened like that last time too. The rain, he figured, must be to ward off any passersby from seeing or overhearing anything.

Suddenly, there was movement in the trees in front of him and he saw someone other than who he expected. Two figures moved far enough out that he could see them. Then they waited expectantly for him to approach them, so he did.

"It has been a long time. Am I to speak with you?" Finn asked reluctantly. They both nodded at him in silence. He had forgotten how childlike these creatures were in appearance and also in mind. They were extremely simple. Similar to a dwarf in height, but angelic looking in nature, with the eyes so blue they practically glowed. This race had not chosen a side in the last great battle and were therefore neutral, often providing services as messengers.

"I need a message sent," he said. Then he adjusted his wording, remembering to keep it short so these creatures could remember it, "Time is up. *They* have come. How to proceed if she goes? Who has been sent?" He looked at them to make sure they got the message and to whom it be delivered. He dared not say a name out loud, but he knew they telepathically read it in his mind. They nodded again. He gave a slight respectful bow of thanks and they backed into the forest the way they had come. Finn settled back under the tree to wait for a reply. In the past, he had received his responses within a few hours, but not this night. He sat there all night in the cold waiting for an answer, but none came. *Perhaps those incompetent creatures got it wrong.* Frustrated, he went home. Apparently, he was on his own.

Chapter Fifteen

Kaeleigh had jolted awake from another one of the flashes that seemed to have merged with her dreams. This one left her feeling empty and heartbroken, as though a piece of her had been ripped out. She was homesick for a family she never even knew. Randomly, her thoughts turned to her stalker-turned-intruder and wondered for the millionth time what had happened last night and the previous times meeting him. Did it mean something?

Or maybe he was just a crazy psycho stalker that should be locked up?

The more she thought about him and the strange and unbelievable things he had said to her, she found herself oddly curious. One thing was for sure, though, she was getting an additional lock put on her apartment door today. Whether he was a good guy or not, she still had no idea how he got into her place, and she didn't want it to happen again.

Kaeleigh had time to spare before her shift at work that night and wanted to see Chel. Annoyed with Finn for not answering her call the night before, she just wanted some "girl time." Chel agreed to meet Kaeleigh at The Station for a quick coffee, but to Kaeleigh's ears she sounded distant and distracted. *I hope she didn't have another fight with her parents.* Kaeleigh was suddenly concerned for her friend.

Chel tended to fly off the handle with her parents, but things always got patched up. As far as parents went, Chel's were pretty great. After all, they had taken Kaeleigh in when she needed it and they had always been there for her. They were like family, the closest she had to parents anyway, but still they weren't really hers. Kaeleigh had always had this feeling that they knew more about her life, her past, than they let on, but she just left it alone. She didn't want to seem ungrateful for all they had done for her.

Kaeleigh arrived at The Station early. She took a moment, absorbing the calm energy within the atmosphere of the café, and taking in a deep breath luxuriating in the floral aromas from The Flower Depot. Instantly, she was refreshed and approached the counter to order. To Kaeleigh's constant surprise, creative-artistic-Chel always ordered the same thing so Kaeleigh took the liberty of ordering both their drinks. *Guess we all need something stable.*

Chel walked in, searching frantically with her eyes for Kaeleigh until they locked in on her over in a different booth from where they usually sat. Kaeleigh waved her over, suddenly concerned at the odd expression on Chel's face.

"Our booth was taken," Kaeleigh said with a shrug when Chel's raised eyebrow questioned the one she was sliding into. "What's wrong? You look like you've seen a ghost." Kaeleigh frowned as she realized Chel was much paler than normal.

Chel sat down, tried to take off her scarf that she always wore when the weather turned chilly, but ended up getting frustrated as she just kept tying it haphazardly around her neck more until she just gave up with a huff.

"Calm down, you're shaking. Tell me what's going on. You're starting to freak me out."

Chel immediately folded her hands to still them. She took a deep breath and looked Kaeleigh in the eyes and said, "I can't tell you."

"What?! You come in here looking like somebody just died. You're shaking and you're not going to tell me, Chel? Bullshit!" Kaeleigh said, totally freaking out now.

"Wait, just wait a minute. Everyone is all right. I don't even know how to tell you any of this, there's no way you'll believe it; *I'm* still trying to believe it," Chel said, scattered. Then she realized how frustrating this must sound when she saw the look of impatience on Kaeleigh's face. "Okay, I need you to trust me and let me *try* to explain." She looked Kaeleigh in the eyes and waited for her to nod her consent.

"So, I went to my parents' house last night, right?" She didn't wait for Kaeleigh's response. "Oh my gosh, so then I told them about your stalker guy. They seemed way too overly worried about him hanging around," Chel sucked in a deep breath, "and then BOOM!" She gestured big with her hands. "It hits me: they're hiding something." Chel glanced furtively at Kaeleigh.

"Go on, Chel," Kaeleigh encouraged, leaning forward as to not miss anything Chel was about to say.

Nodding, Chel took a deep breath. "Remember, they love you and thought they were doing the right thing by both of us. Even though I'm still trying to believe that one myself—side note, sorry, I'll explain.

"Oh my god, I'm so not going to be able to explain this right." Chel looked around The Station, anywhere but at Kaeleigh, shame coloring her face, switching quickly to confusion and then even to anger. Chel straightened her spine then looked directly at Kaeleigh attempting to get her words just right. When nothing came out, she started to get antsy, fidgeting in her seat.

Concern all over Kaeleigh's face, even reaching out her hand toward Chel for comfort. "Chel, what's going on? You're scaring me."

Resigning that she wouldn't be able to get her thoughts straight, Chel finally just blurted out, "So, apparently my family isn't normal and they came to live here to watch out for you because, oh by the way, you're not entirely normal either. Your stalker guy—he isn't normal either. And when I say 'not entirely normal,' yeah, I mean not entirely *human*!" Not even pausing for reaction, she finished, "And he's been sent here to find you and take you back with him but we're not sure *who* sent him yet. Why? I don't know, but we won't let him take you!" Burying her face in her hands, Chel took a shaky breath. "Oh, this sounds like a cruel joke, and I know this doesn't make any sense, but it's unbelievably true, although I can't tell you how I know that yet. You have no idea how sorry I am." She closed her eyes and swallowed a lump in her throat. "I should have known something. I would've helped prepare you..."

"For what?" Kaeleigh interrupted, but to deaf ears, Chel lost in her own thoughts and ramblings obviously still processing her own secrets.

"I'm drowning," Chel choked on a sob. "This is too much right now..."

And with that, Chel jumped up and ran toward the exit, not knowing how to tell her best friend in the world any more than she already had.

"Chel, wait!" Kaeleigh shouted after her, weighed down, her feet lead encumbrances she remained in her seat.

Kaeleigh sat in her spot in the booth unmoving, staring, thinking. Dumbfounded, Kaeleigh didn't know whether to laugh at the absurdity of it all or cry at the terror of the truth she felt in Chel's words. *Drowning*, that was the word Chel had used—that was exactly how Kaeleigh felt—like someone dumped a tank of water over her head without asking. Unprepared, shivering internally from shock, she worried her necklace between her fingers seeking comfort. She felt betrayed. *How could Chel just dump something like that on me then bolt?*

But then Kaeleigh thought about the kind of friend that Chel was and the people her parents were; they would never mean to hurt her. She didn't know what, but there had to be some kind of truth to what Chel had said, *But WTF!* Something at the back of Kaeleigh's mind told her not to disregard what was said no matter how far-fetched it sounded.

Kaeleigh felt a hodgepodge of emotions—hurt, betrayed, confused, full of doubt... She felt like she was floating on a cloud flitting from one reality to the next. *What's real? What's going on? AND what the hell did Chel mean by "not entirely human"?*

Kaeleigh frowned and clenched her fists on top of the table. Memories of a disconnected past, orphanages and foster homes, separated and lost from family or friends for so long, streamed through her mind. All to find out now, sixteen years later, people out there—people she trusted even—knew who she was, knew at least something of her past, maybe even knew her family if she had one...and they kept it from her, possibly even kept them from her.

How could they betray me this way? After all that I have been through, no one thought it prudent to perhaps tell me, "Oh by the way, we know things about your past that might help you understand all of this," but no. No one did. I'm going to be sick.

She got up and ran out of The Station, heading down the street. She kept running until she ended up near the river. She knew that Chel liked to go there to think so maybe she would too. Kaeleigh didn't have much to go on, but she reflected on all that had been happening lately. Chel had a secret that affected her, but she, herself had been keeping secrets so she could extend Chel understanding. Since her youth, Kaeleigh had had visions, but they had gotten stronger. Finn was hiding something too, but she trusted him as he had been her protector and friend. The surprise stalker, Daegan, was the key to something...she just wasn't sure what yet. And the orchids...they had been a constant companion, but why? All the new things had begun around the time she turned eighteen. *All these things have to be related, pieces to a puzzle that I am involved with, but how they fit together I cannot fathom.*

Exhausted and drained, unable to mull over fragmented information any longer, Kaeleigh headed to work. Her only conclusion was she and her friends had individual, but coinciding, secrets and revelations; but instead of honesty and helping each other, they were pulling away, and now they had a stalker to deal with. At least at work she could be distracted. Only the distraction she found was not what she had in mind.

Chapter Sixteen

Kaeleigh had made it through her first few hours at work without losing her mind and was even capable of friendly conversations with some of the restaurant patrons and the waitstaff. On her break, she stepped out the side door to get some fresh air. Usually there were a couple of others taking a smoke break out there but tonight stood only one—a girl about the same age as Kaeleigh who'd been working there a couple months longer than she had. Her name was Melanie, Kaeleigh remembered; she pretty much kept to herself. Kaeleigh said hello. Melanie simply nodded at her, then focused on the cigarette. The door opened behind her, shining more light on the side street that they were facing. Melanie looked up, stiffened, and glared at whoever was behind Kaeleigh. She put out her cigarette and stormed back inside, slamming the door and taking the light from inside with her. Without even turning, sweat broke out on the back of Kaeleigh's neck, eliciting chills down her arms, drawing the hairs erect. She turned to see her manager, Mr. Delacroix, blocking the doorway sympathy mimicked on his round, pockmarked face, what she saw in his beady eyes struck panic in her guts.

"How are you, Kaeleigh?" he asked lighting his own cigarette, taking a puff. "Any more issues with that guy that was giving you trouble yesterday?" he asked, moving in closer, a predator hunting its prey. Like a viper, he shot his arm around her, gripping her shoulders before she had a chance to move away. Kaeleigh stiffened. Her skin started to crawl. She did not like to be touched. Not only was he invading her space that she had not invited him into, but the level of body odor emitting from him gagged her.

"Mr. Delacroix, I'm fine." Kaeleigh struggled to pull away, but his grip was unrelenting. "Please remove your arm and don't touch me again," Kaeleigh said emboldened, not really caring if her job was now on the fence. *Slime ball! Had he treated Melanie like this?*

The manager responded by pulling her in closer and tighter, pressing her chest up against his body. "You're a good worker, Kaeleigh," he paused, his gaze traveling from her eyes to her cleavage now amply displayed; even with limited amount, his eyes lit with want. "I would hate to see you lose your job because you were too upset that you couldn't concentrate." He took another puff of his cigarette, leaned in closer and exhaled right in front of her face as he perused her goods once more. "I want to be here for you. I would protect you. I could make you happy," his voice gritty and thick with lust.

Kaeleigh's arms trapped at her sides the more he pulled her into himself. His hand holding his cigarette between fingers, traced the collar of her shirt. Panic choked her. Claustrophobia seized Kaeleigh, she went pale. The more she struggled, the tighter he held on. Mr. Delacroix pulled her around flush with the front of his body for a hug that she would NOT be reciprocating. He bent down and leaned in close as he stroked her hair, "I like you, Kaeleigh," he whispered in her ear, his tobacco-ridden breath hot on her neck. "I want to keep you safe and all *mine.*" His fingers tangled in the ends of her hair. "You be good to me and I'll be good to you," he practically crooned to her. "It's a partnership to benefit us both. You understand, don't you?" The fingers in her hair crept with disgusting slowness down her spine.

Kaeleigh thought she might be sick. *Is he possessed?*

But before his hands reached their destination, a mental switch flipped inside Kaeleigh. Outraged, an energy stirred within her core, giving her courage and strength. Kaeleigh had never been an "easy target" and she wasn't one now. Kaeleigh was a fighter; it resonated at the depths of who she was. Kaeleigh grabbed hold of his arms like she was going to give in to his insanity.

Satisfied, he loosened his grip just a little. "That's a good girl, I knew you could play fun," his breath was rank as it fell onto her face.

She looked up at him with innocent eyes and a flirtatious smile. "How dare you! You f-ing pig." She kneed him hard and escaped his proximity. He doubled over, collapsing to the ground gasping and grabbing himself; his face turning green from the pain. She bent over him and whispered into his ear, "That's me being good to you."

He shouted at her with what little breath he could muster, "Don't bother coming back to work, you're fired!" Kaeleigh was already at the mouth of the alley leading to the main road.

What an idiot. Kaeleigh shifted left, not wanting him to see her shaking, and yelled, "Did you miss my resignation, because I can come back to deliver it more formally if you'd like." He quickly cowered in on himself again and she turned the corner, only slightly satisfied.

She couldn't believe what a dirty rotten scumbag her boss was and wondered how many of the girls she worked with he had accosted and maybe even succeeded at raping them. Kaeleigh wouldn't put up with that and she wasn't afraid of defending herself. She was shaking so hard as the realization of what had just happened—what *could've* happened—hit her, that she didn't see him coming around the corner until she bumped smack into him.

"Hey!" Kaeleigh exclaimed and quickly jumped back, not realizing yet who was in front of her. Daegan. He stood there, intimidating and emotionless, as he looked her over, yet asked her with sincerity and concern, "Are you hurt?"

She shook her head, not sure yet what he wanted, but unable to hide the wetness that shone in her eyes. Her stomach fluttered, she held a hand to her abdomen and took a moment to breathe and hope she didn't puke on him. *Oh my God! Now what?* "What are you doing here? Is this gang up on Kaeleigh night and someone forgot to tell me?" she asked sarcastically.

"I was waiting for you to get off work so we could talk further." Daegan stepped toward her with unusual hesitation, concern and a flicker of fear in his eyes, but then he stopped. Kaeleigh took a step back and breathed shakily out her mouth, on the edge of complete breakdown as she refused to meet his eyes.

Daegan's eyes struck the air between them, his hand clearly on the hilt of a well-used dagger of some variety. His anger, a now palpable entity, rose as he took in her fragile state. "I felt your distress," his eyes much-too-strongly focused on her face. "I then also felt your strength so I restrained myself. You were quite capable," he said with a trace of pride. "Are you well?" A virulent wisp of energy zipped between them as she finally looked to him.

Kaeleigh looked at him, trying to understand what he was saying. Horrified that Daegan watched the entire encounter, Kaeleigh felt both shame and hatred. Shame that she'd almost been a victim of this filth of a man. Hatred that men were so wicked.

Daegan's thoughts tracked hers to the thought. His fists were still tightly balled, though his face had relaxed momentarily.

How had he felt my distress?

"Finish him off? Uh, no," Kaeleigh stammered. "That's not necessary, although deserved," she replied. "Thank you, I believe you would have helped me." From behind them, a low moan perforated the momentary calm of the night.

Daegan's head darted toward the alley beyond her. He examined her stability then looked back into the alley, his nostrils flaring and his eyes lit again with flame. "The scum needs finishing off. I can smell the bastard's breath," Daegan sneered, his whisper lethal, though not directed at her. "Stay here." He stalked into the darkness of the alley, drawing the blade that had caught her eye.

*This can't be good. I'm alone, he's rummaging through the alley...*and almost as quickly, she felt herself start to stumble. Daegan. His arms underneath hers, his breath much too close. "You're shaking...let's get you on your feet." He jostled her slightly, trying to get a better grip. "May I assist you home? I vow no harm will come to you. Or if you are more comfortable, please call one of your friends and I will wait with you until they come for you," he added gently.

The gentleness in his voice paralyzed her for a moment. What Kaeleigh saw, almost as if through another's eyes, were eyes that could be trusted, eyes that had her best at heart, eyes full of peace and tranquility.

"What did you do to him?" she squeaked out, not entirely sure she wanted to know but also secretly happy that the pervert got what he deserved.

Daegan snuck a peek her way with a slight smirk. "You really want to know?"

Kaeleigh looked him in the eyes, then nodded resolutely.

"I simply impressed upon him that he would never again be doing something like that and that perhaps he should resign and turn himself in to the local authorities," Daegan stated.

"And why would he just turn himself in?"

"Let's just say I am strongly persuasive when I want to be." He sneered with the same hint of danger she had seen in him before. Satisfied, she left it at that.

The two continued noiselessly through the streets, Kaeleigh's legs still shaking. No matter what she did, she couldn't push the peace she felt when she looked into Daegan's eyes through the rest of her body. After tripping a few times, she felt his strength again. Daegan grabbed her elbow and steadied her, but only until she was balanced again and promptly let go. The second time she stumbled, however, he grabbed her elbow like before but did not let go. Reluctantly, she didn't pull away, realizing that she actually needed, actually wanted his help. He kept her steady the rest of the way to her home. Kaeleigh longed for the moment to continue, the moment of safety being held up by a strength she couldn't place, yet somehow recognized. Then breaking the awkward silence, and with the tiniest bit of levity she pried, "So, any revelations about my shocking new tattoo?"

"Ah, you think this is humorous," he said, more to himself than to her. "To answer your question, no." They walked quietly for another block. Then Daegan stopped gently, turning her toward himself. "There is deep strength in you, Kaeleigh. An almost reckless courage," Daegan said, again looking so deep into her eyes that she felt she was standing in front of a stranger, naked for all to see.

She didn't like feeling examined and on display. Especially when she could feel the heat from his body radiating off of him. Yet she yearned to be wrapped up in that heat, to be enveloped by this strength. *I must still be suffering the effects of shock, because what the hell!*

Instinctively, Kaeleigh jerked her arm away from his reach, feeling the heat dissipate as they fell apart. Chel's dad had instilled the "predator principle" in her: Don't ever back down in front of a predator. Move to the side. Give yourself space. Daegan watched her. Feeling her strength return, Kaeleigh started walking again. She didn't say anything, didn't look behind her to see if he was still there, or if he was following her—she knew he was. Not sure how, but she could sort of *feel* him, *feel* his presence. Their paths entwining closer together. This should have creeped her out but instead it gave her an odd sense of comfort knowing he was there. He wasn't going to hurt her, this she was sure. Maybe this stranger was even there to protect her. From what, she couldn't even imagine.

When she arrived at her apartment building, she stopped before going up the stairs to turn and thank Daegan, but instead she asked the question that had been on her mind since last night.

"What happened when you touched my wrist last night?"

He didn't say anything.

"I know you know *things*. You know about me." *You know me. How does he know me?* She sat on the steps leading up to her apartment and looked down at her wrist as if she could see through the stack of bracelets that covered it. Daegan's eyes followed hers from her wrist back to her own eyes, almost tortured with an internal struggle as he stared at her then at her wrist. Silent rather than peppering him with the many questions filling her mind, Kaeleigh watched as Daegan came to a decision. His body shifted from stiff and controlled like a soldier to relaxed and steady as he let his shoulders down and rested his thumbs through the belt loops of his dark jeans. For the first time, Kaeleigh, rather than seeing a stalker, saw a guy who looked about her age.

He was slightly taller than average and built like an athlete, toned and muscular. His T-shirt under his opened jacket was stretched tight in all the right places revealing muscular ridges. Hair—shorter all around and slightly longer and mussed at the top—the inkiest black she had ever seen. His eyes were like deep vats of chocolate mixed with flecks of spicy jalapeño. Daegan was definitely good looking but less like a model and more *other*. Fighter even... *warrior*, the scar peeking out of his neck collar possibly confirming her thoughts.

Then Daegan cleared his throat, bringing her eyes back to his, which in turn generated a new heat that ran up her neck into her face. Kaeleigh was embarrassed at her unabashed examination of the man. Without commenting on her flushing, he began slowly. "The marking on your wrist is similar to other markings I have seen called *srontas*, which relate to cultural backgrounds; however, I have never seen that particular one before—it's different," he said with a frown. "I don't know what yours means, perhaps it is a mistake." *But it can't be a mistake.* Daegan spoke more to himself than to Kaeleigh.

"Okay..." Kaeleigh began, "So, how did *I* get one of these... snortas marks?"

"*Srontas*," he corrected her, a twinkle in his eyes. Then serious again, "I don't know." He struggled to hide his frustration, but ran his fingers through his hair. Frustrated perhaps that he didn't know, perhaps at the situation, perhaps at her. She couldn't tell which.

Kaeleigh determined to have some answers, pried more. "Well, what happened when you touched mine? Something happened, I felt it. I can't describe it, but it felt strange—electric almost—and now I seem to be oddly aware of you... I mean it's like I know when you're around me."

"You think of me?" Daegan asked.

"Whoa, well, not like *that*," Kaeleigh backpedalled, the stain still on her cheeks darkened.

"Not like what?" Suddenly serious and confused, Daegan furrowed his brow, the thought of what she inferred never had crossed his mind. She was *human*...or was she?

"Just forget it, please," Kaeleigh looked up and down her street, anywhere but at Daegan.

"All right," he replied simply as if it was already forgotten.
Curious.

Before she could blurt out something to distract from the awkward silence of the moment, he started pacing, raking his fingers through his hair again... clearly uncomfortable.

"When I touched you... I've never had that happen before. I have never *heard* of that happening before. I attempted to find out, but my contact was unavailable." He looked her in the eye. "The only thing I can offer is that my touching your mark somehow activated a piece of who you are..." He drifted off, apparently thinking out loud to himself. "In other words, there is something in you that is responding to the energy in me." He was silent for a moment, then quite abruptly said, "Kaeleigh, I need to take you back with me, to my realm. No harm will come to you while under my protection. I give you my word."

Kaeleigh stood up, wiped off the back of her jeans, and calmly looked him straight in the eye. There was a part of her that leapt at the idea finding answers. She truly believed he would not hurt her, but still he was talking about being from another realm. "I don't know you or this place you say you're from," she said. "Could you show me on a map? Would my friends know where I was?" Kaeleigh ran her hands down her face. "Ugh, this is crazy. It's been a long and rough night. I need some time. I'm sorry, but I can't go anywhere with you," she said softly then started up the stairs. As much as she wanted to go in her heart, she was wary, the unknown still more fearful than the satisfaction of getting answers. Half-way up, she turned back around and said with meaning, "Thank you for walking me home."

He nodded and turned to tell her one last thing before he left, "It will take trust on your part. While you remain here, for your safety, you must stay close to your guardian and take his advice. Goodbye for now, Kaeleigh." He smiled a sincerely handsome smile that made her heart do a little flip, and then he walked away.

Confused, Kaeleigh ran back down the several stairs she had climbed to ask who he thought her "guardian" was, stopping at the street corner. She was about to open her mouth when she saw Daegan disappear... *DISAPPEAR?* And not just disappear as in "losing sight of him as he walked off into the darkness of night," but as in "poof, gone." *WTF?* She blinked several times, shook her head, and headed back up the stairs and into the safety of her apartment. *Great! As if the weird flashes and the cryptic messages from the good-looking stranger weren't crazy enough, he now had disappeared! He actually disappeared!! My friends are going to love this—if they don't kill me, that is.*

Her thoughts were such a blur she didn't even remember the climb up to her apartment. When she reached her front door, she paused, looked around, took a deep breath, then reached down to pick up the beautiful single-stemmed orchid that was lying across her doormat. Tears began to run down her face.

Kaeleigh stood at her front door cradling the delicate and beautiful flower, crying tears of frustration, fear, confusion, and even loneliness. Hearing footsteps, Kaeleigh turned to see Finn walking up the stairs.

"What's wrong?" he asked, concern mapped all over his face, and breathing hard as he sprinted up the remaining steps.

"THIS!" She strained her voice so he could hear through her tears as she showed him the orchid. *And a lot more,* she amended internally.

Finn looked at the flower and then into her eyes. "Let's go inside," he said calmly as he escorted her into her apartment. After sitting her down on her couch, he went into her little kitchen to make her some tea. He came back to where he left her and handed her the steaming cup of tea.

"Mmmm, smells good." Kaeleigh inhaled deeply, letting the soothing aroma calm her frayed emotions. "It's not your usual recipe."

"It's just chamomile with a touch of vanilla," then looking intently at her, "What's wrong? Did you see *him* again?" Kaeleigh nodded as she pulled herself together to tell Finn what happened at the restaurant, but he interrupted with his own outburst.

"What did he do to you? You're not going anywhere alone again!" Finn burst out in anger as he paced back and forth across Kaeleigh's living room, which was not that spacious to begin with. He looked wild and ferocious and reminded Kaeleigh of a caged cat. He was actually starting to make her nervous, which in turn angered her more.

Kaeleigh stood up and marched into the kitchen. "Where are you going?" Finn asked, paranoid.

Kaeleigh turned around and looked at him. "You didn't even listen to me! Get a grip, Finn. I appreciate your concern but I might feel safer with you if you actually paid attention to me and listened to what I say. I think Daegan listened to me better, and he's a total stranger. What is going on with you, Finn?"

Finn looked at Kaeleigh with one eyebrow raised and steam practically coming out of his nostrils. "Daegan?"

"The stalker guy," she started. "You know, Daegan. Yeah, so if you had let me tell you about it, that my boss tried to seduce me..." She took a drink of tea and gulped loudly, "dominate, probably rape me...if you had let me tell you, then I would have told you how Daegan came to my rescue and handed out his form of justice—even though I had already dealt with the boss-man—and how he walked me home to make sure I was okay. He was decent, and genuinely offered to protect me."

Again, Finn looked at her, but this time his features were softer and his shoulders that were set and indignant now lowered in defeat. He sighed, dropped his eyes, and dropped next to her on the couch putting his arm around her. "Oh god, Kae, are you all right?" he asked truly concerned.

Kaeleigh nodded, "I was so scared, Finn."

He drew closer and warmly gripped her shoulders. "I'm sorry. I'm sorry I wasn't there for you. I'm sorry I didn't listen." He kissed her temple.

"Why are you so angry about Daegan and, well, everything lately?" Kaeleigh asked as she wiped dried tear tracks off her face.

Finn sighed deeply and gazed openly at her, tucking a loose curl behind her ear, "I'm not angry at you, Kaeleigh, know that... never at you. I'm angry at myself, at the situation, at the unknown and how I'm supposed to move forward with it all, but never at you." He paused and turned away from her toward the window. "There's a lot going on that I wasn't prepared for, that I didn't prepare you for..." he stood up and walked to the slider door window, staring absently out into the darkness of night, "I got comfortable in our life here, I didn't want it to change, I didn't think this day would come so soon," he muttered quietly, but she heard.

"You know something, Finn. Why won't you tell me? Prepare me now," Kaeleigh pleaded, sitting on the edge of her seat, expectation in her eyes.

"I don't know enough. I don't know who this guy is and what he wants. He's here for a reason, but I don't know which side he is on," he rambled more to himself. Finn turned abruptly in Kaeleigh's direction, "I don't want you around this Daegan, though. Even if he seems like a decent guy."

Kaeleigh gulped, fidgeting with a loose string on the couch. "It's not like I plan on hanging out with him, Finn. I don't even know him. Plus, he's not all there," she said as she tapped her finger to her head. "Remember, he thinks I'm 'the one' or something and wants to take me back to where he's from, Alandria—wherever that is... probably outer space," Kaeleigh said as she rolled her eyes and shrugged. But something about what she was saying began stirring a longing buried deep within her. She looked at Finn, who now looked like he had seen a ghost. "Finn?"

Finn dropped his hands, backed up to the couch and sat down. "He wants to take you back? You didn't tell me that part. He can't... You can't... You can't go anywhere with him, it's not safe," Finn said, now rambling, lost in his own thoughts. "We have to leave! We should go on vacation. You aren't going back to that job anyway after what happened, right? Let's get Chel and go on a trip to... well, I don't know where yet but it doesn't matter." Finn was once again pacing and now rubbing his hands together over and over, mentally forming some kind of plan.

Kaeleigh moved to stand against the wall to the kitchen with her arms folded over her chest, watching Finn in bewilderment having what seemed to be some kind of breakdown. "Finn?" He didn't look at her but kept pacing, "FINN!" Kaeleigh now shouted at him, which shocked him out of his little tirade. "What are you talking about? You're acting crazy. God, you and Chel both are acting crazy, and I am not going anywhere. End of story."

Chapter Seventeen

Exhile. The Realm of the Unforgiven Dead

"A gate has been opened," a monotone voice in the dimly lit cavern spoke.

Hope flared. Cley-una concentrated her magic—what was left of it—with all her strength. She, as well as several others among her with similar powers, was desperately trying to connect, to communicate with others outside their cave. She could have accomplished it effortlessly when her soul had been free, but in Exhile their powers were muted. It took their collective energy to push enough magic through to force what little connection they were making. Cley-una, being the Ferrishyn that she was, felt she should have had a greater ability to connect, but unfortunately she had been fighting to get through a clear message with no sustained success.

"I can't get through." Frustrated, Cley-una collapsed the connection she had been maintaining until then. "He is so closed off and guarded. It makes it even harder to break through. Although it is not him alone, there is an outside force that has a connection rooted within him." She sighed sadly. "I am only able to get through to the girl with images and feelings. If she is vulnerable, she will connect with my words, but it's harder in the mortal realm and even then I could only make contact with Eva's added help."

A tall Ferrishyn warrior stepped up behind Cley-una and put his hands on her shoulders, looking at her with deep love and confidence. "Arileas explained to Daegan he needed to contact us. We will just have to wait for the opportune moment to try again."

"He is stubborn," an older Faerie woman with bluish hair piped up.

"No, he just can't hear us, Tylna." An older Elvish woman flippantly contradicted the other woman with a bored wave of her hand, having been over it many times before.

Caves and tunnels in various degrees of jutting out and hiding, populated the mountain ridges in the forsaken realm. The trapped resided somewhere, lost within one of those mountains. Small groups of mostly Shifters had gone scouting to find a way out, but always ended right back where they started. The cave they had called home for many years opened at one end to look outside but an invisible barrier sealed them inside, impenetrable to escape. Outside was always overcast with an eerie reddish glow, allowing barely enough light to see the outlines of the other mountain ranges. Inside, the cave was cold and dark, but for the few torches that were never snuffed out. Never needing sustenance, somehow stuck in an in-between form—not entirely dead, but not truly alive—they were trapped in an inexcusable form of existence, not able to move on. Not only were they prevented from leaving, but their magic was being suppressed. It felt like a tremendous weight compressing and binding the very core fibers of their magical energies.

A small number of ten—though ten too many—consisting of Faeries, Elves, and Shifters were all trapped. It had been over fifteen years for the newest of them, but for others it had been much, much longer. They knew who their captor was, although they never saw her, but they hadn't figured out how *she* had managed to accomplish it. It shouldn't have been possible, but it had happened and they were forced to work within their means to still try to help Alandria.

Cley-una gasped, feeling an evil stir. "They are coming for her." She looked around at the others. "We must find a way to get through to Daegan," desperation rang in her voice.

"The time is now. He is coming to us," the same monotone voice floated from the back of the group. "The words of the prophecy are coming to life. Let them help us break through."

One man in particular, a large Ferrishyn dressed in warrior's garb from an earlier time, stepped forward. His long black hair was pulled back in a knot at the nape of his neck, a torque around one bicep and his mark on the other. Broad and muscular, he stood regal and authoritative, his eyes focused.

"Together. Now. We must focus all our energies on the words of the prophecy. Our time of restlessness is almost over. Our time of being silenced is being brought to an end and our voices will once again be heard. This darkness will suffer the light." He paused, looking at each individual, infusing them with strength and courage, willing them to remember who they were as he extended his sword outward toward his fellow captives. "We will not be stopped in death as in life. We are the Orchids. The new age of Alandria has begun. We will be silenced no more!" He struck the ground, driving his sword deep into it.

Chapter Eighteen

Daegan needed direction. He took a watchful post in the only tree he could find that gave him direct sight of Kaeleigh's apartment. In this realm, his powers were limited, but sitting in this tree, he could feel the earth's energy pulsing within it. He felt more himself sitting invisible to the world around him perched up in the tree. He would protect her. He believed she was the one—the Sol-lumieth—whether she believed it or not. He had now given his word—and that meant something to him. He could also not deny that he felt something shifting in the air, a slight stirring that no one but perhaps himself in this realm would even notice. The kind of stirring caused when the gates between realms were opened. Rumors traveled of more gates existing than the one he commonly used to and from Alandria and the mortal realm; however, he had not yet discovered them. He had a sense that his presence might be needed again soon, but this time he planned on being there in time to act. Daegan centered his magic with all his might once more, seeking a connection with the Orchids.

A storm of red stains the skies of Alandria
The darkness brings cleansing to a world run thick
with confusion and conspiracy.
Behold, a union of strength rises.
Mystery comes with strength and compassion.
The shadow gives way as the Orchids bloom.
Seats of power are set to the right.
As things once held in sleep and night
Have now crossed over.
Awake, Alandria!

The sword is upon you.
There is hope in the hidden,
Destiny revealed in the unknown.
Awake.

Daegan heard the whispered voices in unison chanting what he assumed had to be the ancient prophecy he was told about. Over and over again the whispered chants rang in his mind until Daegan, hands clutching his head to keep it from exploding, couldn't take it anymore and yelled out loud, "Silence!" A man a block away turned to see where the shout had come. He could not see Daegan, but apparently he could hear him.

Daegan couldn't think straight. *What is going on?* Instantly, the thought ran through his mind: The Orchids. They *were* speaking to him. The words of the prophecy cycled through his head. This time he controlled it. He paid attention to the words, making every effort to make sense of them. Sadness and despair were heavy in the undertones of the voices, but as the chant went on they gained strength... and hope. As Daegan reflected upon what his part could be, for the first time in a long time, he dared to believe... and to hope.

All was silent again in his head, just in time for the whisperings of the wind to carry the last words he heard the Orchids speak, "They are coming for her." And with it the faintest scent of something familiar danced past Daegan's nose. He inhaled deeply then exhaled with a sigh. The smells of Alandria. Home. But also danger. Then he heard the crack of thunder from a storm less sky.

A gate had opened.

Instantly, his defenses were up. The hum of electricity skated across his skin; hairs on the back of his neck bristled, a feeling of danger he was accustomed to. This feeling, however, was accompanied by another he was all too familiar with, but carried out upon the undeserving, sentenced by Maleina. It felt... *wrong.* Daegan jumped down out of the tree from the highest branch with ease. He startled the man on the corner assumed to be alone when Daegan, no longer invisible to this realm, landed and ran past him. Drawing a knife that was sheathed at his wrist, he ran up the stairs to Kaeleigh's apartment and without knocking, he flung the door open.

"What the...?" Finn shouted as he grabbed Kaeleigh and shoved her behind him. At the same time Kaeleigh shouted, "Oh my god, Daegan!"

"We don't have time for pleasantries or explanations. Others have come. I will not let harm come to her," Daegan said as he strode into the room extending his knife.

Finn turned toward Daegan, keeping himself between Kaeleigh and who he viewed as the potential danger: *Daegan.*

Kaeleigh gripped Finn's arm from where she stood behind him. "Finn, stop this. Daegan has already proven he's not here to hurt me." She looked at Daegan. "Daegan, this is Finn."

Finn, never taking his eyes off of Daegan, said with sarcasm, "You're going to protect her with that little knife?"

Daegan stared intently at Finn, then with a small smirk he replied, "This knife has been through a lot, but no, not just this..." He slipped out from under his other sleeve a second knife. He twirled them both around effortlessly and fluidly in his hands almost like a choreographed performance. "If those don't work, I also have this," and from where it must have been sheathed under his jacket at his back, he reverently pulled out a very wickedly dangerous-looking sword with some kind of runes etched into the hilt. Lethal, magnificent, and *otherworldly* were the only words to describe what was before them.

Finn took in the weaponry, a glint in his eyes, nodding his approval even though he knew Daegan didn't wait for it. He pulled out his own knife—which was really more of a short sword—that had been sheathed inconspicuously under his pant leg. Daegan nodded to Finn and took his position on the opposite side of Kaeleigh so she was in between them both. Kaeleigh stood in shock, her mouth agape.

"Finn, why on earth have you been hiding a knife like that?" she asked, still in shock. Kaeleigh did not believe that she was truly in danger. *They are totally overreacting. They have to be. Aren't they?*

"And *who* is 'coming for me'?" She shot a look at Daegan, but Finn shushed her and pushed her behind him again.

For the first time in a very long time, Finn could *feel* the darkness in others from the other realm. His realm. It had been too long. Drawing his knife out in front of him, Finn stiffened. "They're here," he whispered.

Kaeleigh was about to ask again "Who is here?" but Finn's intense reaction silenced her. *And WHO are you?* she thought, looking at Finn poised to fight, his knife comfortably at the ready. She had never seen him like this. Now she was getting scared. Nothing but eerie silence hung in the air. Kaeleigh's breathing grew labored and heavy. The temperature in the room suddenly dropped, creating a freakish chill. She grabbed Finn's free arm nervously and looked around, not moving, waiting to see who would come through the door. Only they didn't.

A snap broke the silence then three of the ugliest creatures Kaeleigh could ever imagine appeared out of nowhere. Kaeleigh stifled a scream, gripping onto Finn that much tighter. About four feet tall, they looked like old men with shriveled faces, big noses, and Einstein-like crazy white hair and eyebrows. They also looked part feral cat with pointy ears, long sharp claws, furry arms, and long tails. They dressed in very simple but homely robes. Each held a jagged, evil-looking dagger as though they were ready to gut open a pig. Huffing heavily and drooling, they looked around the room with wild eyes until they landed on Kaeleigh. One stepped forward from the group.

"Are you the one we search for?" he asked in a low, gruff, inhuman voice.

Kaeleigh's guards stood poised and ready for action. They stepped together in unison, creating a shield in front of Kaeleigh. She took a deep breath, gained her composure best she could, and stood up straight, not wanting to show fear, for she had no idea what these creatures were or what they would do to her. Tending to ramble when she was nervous she spoke without thinking. "I'm really getting sick of that question," she said, trying to put all her strength behind her voice. "How am I supposed to know who you are looking for?"

Finn released a very low growl in the back of his throat that she knew meant for her to shut up and let him handle it. She saw the tiniest twitch of the corner of Daegan's mouth and suddenly her bravado returned. She was about to say something else to the tune of *Get the hell out of my house!* when Finn interjected, almost assuredly to keep her from saying something stupid.

"What do you want?" Finn asked. Daegan gave him a brief look of annoyance but didn't say anything.

The one that had stepped forward came a couple steps closer, sniffing the air like some kind of animal. Which she supposed wasn't too far off. The boys closed the gap in front of Kaeleigh. Ugly Leader got a sly grin on his face. He looked back at his groupies, who were panting in expectation, and laughed as he said, "She must be it! They guard her too well for a mere *human*."

Kaeleigh inhaled deeply as Daegan took a step forward to address Ugly Leader. "What is your purpose with the girl?" He stood casually, yet absolutely nothing about the way that he asked or the intensity in his eyes was casual. The leader of the uglies seemed to notice and backed up.

Ugly Leader replied with his eyes lowered enough to still see Daegan, but not look directly in his eyes. "We are to take her to *her* alive... or not," he said with a bit of a snicker, pointing at Kaeleigh. She gasped.

With that Finn started to rush the uglies, but Daegan jerked him back with a glare and whispered out of the corer of his mouth, "Not yet." The uglies snickered again, making Finn furious.

Daegan spoke again. "Who is this *her*? Who sent you?" The uglies snickered again, reminding Kaeleigh of a pack of hyenas. In a flash, Daegan rushed Ugly Leader and had one hand pulling his hair back forcing his head up and the other pointing his extremely sharp knife into his throat, drawing a bead of blackish liquid. Kaeleigh gasped again, struggling to keep down the bile that threatened at the back of her throat.

"Try again," Daegan growled out. "Who is *she*? Did Maleina send you?" Daegan spoke with a deadly power in his voice that was not there before. Ugly Leader cowered and said, "No, no, no. Not her, the other one, the other *her*. I do not know what she is called, only that she is not good, she is EEEVI..." The word was cut off as he tilted his head back and started to scream and choke all at the same time. Daegan took a step back, confused. Finn had come up beside him, knife drawn, ready to assist if needed. Daegan had not even scratched much more than a surface wound, but the Ugly dropped to his knees, starting to disintegrate, then vanished. The other Uglies gasped in terror. "It's *her*." They too vanished.

Finn, Daegan, and Kaeleigh stood still, not saying anything. Neither of the boys lowered their weapons... just in case. Once Kaeleigh saw Finn drop his soldier stature and Daegan subtly relax his shoulders, she started in on them. But what she intended to be an angry interrogation came out more like a breathy, shaky stammer. "What...? What... were those *things*? What...? Who... *are* you?" She spun, speaking directly to Daegan, but then looked at Finn with utter confusion and betrayal. "And you! *Who* are you?" Kaeleigh had composed herself pretty well, but now that the immediate threat had subsided she felt herself start to crumble. As she pointed at Finn she realized her hand was shaking. She yanked her hand down trying to hide it. Taking in a deep breath, she took note that both the boys were staring at her, sure she was going to lose it, but she wasn't about to fall apart again today. She was fine. "I'm fine."

Turning around, she walked into the kitchen. She was controlled. She was fine. Kaeleigh washed her hands over and over. She splashed her face with water, trying to contain her emotions. Fine. She was fine. Hands still shaking, she filled a glass with water but suddenly dropped it, shattering it all over the floor. She was not fine. Nothing about this was fine. Too much had happened in too short a period of time. Sobbing uncontrollably, she fell to her knees. She was not fine.

Kaeleigh felt strong arms pick her up off the floor and out of the shards of scattered glass. Finn cradled her close to his chest. She felt comforted by his closeness and breathed in the smell that was signature to him—spring and mowed grass after a fresh rain. As he moved her through the apartment, she could see Daegan out of the corner of her eye frowning. He laid her on her bed and she curled on her side. Gently he brushed the hair out of her face, tucking it behind her ear. She looked at him but all he could see was hurt and fear and it broke his heart. Tucking her in, he murmured that he would be in the other room and left her to herself.

❁❁❁

Kaeleigh woke up, her mind a blur and yet weighed down with the gravity of something dark having just happened. She yawned and wiped the sleep away from her face, zombie-like her limbs were slow and sluggish as she walked into the living room. Kaeleigh looked into the kitchen to the floor where shattered glass gave way to the outburst of emotion she could no longer contain. Shame crept into her face, her strength had failed her. Or did it at all? Lighter than she had been earlier her emotions, she realized, were stable for now. Finn's back was to her as he looked out the slider door to the balcony, his hands clasped behind his back. She knew he was aware of her; he always was. Without even looking at her he sighed then said, "I know you have questions and no idea what is going on. There is little I'm able to say at this point, but first..." Then he turned around to look at Kaeleigh with soft eyes. "Are you all right?"

Kaeleigh put her hands on her hips, dropped her head, took another deep breath, then looked up at Finn and gave him a curt nod. He understood she was trying to process everything and wasn't quite ready to talk about her feelings. He simply reciprocated her nod.

"Who are you, Finn? *What* are you?" she pleaded softly.

"I'm your friend and I'll protect you with my life. I am also a..." he sighed with frustration or possibly relief of the interruption, "Chel's here." Just before Chel rattled the door handle, he added, "I thought you might need someone you trusted." He sounded dejected. Chel came hesitantly through the door, as if not sure what she was walking into.

"Where's Daegan?" Kaeleigh asked after a deep breath, looking around her apartment.

"He's doing a perimeter search outside... or he left," Finn answered with a casual shrug of his shoulders. Answering the questioning look on Kaeleigh's face, he continued, "I don't trust him, Kae." Then he shifted his gaze slightly over her head as Daegan walked back into the apartment.

"You shouldn't," Daegan said flatly. Finn could have been embarrassed that Daegan heard what he said, but he wasn't. He looked at him as if he had been telling it straight to his face.

"Not to ruin this lovely tension-filled moment, but Kaeleigh and I need a minute," Chel said as she implored Kaeleigh with questioning eyes. Kaeleigh nodded and Chel grabbed her arm, tugging her back into Kaeleigh's bedroom.

❆❆❆

Chel looked around the room that she used to share with Kaeleigh. Sadness flooded her eyes as she realized how much she missed living with her friend. She was also sad at the loss of closeness she felt caused by the rift her new secret had caused. Chel needed to find a way to not lose Kaeleigh without betraying her family in the process.

It made her smile to see that Kaeleigh hadn't taken down all her posters and pieces of artwork that she had pinned haphazardly around the room. Kaeleigh liked order; it gave her some sense of control, Chel knew. But Chel was abstract when it came to her art and things that *spoke* to her. Random symbols and runes that she had been studying were sketched and painted in various sizes and colors scattered amidst forest scenes, moons in various stages, and sketches of animals in transitional evolutionary stages. She hadn't realized what these particular pieces had really meant to her until seeing them here again today.

Taking a deep breath, she faced Kaeleigh, who was patiently sitting on her bed, waiting. Chel cleared her throat, trying to figure out where to begin. "I'm so sorry for running out on you earlier," she said with tears streaming down her face. "I didn't handle that well at all. I was a coward and I left you alone after my selfish rant." Chel started pacing the bedroom. "Kaeleigh, there are some things that I want to share with you because it does pertain to you, but it's not my secret to tell and I have to respect that. My parents had their reasons for keeping things from me and from you. I may not agree with how they chose to do that and I still don't understand everything, but I am not able to share it. I'm so sorry. I can't imagine how that feels." She looked at Kaeleigh to see how she was taking what she was saying, but Kaeleigh remained still yet soft, processing.

"I also need you to know that I will never leave you like that again. I will stand by you and help you if I can as you search for the answers that I know you are looking for. Things are going to change, I can feel it, but I want to be there with you... wherever that is." Chel willed Kaeleigh to understand what she was trying to say.

Kaeleigh looked into Chel's eyes. "I know you and your parents would never do anything to harm me. I admit I felt betrayed and hurt and confused—I'm still confused, by the way—but too much has happened lately and I don't want to lose you." Tears started to trail down Kaeleigh's face. She stood and embraced Chel tightly. "I'm mad at you for keeping secrets from me, but I haven't been the most forthcoming with mine either. You've always been patient with me when I have been slow to share things with you. I trust your parents too, they must have a good reason."

"Where do we go from here, Kaeleigh?"

"There is too much to just forget it and move on so... we move forward. It's time for some answers." Kaeleigh looked at Chel with a new resolve in her spirit.

She knew what she needed to do. Dragging Chel behind her into the living room, they stopped each of them eyeing Daegan at one end of the room and Finn up against the wall at the opposite end. This was going to be harder than Kaeleigh thought.

"I..." Kaeleigh began.

"We," Chel interrupted.

"We," Kaeleigh corrected with a small grateful smile. "We need answers and we believe we need to go with Daegan to this other realm to find them."

Finn kicked off the wall, standing immovable, his arms folded across his chest his silent debate evident.

"I wanted to tell you," Chel whispered out the side of her mouth, clearly unsure what Finn might do, "my parents had a map of Alandria. It exists...in case you weren't sure." Kaeleigh's eyes were wide, but only nodded.

"I vow to you to keep you safe until our journey parts," Daegan said moving into the room.

Finn watched him closely. "I am against her going, but how do we trust you to stay true to your word? Who sent you to her?"

"Opposing sides have requested her presence, one with more knowledge than the other. I am simply the sent," Daegan's words exposing a cadence not from this area. "More will come for her, this you know. She will be hunted in her own realm. Are you prepared to continue to fight off all that will be sent for her? Will you remain at her side every moment?" Daegan searched Finn's face for his truth. "She will be safer there for now than she would be here where they could find her at any turn. Her signature energy has begun to break through her glamoured shell, a beacon for any looking."

Kaeleigh and Chel stared between Daegan and Finn, confused and not even sure how to catch up. Finn was clearly upset, but challenged at what might be the lesser of two evils. He looked to Kaeleigh, hope gleaming in her eyes, and prayed to whoever might hear that he was making the right choice for her, of course he couldn't force her but he would've tried if he thought he had a chance. He hadn't been given much instruction and his source was no longer offering insight; he was on his own. Plus when Kaeleigh made up her mind, he knew there was no stopping her, but at least they could join her—and they did.

Chapter Nineteen

The group took a two-hour car ride that seemed like forever with the heavy silence that weighed upon them into and through White-fish, driving as far as they could up the mountain. They pulled into a driveway of a cabin hidden away back in the trees. They all got out as Daegan pulled his truck into the garage at the back. They were looking around upon his return.

"Daegan? Whose place is this?" Chel asked.

"It belongs to the Ferrishyn—my people—and is used as needed when crossing the realms," Daegan answered.

"It looks like someone is home. Are there others here?" Kaeleigh spoke while trying to see in the windows from a distance.

"There are." Daegan spoke flatly, ending any further conversation.

Taken aback by his toneless and harsh reply, she grabbed onto Chel's arm. Pretending that what he said hadn't affected her, they passed the cabin and set about hiking up a trail hidden in the thick trees. Stopping to take a break, Kaeleigh cautiously approached the edge where forest met cliffside. She inhaled deep; the chill in the air, though fresh and breathtaking in more ways than the effects of the altitude, cut through her lungs. They had packed accordingly with a backpack each. The mountains outside of Whitefish were absolutely beautiful. Kaeleigh had come to the mountains several times, but she had never been up this high. By the time they got there the colors of the sky were rich with pinks and golds as the sun began its descent.

Chel walked up next to Kaeleigh, staring out at the majesty that was before them. "It's amazing," Chel breathed out in awe.

"It's not much farther," Daegan spoke as he walked up next to the girls. "Let's get moving before it gets dark out here."

"Are there things that go bump in the night out here?" Chel said warily looking around.

"Well, yes, probably, but it's also going to get extremely cold once the sun goes down," Daegan said with a shrug as he walked off.

Both girls rolled their eyes but fell into step behind him with Finn bringing up the rear.

❋❋❋

"'Not much farther' sure seems like quite a bit farther, if you ask me," Chel huffed out under her breath. Kaeleigh heard and snorted her agreement. They suddenly stopped as their "guide" in front of them abruptly halted.

Daegan looked back at the girls over his shoulder with a smirk. "'Not much farther,'" he repeated, as if he were saying "See?!" And he nodded at the ominous rock that was suddenly before them.

Kaeleigh and Chel looked around, confused. They could have sworn that rock wasn't there only moments ago. They had felt like they were going in circles and for all they knew maybe they had been.

The four of them stood staring for what seemed like forever at a patch of tightly woven trees guarding the front of a large wall of old rock chiseled out of the mountain itself. It looked archaic. Etched into the rock, but barely visible from the wearing of time and erosion, were what looked like drawings or symbols. Shifting her weight from one foot to the other, Kaeleigh was filled with a nervous energy but also a "rightness" about her decision. Still unsure if she even believed in what or where they were supposed to be going, she could feel something, a low hum of a vibration, coming from that rock wall or from deep within the earth; she wasn't quite sure. Chel, Kaeleigh, Daegan, and Finn—against his better judgment—stood on the precipice between what she knew to be real and the possibility of what shouldn't be real.

Looking around at the little group, Kaeleigh saw an assortment of expressions. Chel, a little unsure and apprehensive but also intrigued as she stared intently at the odd symbols. Finn, unexpressive, protective, but something else flashing in his eyes... anxiety or fear maybe? Daegan standing tall and strong, never once removing his eyes from that rock wall.

What is he looking at? Kaeleigh wondered. She stepped up to him, about to touch him, when his arm swung back with his hand lifted, giving her the universal sign to wait or halt. She stopped, frozen, unsure what to do and feeling slightly awkward.

"What are we..." *waiting for? looking at? doing?* Any number of phrases to finish that sentence left hanging in the air when he gave her a sharp side look telling her not to interrupt. Then he sighed and softened just a fraction and answered her unasked question.

"We are waiting for the precise moment at twilight when the gates are unveiled allowing entrance. Can you not feel it?" he asked. He finally looked at her, but his intense gaze looked right through her. He seemed to notice something in her and then more seriously he asked, "Do you feel it?"

"I don't know what I feel, but I feel... vibrations," she replied sheepishly.

Unexpectedly, a bird cried from far above. A raven, actually, black as night and big, soaring in a circle above the little patch of trees that they were in. At the same time, something stirred in the air even though no breeze was present. A shimmering expansion like the opening of an invisible barrier suddenly became visible. The atmosphere seemed to take on a different pressure: thicker or tighter, restricting their efforts to breathe or even to move.

Daegan looked them over and said, "If you're ready, follow me, but it's not open long so do not take too much time." But before he started to move he added with a sharp snap, "And stay close!"

With that, he turned without looking back and walked toward the rock wall. He took out his knife and carved a strange symbol onto the rock, then pricked his thumb and smeared his blood on top of the symbol.

Handling his knife with great care, he handed it hilt first to Kaeleigh, who looked shocked. After a few seconds of hesitation, she took the knife and ran it along the meat of her thumb. She smeared the blood on the rock with barely a wince, refusing to show her fear. Daegan's eyes widened the slightest with surprise. Or was it admiration? She wouldn't have even noticed except that she was, well, noticing and not too subtly either, she realized. *Oh well.*

She handed the knife to Chel, whose eyes looked like they were about to explode, but without question or comment she followed Kaeleigh's example. She handed it to Finn, who did the same after a moment of hesitation. Then they watched silently as Daegan walked INTO the rock wall and disappeared.

With one last look at her friends before she went through, Kaeleigh shrugged her shoulders, took a deep breath, then started to walk in.

Finn grabbed her arm before she finished crossing the threshold. "Wait, it's not too late. You don't have to do this. We can still go home," he said desperately.

"No," she said, resigning herself to her fate, "I don't think I can stop now, but if you don't want to follow I understand."

She turned and walked straight through the wall. Her friends followed. They wouldn't leave her, not now. Kaeleigh felt guilty leading them into something that could be—probably was—dangerous, not even knowing when, or if, they'd get home. But she was also relieved they were with her—they were everything she had and knew she would need them. Too many questions needed answers. Deep inside, Kaeleigh felt this was the way to find them; the only way.

CHAPTER TWENTY

ALANDRIA

Daegan's description of the entrance was precise when he had given them instructions before passing through the wall. *Once you get through the entrance—IF it allowed you in* (apparently, most mortals were not welcome)—*there is a short tunnel that is dark and musty. Oh, and it's pitch-black, so don't touch anything, it might not let you go. Keep walking straight until it allows you out. Don't stop. If you don't keep walking, you might not come out the other side.*

He had spoken of the tunnel and the darkness like it had a mind of its own. Like it was *alive*. Shivers ran up Kaeleigh's spine and the hairs on her arms stood straight up. The oppressive darkness wore on her eyes, her mind, her soul. Swallowed in it, she couldn't help but want to be immediately out of it. The uncertainty of what was ahead of them only made it that much more so.

As they walked, they held tightly onto each other's hands, willing themselves to make it to the other side. As soon as Kaeleigh had grabbed Daegan's hand, which he had been reluctant to give her, a spark like a low-wattage electric current hummed between them. She had automatically jerked her hand back, but he gripped her tighter as he said gruffly to keep walking and stay together. Before he moved forward, both he and Kaeleigh had a moment where they looked down at their hands, then at each other. Before she could ask what it was, he was pulling them along.

What is that? Can the others see it? The small, but subtle source of light in the darkness sparked a flicker of peace in her gut, easing her fears. Unfortunately, the feeling was short-lived as she heard scuttling noises to the right of her head. She shrieked a girly shriek and jumped to the side, causing the others behind her to be yanked with her. *Great, I screamed like a girl. But hello! I am a girl—a girl who doesn't like creepy crawly things in dark tunnels!*

"What is that?" Chel loudly whispered nervously from behind her.

"Um... uh... it's probably nothing," Kaeleigh stammered, remembering Chel was even more jumpy than she was, attempting to keep her friend calm.

"Oh great! There's something in here, isn't there?" Chel asked suddenly, much more calmly than Kaeleigh would've given her credit for. Not even a second later, Chel inhaled sharply. "I think the *something* just ran over my foot!" she whispered, trying not to freak out but on the verge of not succeeding.

"I'm sure it's not—" Kaeleigh started but cut herself off with her own sharp intake of breath. "It just ran over mine too!"

Chel huddled as close to Kaeleigh as she could, pulling Finn along behind her.

"Be quiet!" Daegan growled, still trying to drag them along behind him with difficulty.

Kaeleigh could hear Finn irritated as well but also laughing under his breath, probably at how irritated they had made Daegan. The girls were squirming and jumping, not wanting to walk on the ground for long enough to let anything else reach them. At least they hadn't screamed.

At least not until something grabbed or latched onto Chel's ankle and caused her to stumble into Kaeleigh's back, which in turn made her stumble into Daegan's back. That's when the screaming began. Daegan turned abruptly. Fire lit his eyes again. Kaeleigh didn't know if the others could see it but she figured they probably could when instantly Chel's screams stopped and Finn's calming words fell flat. However, she knew they couldn't see him eye the snake of a vine that slithered out from the wall of the tunnel. Or when he slashed it in half with his sword, severing its connection to Chel's ankle. Only because of the low-wattage energy coming from where their hands met could she see anything.

"You are released, Chel. Please, we must hurry, unless you want to spend eternity circling this tunnel never to see the light of day." He tugged Kaeleigh's hand and they all began to move again.

"Thank you," Chel managed to get out while trying to catch her breath.

After what seemed like forever walking in utter silence, the pressure shifted again as though they had walked out of an atmospheric bubble. They stumbled into each other as they were spit out into another forest. This forest, however, was unusually all-encompassing, so dense all you could see were trees upon trees. This forest, different than the one they left, was old as time. It felt mysterious and *alive*... very alive.

They all stood there for several minutes taking it in. Kaeleigh took a deep, invigorating breath soaking in the natural scent. Renewed energy shot through her faster than ever before in a natural environment. A weight lifted off her; she felt alive and refreshed for the first time... well, ever.

"We got through!" Chel exclaimed, stating the obvious but excited nonetheless.

Daegan looked at all of them, his eyes finally landing on Chel with a thoughtful expression, and said, "Yes, you did. Interesting. I will admit I was unsure if you would make it, but now that you have, we continue on."

Kaeleigh looked at his expression, realizing he was trying to figure Chel out. He turned and started to walk. Then what he said registered in her brain. He had been addressing Chel specifically.

"Wait." Kaeleigh held up her hand. "You didn't think she would make it, but you still led her through?" Her volume was beginning to rise. "So if she hadn't made it, what would've happened? She'd get bounced back to where we came from?" She looked from Daegan expressionless face to Finn's stony face then back to Daegan's.

He shrugged. "No. She'd die."

Kaeleigh was livid. Finn's hand on her forearm stopped her from going any further with her thoughts. "I wouldn't have let her go through if I thought she wouldn't have made it," Finn said, speaking for the first time since they had arrived at the mountain.

Looking at Chel, now having wandered about ten yards ahead of all of them, Kaeleigh lost her anger, only to replace it with apprehension. Head cocked and eyes closed, Kaeleigh could see her friend paying attention to something else entirely. Very unusual for Chel. Something was stirring.

A warm breeze came upon them, carrying with it the subtle tinkling sound of soft chimes. It circled playfully around each of them.

As suddenly as the sound rushed through, it departed. A rustling above them drew their attention as old oaks, cedars, and other pillars of the earth began to sway their branches and creak with the wind. Daegan was stiff—but when wasn't he—his gaze alert and searching. He turned in a slow cautious circle, as did the rest of the group trying to see what had alerted his senses.

All except Kaeleigh. She stood very still as a small ball of brilliantly bright white light floated slowly down from high in the trees to right before her face. Kaeleigh strived to call out to Daegan, but she had no voice. Panic welled up inside her as she realized she couldn't move. A moment later a serene feeling of peace flooded her and she relaxed. Everyone else had stopped moving and was staring at her, well at it—the light—as it then moved to hover in front of Daegan. He bowed gracefully as it flitted in front of him then swirled back around Kaeleigh on its way back up into the trees from whence it came. It made a beautiful sound like a song of the most delicate wind chimes as it departed.

There had been a subtle subtext almost like a whispered voice in her mind underlying the chimes. The words were spoken softly in an alluringly beautiful and hypnotic sound with many voices that were individual yet one: *"Welcome, Kaeleighnna, daughter of the Orchids. Welcome back to Alandria."* The voice continued as it slowly moved back into the trees, *"Take warning; you are in danger as you stand. Hunters are coming."*

Kaeleigh was captivated so much so that she forgot to breathe. She almost fell over, but Daegan caught her arm and held her steady. Her head was spinning. Did everyone hear the voice? Or was it just in her mind?

Chel was the first to speak as she rushed to Kaeleigh's other arm. "Kaeleigh, are you okay?" Kaeleigh nodded, still confused. She looked at Daegan as if she knew he was going to speak.

"What did she say to you?" he asked her.

"She?" Finn and Chel asked at the same time.

"*She* is the priestess of the forest. She is of the trees and one with the trees. Elders have said she is of the Dryads. She is keeper of the forest. If she spoke to you, it is not to be taken lightly. What did she say?" Daegan asked again with impatience.

Kaeleigh took a deep breath. So the voice had only been in her head. "She said, 'Welcome *back* to Alandria,' but I've never been here before. How does she know me?" Kaeleigh said, not wanting to mention the name she called her yet for some reason. It felt very personal. She wasn't sure why but she wanted to keep it to herself for now.

Daegan interjected, "She is old as Alandria and knows many things. The trees tell her all the goings-on in our realm. She does not speak to many, it is a great honor."

Kaeleigh was not quite sure what she should do to show her gratitude for the honor, but she did not want to offend her. Kaeleigh looked up into the trees where that last glow of light had been, said thank you, and gave a little curtsy of respect. Suddenly she remembered the looming threat to their lives at the moment; all the rest would have to wait. "Oh! She said we were in danger. Something about hunters were coming."

Daegan and Finn, having the same reaction, reached for their swords and knives respectively. Kaeleigh couldn't help but notice their warrior-like stature. Both were extremely intimidating and fierce in their individual ways. It really was a magnificent sight to behold, were they not all in mortal danger.

Daegan spoke. "We must move now!" He began walking quickly with an intense purpose. Not for the first time, Kaeleigh wondered what he was hiding under his stone exterior.

"Who is *hunting* us?" Chel asked as she came to walk next to Kaeleigh. "Do we get swords too?" she added with an excited gleam in her eyes that Kaeleigh hadn't seen before. Chel had always been adventurous and feisty, but the intensity and confidence in the face of real possible danger—this was new. *What is going on with her?*

"I want a knife or something sharp if we are going to be attacked," Kaeleigh jumped in.

Without turning to look at Chel, Daegan said, "I think you will discover that you have your own weapons at your disposal when you are in need of them most." About to argue that she had no idea what he was talking about, Kaeleigh saw Chel look down at herself as if to see if a weapon magically appeared. Kaeleigh frowned, sure that wasn't what he meant, but mimicked Chel by patting down her legs—after all, this was a place of magic. But no such luck. After a few minutes, Kaeleigh noticed out of the corner of her eyes that her friend appeared to be confused and deep in thought, as though trying to puzzle out what Daegan had said to her.

Minutes or hours, time passed slowly, but the group remained alert and ready for something to jump out at them, Kaeleigh couldn't stand the quiet any longer. She walked closer to Daegan to ask him about the priestess.

"Where are we?" she asked as a conversation starter.

"This is the Forest of Dul-Isteach," he replied. Anticipating her next question he added, "It means Forest of Entry."

"Has she, the priestess, ever spoken with you before?"

After a minute with no response she thought perhaps he was actually going to ignore her. Her irritation grew, but then he sighed. He seemed to be distant in his gaze, still not looking at her as he spoke. "Yes, once, not that long ago and then just now." He seemed conflicted. An inner struggle waged behind his eyes. About what the priestess had said? Or if he was going to tell her what was said? He didn't have to make that decision just now, though, as his thoughts were interrupted.

Grabbing Kaeleigh's arm, Daegan swung her behind him, holding out his sword. In swift movements that appeared practiced and conditioned, Finn and Daegan simultaneously backed the girls up behind them, creating a makeshift circle of protection. Nothing moved against them, but an eerie stillness had settled. They were being surrounded, enclosed upon, by something they couldn't see but which carried with it darkness and evil.

The weight of a stare was heavy upon Kaeleigh, pressing in and suffocating her peace from every side. Seeking something, but what, she didn't know. Gripping the back of Daegan's shirt in one fist and Chel's hand in the other, she kept her eyes and ears open. Out of the corner of her eyes she saw Daegan lift his hand that wasn't gripping the sword, touch his ring on the opposite hand, and mutter something under his breath in a language she didn't know. Immediately, she felt a cushioning of warm air surround them that carried peace with it. The surrounding darkness swirled around them faster and faster, suddenly confused and aimless it left, lifting the translucent veil of darkness as it went.

"What just happened?" Kaeleigh asked. "Is it gone?"

"For now, but not for long if we don't get moving. I constructed a temporary shield that will throw it off our scent," Daegan said. His voice was once again matter of fact, but also carried the barest hint of confusion.

Kaeleigh looked to Finn, who hadn't yet dropped his knives. His eyes were cautious and guarded but also fearful. Whatever was out there, he was also afraid... for her? for himself? He looked back at her. "Let's get going!"

The unseen "path" they traveled on took them deeper and deeper into the forest. The sun was going down, bathing them in twilight. The trees were growing tighter, causing their canopy to knit together, creating a patchwork quilt of various greens and browns splashed with beautiful colors from mixed-in flowers and leaves. Long draping moss, resembling Spanish moss from the mortal realm, trailed down from the branches while ivy climbed their trunks, giving the forest an enchanted and mysterious feeling. The trunks of some of the trees were so massive it took a while to go around them; and their roots clawed their way out from below the ground, making them an obstacle to climb over.

Finn was helping Chel climb over one of the massive root systems. They followed the roots up some kind of embankment and began climbing. Kaeleigh went around them and climbed up her own roots. She struggled on her own, but didn't want to ask Daegan; he didn't seem like he wanted to touch her more than he had to. The energies that flowed between their connection before had created an awkward situation. Her footing slipped and she huffed out in frustration. Daegan peered down at her from the top of the ridge. Frowning and looking like he was trying to decide something, he hesitantly extended his hand to her.

"I don't need your help, thank you," she said flatly, irritated that he had to think about it. She reached and grabbed the next root on her own then stepped up to begin her climb once again. He waited half a heartbeat, then reached down, grasped her wrist tightly, and gave a good pull. She landed a little unsteadily but, to her surprise, on her feet. Glaring at him she spewed, "I could've done it myself." He kept walking, not giving her childish tantrum the time of day. With her hands on her hips, catching her breath, she softened and sighed. "Thank you." And she meant it. He gave her the briefest nod, took stock of their group, and kept walking. *Man of many words.*

She pushed herself to keep up with him, not wanting to show any further weakness in his eyes—why she should care, she couldn't figure out. "Daegan," she asked a little hesitantly, and saw the briefest tensing of his back muscles as if she had spat his name. She sighed, frustrated at his reaction, but she was not about to back down. "Are we going to make it to wherever we are going tonight or will we have to camp somewhere and continue tomorrow?"

"We will not make it there tonight. Neither will we stop and make camp for the night. We have a long journey and best to keep moving." With that, he kept moving.

"Daegan, it's been a long day. I think we could all use a little rest and some food," Kaeleigh snapped back yet trying not to sound like she was whining either. He turned around and looked directly into her eyes again. *Searching for something? Go ahead, take a good look, I have nothing to hide.* His eyes widened as if he could sense what she was thinking. Finn stepped up to Kaeleigh's side, sensing the tension.

Kaeleigh, realizing what was happening, rested her hand on Finn's arm and stepped forward. "I am not challenging you or your decisions. I merely had concerns for the well-being of my friends and frankly, I'm tired." *Okay, so maybe I was challenging him just a little. Oops, too late now.* She could feel Finn and Chel's eyes on her, but she didn't take her eyes from Daegan's. Kaeleigh had gotten into a few stare-downs with Chel's parents over the years, both for challenge and for practice, which she often won, but always had wondered if they let her. Now she was not so sure, but the practice had helped her confidence. Daegan inclined his head toward her in concession, but did not drop his eyes in defeat. She acknowledged.

"There is a home of a *friend* that is not much further. He will give us shelter," Daegan said thoughtfully and gave a curt nod to Kaeleigh.

She smiled. "Thank you, Daegan."

He shrugged. "It benefits us to go that direction, it is merely convenient."

Kaeleigh rolled her eyes and stalked passed him. "Seriously? A 'you're welcome' would have been more 'convenient.' Less words used," she replied sarcastically.

"You couldn't just let it go, could you?" Finn to Daegan. "Now she's pissed."

"That is not my problem," he retorted.

"Oh, it will be."

Daegan's gruff sigh sounded more like a low growl. "There are things she should know," Daegan whispered to Finn. "Things you should have prepared her for. *You* should have instructed her. Instead, she knows nothing!" he spat out. Finn clenched his jaw, trying not to start a fight.

"I'm right here and I can hear you!" Kaeleigh yelled. "Finn has his reasons for not sharing more than he has," she defended, but suddenly caught what she was saying, as if the words finally took hold that Finn really had withheld important information from her. A prick of pain stabbed her heart as she kept walking.

Daegan and Finn looked at each other, surprised that she could hear them. They were far enough away from her and had used such hushed tones that a normal person wouldn't have made out a word. Finn glared at Daegan, then even softer he growled out, "Let's keep moving."

"Yes, shall we?" She smiled tightly and kept walking as Chel jogged up beside her.

Daegan stared after her with his own little smirk and replied softly, "Very good." Kaeleigh barely turned her head in confusion, acknowledging that she had heard him. "Interesting," he mused.

Chapter Twenty-One

Daegan finally regained his position at the head of the group. He directed a brief gaze her way, studying her. Long-distance hearing was a very rare gift. In fact, he didn't know of anyone other than himself and the Elders.

"Have you always been able to hear so well?" Daegan asked, genuinely curious.

Kaeleigh thought about his question. "Um, actually no. Now that you mention it, it's only been since we have been here. That's... odd," she finished more to herself than in response to him.

"Yes, it is odd. It is actually a rare gift in these parts. I would advise you to keep it to yourself," he said as he lowered his voice. "There are those that would not hesitate to try and take gifts such as that for themselves."

Kaeleigh stopped abruptly. "What do you mean? How could someone take something that is a part of me?"

"This is not a world without dangers, Kaeleigh, and it is much different than where you come from. There are creatures who have ways of extracting one's soul, the part that gifts are made from. Or at least, force you to use it against your will," he said. Genuine concern and a hint of true regret showed briefly through his hard mask, but then vanished.

She shuddered with fear and revulsion, while at the same time feeling a foreign warmth that wrapped around her at the way Daegan said her name. Indignant, she straightened her back. "Let them try and take anything from me!" She turned with a huff to storm off with a perfectly timed exit only to trip on a large vine that she didn't see in front of her. About to fall on her face, in what could only be described as one of the most graceful falls ever (not!), she felt two steady strong arms grab her arms from behind to steady her back onto her feet. A flush rose on her face as she brushed off the imaginary dust along with her dignity trying to regain her composure once again.

Chel ran up beside her friend and looped her arm through Kaeleigh's to help support her friend. Kaeleigh patted her friend's arm. They both put noses to the sky, sarcastic in their regal strides trying to make light of her misstep, and giggled. Kaeleigh knew she wasn't the most graceful, but she appreciated her friend joining her.

Daegan found himself feeling irritably endeared. He was also surprised by her stubbornness and recklessness; that could be to her both an advantage and a disadvantage—that mouth could get her into tr ouble... as it could him. He was already unsure of how bringing this group to Maleina would be received. Maleina would not be happy about the "tagalongs." He was pretty sure he was going to have to ditch the other two somehow, but that could be tricky— they were a very close group, except for the secrets that both Chel and Finn were keeping from Kaeleigh. Daegan knew what race each of her friends hailed from by their signature energy. Chel, he also recognized by her scent, but only in part as if she wasn't quite whole similar to the younger Shifters who hadn't yet shifted.

Daegan knew the Elder hadn't wanted him to take Kaeleigh to see Maleina, but he was bound. He was curious to know Maleina's true intentions. Unfortunately, that could be problematic as well. He hoped Hal would be able to help him help her leave their territory unscathed and send her back to the mortal realm where she came from and be-longed. Even if she was from here once, she didn't belong here anymore. She had no idea what it took to survive here.

Chapter Twenty-Two

Finn scanned his surroundings suspiciously. He recognized this area of the forest, although it had been a long time since he had seen these parts, sixteen years to be precise. Memories flooded his mind, panic seized his chest, but his need to protect Kaeleigh at all costs consumed him. He was simmering underneath his skin; agitated, restless, wanting nothing more than to drive his knife into something, hearing the tearing of flesh and the cracking of bone. Being back in this place set his bloodlust on edge. He had not felt the intensity of the need for a fight in a very long time, since the last time he walked through these very woods. To add to all of that, he had not a shred of trust in Daegan, not yet understanding his motives. Nerves kept him on edge as he surveyed as far as his eyes could see, which happened to be farther than the average mortal. Picking up his pace, he came alongside Kaeleigh, his posture rigid and wound so tight he thought he might explode.

Kaeleigh sensed his tension next to her and shot a questioning glance up at his face. Finn towered over her by half a head. Knowing now she could hear him, he whispered, "I have a bad feeling. Something is amiss and I don't trust where *he* is leading us." Finn did nothing to acknowledge he'd spoken to her, keeping his eyes focused straight ahead, but Kaeleigh watched his muscles twitch with almost new eyes. His hands flexed into tight fists, only to splay wide once again, and then reflexively felt for his daggers at his hips. Kaeleigh felt she was seeing Finn for what he might truly be. *A killer.*

Then breaking both Kaeleigh's and Finn's thoughts, almost as if on cue, Daegan's voice came over the space between them.

"Steady, Guardian, I am not who your fight is to be directed at this time," Daegan said in that calming tone. "Do not draw unnecessary attention, but be prepared on the count of three."

Kaeleigh and Chel sucked in two quick, surprised breaths. Finn, angry and not a little surprised that Daegan could hear him too, un-flinchingly responded by drawing one of his daggers. Kaeleigh was his primary concern right now, and he would keep her safe. His nod of ac-knowledgment was seen but did not break his stride or forward motion as he prepared for what he wasn't sure.

A twig behind them snapped. Chel jolted silently, gripping Kaeleigh's arm more tightly.

Daegan began to whisper a count as both he and Finn stepped close to the girls, ready to surround them. "... Three!" Then in what appeared practice perfect they both whipped around, drawing their weapons out, and encircling Chel and Kaeleigh as best they could without a third anchor to complete the protective triad. Silence met them all.

Eyes searching. Nothing. Stances poised and ready for a fight. Still nothing. "Show yourself!" Daegan commanded with absolute authority. Still nothing.

Kaeleigh was watching something off to the right of the path they had just come from. Her watch turned to an intense stare, which Finn could sense. "What do you see?" he asked her.

"I'm not sure, but I think that boulder moved," Kaeleigh's eyes squinted trying to reason away the implausible. "But that would be impossible though, wouldn't it?"

"Not necessarily," Finn replied.

Daegan immediately took several steps toward the boulder in ques-tion, trained his sword toward it, and cautiously nudged it with his boot. The girls shrieked in unison as the boulder clearly rolled away from Daegan's sword and transformed into a small, bear-like creature. It had the body and fur of a brown bear, but with an elongated face and tusk of a rhino. The creature had long, razor-sharp claws that could shred an animal—or person—easily in half. He growled, crouching, ready to spring and devour his prey before him. His eyes glowed a murderous red while smoke puffed from his nostrils. The creature stood there, snorting in disgust, looking at Daegan readying itself to charge. Daegan, on the other hand, steadied his weapon and his stance as Finn, side daggers in hand and ready to go, slowly approached.

Despite the fear coursing through her, Kaeleigh felt a new strength stirring within her, a fierce protectiveness that she had never experienced before. She would not allow death to come to these warriors, nor her dear friend. Not when they'd come this far and not when they still had so far to go to find the answers she'd been looking for all her life. Kaeleigh pulled out of Chel's strong grasp and boldly, silently stepped forward until she was right behind Daegan and Finn.

Daegan sensed her approach. "Get back, Kaeleigh! You do not know what you are doing," he spat out fiercely. She stopped but refused to back down and glared at the back of his head. Strangely, and as if picking up her own weapon, she took her stare and pointed it at the creature before them. It shifted his murderous eyes of fire from Daegan's to hers, sniffing the air for the new scent that she brought. His growl deepened and intensified at this new threat... his new prey. She stiffened but still did not back down. A primal and deeply hidden surge tore through her body as she shot her finger out at the beast and shouted with an authority she had never known before, "NO! You will not harm us." In front of her, both Finn and Daegan flinched at the command in her voice. Despite their surprise, they were strong enough to keep the protective barrier intact.

The beast snorted and twitched as if something had smacked him on his muzzle, and immediately began to back away with his head low to the ground. Daegan raised his sword, ready to end the creature. Chel gasped behind her, then in anguish cried out, "NO! Don't!" Daegan restrained himself with frustrated exasperation. Kaeleigh, afraid to lose eye contact with the beast, kept her gaze on the creature strong. No need to find out if loosing eye contact would somehow release its submission to her... *to me! Ha! Never would've believed that.*

"We have to finish him off, Kaeleigh," Daegan said in a low tone, oblivious to Chel's protest.

"NO!!!!" Chel began to shriek! You can't! You can't!"

"What is it, Chel?" Kaeleigh bit out more sharply than she meant. "Clearly the thing wants to kill us."

"No, don't kill him, please. He means no real harm," she rushed out all in one breath.

Daegan gritted his teeth and growled deeply in his chest. Kaeleigh shifted her feet and pushed her will into her next words directed at the creature, "Stay. Do not move." Daegan and Finn, both fierce in their protective stances, glanced her way and each shot her "what now?" expressions. Kaeleigh eyed the beast once more, then slowly turned, looking back to see her friend on her knees. Kaeleigh watched Chel, her face now a sheet of white and her arms up by her head holding it like she was in pain. Kaeleigh had never seen her friend this way. The creature perhaps perplexed too, held its position, but watched them curiously. Assured the creature was going to stay, Kaeleigh moved cautiously to Chel's side with a softer tone.

"Chel, what's wrong?" she urged.

Chel turned her eyes up to Kaeleigh with what seemed like intense effort. "Don't hurt him, he's scared and all alone. His mother was killed. He's young and impulsive and... and sorry," she spewed out in a new, almost tortured way. Chel usually talked fast when she got on a roll, but not like this. Kaeleigh looked at her friend and stroked her hair, not knowing what else to do.

"How do you know that, Chel?" Kaeleigh asked gently with concern in her voice.

"I... I can hear him," she stammered. Out of fear, she raised her voice desperately. "Why can I hear him?"

Finn, although startled with the revelation, kept his daggers pointed at the beast. Daegan, on the other hand, lowered his own with a sigh and turned sideways so he could see both the creature and the girls behind him now huddled on the ground.

"It seems to be part of your gift, although it is unusual in your kind to hear another kind."

Three pairs of eyes swung up to meet Daegan's; but Chel's were first surprised then beseeching him at the same time to not reveal anything. Chel didn't know what Daegan might know about her, but he seemed to know more than she had let on. Daegan glanced at Kaeleigh, understanding that she wanted to tell Kaeleigh herself, but still he shot her a perturbed glare.

Kaeleigh bit his head off, misunderstanding his words to being condescending, once again, toward humans—as if they were really that different from him and his "kind." Chel relaxed at Kaeleigh's blunder. If only Kaeleigh knew the truth of what she said, at least where Chel was concerned.

"Can you... well, can you talk back to it— the creature?" Kaeleigh said as she pointed toward the beast, switching gears.

"Um, I don't know. Let me try," she said, a bit shaky as she focused her eyes on the beast and squinted her eyes in concentration. "Hmm, nothing. Maybe it's one way, maybe he can't hear me." Chel sounded a little disappointed. The beast snorted and shook its head. "Let me try again, out loud," Chel said. "Sit," she commanded. The beast glared at her. Chel, rose to her feet and inhaled. "Will you sit...please?" The bear-like creature wiggled some then sat on its hind legs. "Oh!" Chel said, a bit surprised. "He can hear and understand us just fine, I guess. He prefers to hear our voices." She sounded a little embarrassed.

Kaeleigh had risen with her friend. "Don't worry, Chel, you've always been sensitive to animals. Maybe your gift is just amplified here." Chel slowly nodded.

"Send it on its way, Chel," Kaeleigh encouraged.

Chel stood up straight, trying to look taller and full of authority that she didn't have here in this place. "We will not harm you if you do not harm us. Move away slowly and be on your way." The beast lowered its head and slowly crouched forward to Chel. Everyone held perfectly still. It stopped right in front of her and bowed his head further. "You are welcome. Go and be safe." Chel held her hand out, and the creature pushed his nose to her hand and then licked her. Chel giggled and they watched as the cub scampered into the trees.

Finn didn't lower his daggers until the beast was far into the trees, beyond their sight. Daegan looked at Kaeleigh with one eyebrow raised in that cocky way that was also a bit of a breath-taker. He nodded at her. "Well done, Kaeleigh. We need to make camp for the night. We will not make it to my friend tonight. I hear a stream up ahead, let us press on only a bit further."

Well done, Kaeleigh, was all he said, and yet it sent flutters all through her stomach. It shouldn't have. Daegan led the way, while she and Chel walked together in the middle and Finn brought up the rear. *Lovely, a gender sandwich.*

They were still deep in the forest but had found a small and unusual clearing. It was surrounded by giant trees tall and proud, alongside quite a few smaller, clearly newer ones—all of them draped in greenery, as each clung tree to tree and branch to branch, as if stitched together. Large boulders and other smaller brush and newer growth were scattered amidst the clearing. The ground was mostly dirt but scattered patches of grasses, flowers, and various other coverings gave it a comfortable, peaceful atmosphere.

Kaeleigh took it all in thoughtfully. "There is something oddly familiar about this place," she said to no one in particular. "It looks like it was used for something. Those boulders don't look naturally placed the way they are. It's like they were put there to circle something."

Finn, too, looked around at what she was seeing and then stiffened. In a memory flash he was instantly taken back to a time many years ago. He had been here before... *But why would Kaeleigh find it familiar? Unless... could this have been in her visions?* Finn's hands at his sides began shaking.

Kaeleigh, closing the gap between them, asked, "Finn, are you okay? Did you hear something? Is someone coming?"

He quickly regained his composure and used her out. "I did think I heard something, but I must be too sensitive." *You would have heard it long before I did with that new hearing of yours,* he thought to himself. He inconspicuously tried to gauge Daegan's reaction as he no doubt heard their entire interaction.

Daegan's face remained impassive. He eyed the boulders, the layout of the clearing, the line of the trees, even the earth beneath their feet. Grim, but inflexible he looked at the group. "We should move on."

"What? Why?" Kaeleigh demanded.

"Yeah, why?" Chel asked at the same time, her eyes locked hard onto Daegan's and her arms stubbornly crossed at her chest. Her eyes though, immediately retreated when he returned her stare.

Because I have a job to do. I was sent on this mission for one person, it was not to be a group effort, Daegan's thoughts flooded his mind, not for the first time.

Finn remained quiet, but undoubtedly looked uncomfortable. Daegan looked to him, studying his face. *For what? Support? Allegiance? Well, he isn't going to get it from me even though I would do almost anything to not stay the night here,* Finn added nothing to the conversation, *Why would I give him the pleasure?*

A little smirk appeared at the side of Daegan's mouth as he suddenly came to some internal decision. "All right, after further thought, we will stay here as planned. You still good with that, *Finn*?"

All eyes shifted to Finn. He shifted his posture from defensive to casual, leaning against one of the boulders. He met the challenge. "Of course, fine," he said stronger than he felt at present. Finn wasn't going to give Daegan the satisfaction he was looking for. After all it had been ages since he had last been in this place—all it held were memories. "I'll get wood for a fire," Finn said casually as he exited the clearing.

The girls sagged against each other on a large boulder that was roughly flattened on top, making a nice place to sit. Kaeleigh hugged her knees up to her chest. "Now what?" Chel shrugged as they finally had gotten comfortable. Daegan studied several of the large boulders at the edge of the clearing, while occasionally picking up twigs and brush for kindling.

Despite his pretense and even some attempts to convince himself of the clearing's now benign nature, Finn's nerves were still high. They spiked even higher when he realized just where the girls were sitting. Panicked and unable to stifle it, he dropped the firewood in his arms. "Get off the rock," he choked out, voice barely above a whisper. "Get off NOW."

The *now* had a ring of authority but something more... blood-curdling fear. Kaeleigh and Chel jumped up as if their asses were on fire, remembering the last rock they thought was a boulder, but turned out to be a large beast of a creature.

"What? What?" they cried, flailing about as if something creepy crawly had climbed on them they were trying to get off.

Finn, white as a ghost, shook his head quickly and wiped a hand down his face to shake off the memories. He then kicked the rock to cover up the fear he'd let out. Intent on not making eye contact with Kaeleigh and not sounding either too concerned or too indifferent, he rebounded, "Okay, so I *might* have overreacted." He laughed it off like it was nothing.

His laugh was a little too forced, Kaeleigh thought, *but why?*

"I thought the rock moved, like it did right before we scared off the bear-like creature," Finn added lifting one shoulder, brushing it off, and closing further discussion and his expression down. "All the same, stay off those kinds of rocks—we don't want any more encounters." He then stormed back into the forest to get more firewood and blow off a little steam. If he was wound any more tightly, he was going to explode.

Daegan watched the charade with little interest at first. He had his own memories of this place, but Finn seemed to be much more haunted than he was letting on. The girls seemed to be oblivious—well at least Chel did—and Kaeleigh appeared to be putting on a bit of her own show for Finn, probably buying time while she puzzled it out. Daegan sensed that she was seeing something, but he wasn't sure what it was. Not that he cared. He didn't need to know anything about these people, as he was just delivering them amongst his other duties, but things were becoming more intriguing as well as complicated the further into Alandria they got. He must not get involved though. His arm had burned him a couple times already; a warning.

❈❈❈

The fire crackled and flared, emitting waves of heat as Kaeleigh, Chel, and Finn snuggled close together and warmed their hands and bodies by the hot flames. Daegan had returned from a quick hunting trip with a couple of rabbits that they cooked up for dinner. Kaeleigh had never eaten rabbit nor did she want to, but she was starving and stomached the new fare by pretending it was chicken. Chel, on the other hand, who had been sensitive to animals all her life, would have rather starved herself into an early grave before she ate Bambi or his friend Thumper. Luckily for her, they had packed some of their own snacks in their backpacks, which she eagerly opened and ate—fending off at least for one night the need to eat meat.

Night had fallen and with it a cool breeze. Daegan stood off a bit from their group as a sentinel, close enough that he could still feel the fire, but far enough not to be considered a part of the group. Isolated. His hand rested on the pommel of his sword strapped at his hip. His eyes scanned the forest, constantly on alert. Kaeleigh felt safe with him there, whether he was really there for their safety or just keeping them safe long enough to get *somewhere*—hopefully, somewhere with answers.

Finally resting in this place, she was able to give way to some of her thoughts. Finn didn't trust Daegan and she didn't completely either, but she wanted—no, *needed*—some answers, and right now that outweighed her uneasy feeling. Something strange was happening with her friends too, but she didn't know how to approach it, especially with Daegan around. Each time she felt like the time was right to say something to Finn or Chel, she'd clam up. She didn't want to expose her friends to a stranger. *Even though it seems he knows more about them than I do right now.* He had all but proven that he could hear extremely well too. There was that—her own enhanced hearing. This among the other surprising "gifts" she was discovering were hard to process for her. Most of all, this new energy stirring and fluttering up inside her body was exciting but also scary—she didn't know what to make of it.

Glancing back to where Daegan stood, she felt another emotion stir... sadness. He seemed not only distant and cold, but also alone. As if sensing her thoughts, he turned sharply to look at her with anger—no! hatred—in his eyes. She shrank back, taken off guard, and bumping into Chel in the process. Assuring Chel she was okay, she quickly glanced at Daegan again, to find him not looking at her but head down with a frown, pinching the bridge of his nose as if to relieve a headache. Something seemed off. There was an odd, faint green aura around him that she didn't remember seeing before. Well, she was not going to be some weak, helpless little girl that let some big mean guy bully her around. She didn't understand what she often saw storming in his eyes, but she would not be made to be afraid. Not again.

Kaeleigh got up and gathered her inner courage with her. *Come on, Kaeleigh, pull up those big-girl panties.* She didn't march like an entitled brat over to get in his face; she simply walked. Boldly. He didn't turn at her approach, although he knew she was coming. Rather, he ignored her, the ultimate insult. Kaeleigh got close, close enough that she could feel the heat radiating off of his chest but not so close that she couldn't look up to his face. Shaking inside, her heart beating loudly and out of control, she thought she might be sick, but took a deep breath to gather her control. Feeling that unfamiliar energy stirring within, her soul awakening to give her courage once again, she clenched and unclenched her fists, trying to regain control of her racing heart. She would not let him intimidate her. She would not back down until he acknowledged her.

Kaeleigh instinctively let go of the pressure that had been building inside her petite frame and directed it at Daegan. He flinched, though just barely. She wasn't even sure what had happened. Apparently, neither was he as he looked down at her with confusion then instinctively took the smallest step back. She had won. He looked even angrier, but she knew it wasn't at her, but at himself. Not wanting to pursue a challenge, she too took one step back. Daegan acknowledged her with the curtest nod. His eyes found hers, and she felt her breath hitch. There was connection. She had never felt that before. Kaeleigh could feel the energy surrounding her—his energy—reaching out and pulling her closer; a foreign feeling igniting a spark, her soul desiring to touch it. Kaeleigh didn't think he did it on purpose. When she remembered why she approached him, the connection broke. She felt empty and confused.

Shaking off the loss, Kaeleigh breathed deeply. "Right now, you are the key. You are the only thing leading me to what could be some understanding of who I am and what I've been searching for." She looked at him with carefully guarded hope. *What is it I should say... or not say?* "So I'm trusting you, for now, with our protection, which you have offered. I'm sure we are an inconvenience to your traveling, but I wanted to say... I appreciate it," she said, not really even sure why she did. Oddly, he stared at her with even more confusion and possibly anger. "Why are you so angry with me?" she said, slightly hurt. "I don't understand why you are so hostile toward me. Or are you always like this?"

To her surprise he answered her. "You may not ever understand who you truly are, and you must be prepared to be let down." He turned his head to gaze out past her. "Yes, I am pretty much always like this. And I am not angry with *you*," he shared in a rare moment of vulnerability. He closed his mouth, done discussing it, swallowing his own feelings and returning the mask of indifference, even anger. She wasn't entirely sure his answer was in regards to her at all.

Kaeleigh looked up at the small opening in the tree canopy that was above their little clearing. Stars were bursting everywhere. It was the most beautiful sight she had ever seen. "Everything is so much more vivid here. The night sky is unbelievable!"

In the same instant, Kaeleigh looked back frantically. Daegan stared at her in confusion and reached for his sword instinctively. "What? Do you hear something? See something?" Daegan strained to see or hear what Kaeleigh must be sensing, looking all around them. He was surprised she would hear something before his trained and sensitive ears would.

"Don't you hear it?" Kaeleigh asked, now holding a hand over one of her ears. "It's getting louder, what is it?"

Daegan, staring in bewilderment, then looked to her other friends. "Do you hear anything over there?" They both shook their heads and headed toward them. "We don't hear it, Kaeleigh. What do you hear?" Daegan said close to her ear, not sure if she could even hear him. She had both hands over her ears now and was starting to crumple to the ground. The anguish etched in her face showed obvious pain. It made him cringe and tore at something deep inside him.

"The buzzing, it's getting louder! Make it stop... head hurts... dizzy... who are they?" Kaeleigh said breathlessly, trying to get words out. Finn and Chel each grabbed one of her elbows, guiding her gently to the ground. Worried, they looked at each other and then at Daegan.

"Kaeleigh? What's wrong?" Chel asked. She looked up at Daegan with panic in her eyes, "What's wrong with her?"

Finn looked her over, trying to determine the cause. He placed his hand on her head and closed his eyes only to open them again. Frustrated and worried he yelled, "What are you doing to her?"

Daegan's eyes widened with instant fury and stepped toward Finn. "I did nothing to her!" he spat.

Chel grabbed Finn's arm and looked between them. "STOP IT! *Both* of you. Kaeleigh needs help, what do we do?" Chel yelled and pleaded at the same time. A trickle of blood dripped from Kaeleigh's nose, staining its trail down her face.

Daegan, not knowing if he could do anything to help, instinctively reached out and touched the side of her face with just the tips of his fingers. Kaeleigh stilled at his touch. He hadn't realized that she had been shaking. Daegan wasn't a healer. He didn't know what to do, but this seemed natural; it felt right. His empathic gift allowed him to read others. Strengthened through physical contact, he picked up some kind of static, LOUD static. Tremors crept up through his arm stemming from where he touched her. His eyes widened in surprise, but Daegan placed his other hand on the opposite side of her face, seeking a deeper connection. Slowly, she relaxed little by little into his hands and opened her eyes.

The first thing Kaeleigh saw were deep chocolate-brown eyes boring into hers. She locked on to the strength and intensity from them. Daegan was straining with his head tilted slightly to the right. Eyes still open, always on alert. Chel's expression had gone from fear for her friend to amazement at what she was seeing. Finn, on the other hand, now paced with agitation, looking on with skepticism, worry, and protection. At her sigh, he quickly moved close to her side. Seeing the color return to her face, the relaxation in her body, and that she was now all right, his eyes zeroed in on where Daegan's fingers cradled her face.

Then Kaeleigh's whole body suddenly relaxed as the buzzing ceased. Daegan removed his hands and took a step back to give her room. She could barely raise her head, but uttered an almost inaudible "Thank you." Her world tilted on its axis before she collapsed and passed out.

❃❃❃

Kaeleigh woke up slowly, limb by limb. She had no idea how long she had been out. It was dark now but that only told her it wasn't morning yet. The fire still crackled and Chel was huddled close to her, asleep. Light from the fire danced off the large boulder that sat at their back, making engrossing shadows to look at as she lay on the ground covered in a duster-style jacket that she recognized as Daegan's. She slowly raised her head, rolled to her side, and pushed herself up to sitting, but got woozy immediately and had to lay back down.

Daegan's voice, quiet but across the fire from them, carried to her. "Go easy or you'll just pass out again." She could almost hear the smirk at the end of that sentence.

Slowly, Kaeleigh tried to sit up once again, her hand holding her head. "How long was I out? Where's Finn?" she asked, noticing that he wasn't by the fire. Her head was pounding from a headache but not near the pain from last night or whenever it was. She sat cross-legged, rubbing her head and pinching the bridge of her nose.

"Not too long, maybe a few hours." Daegan's voice sounded strained and tired. "Finn is getting more firewood. He is keeping watch for a while."

Daegan's head was down, resting on his arms as he sat with his knees propped up. He didn't look too good. "Are you all right?" She was sure he wouldn't like being asked, but she had to ask anyway.

He lifted his head to look at her, offering a tight smile. "I will be fine. The question is *how are you*?" He stretched across the space separating them and handed her a flask of water, then leaned his head back against the rock that was holding him up.

Kaeleigh took a sip of the water, soothing her parched throat. "My head still hurts, but more like a headache and less like whatever happened before. I'm not sure what you did, but... thank you," Kaeleigh said remembering his hands, rough and calloused, but gentle on her face, easing the tension as soon as he touched her. "Are you some kind of healer?" She passed the flask back to him.

"A healer?" he laughed out. "No, I'm not." He closed his eyes and relaxed for a whole minute—something very unlike him. He seemed softer. Kaeleigh wished she could see more of that side of him. She didn't think he would say more, but then he did. "It is more an absorbing of your emotions to feel what you are feeling, not unlike an empath, but it seems I can also provide a little relief as well." He hesitated, "I—I did not know I could do that. It has never happened that way before." Daegan seemed confused or trying to work something out as he said it.

"Could you hear the buzzing? Do you know what it was? Are you sure you're okay, because you don't look too great. Did helping me take strength from you?"

Daegan sighed and looked over at her through heavy lids. "So many questions," he said with only a fraction of the exasperation he usually showed her.

"I'm sorr... " she started to say.

He held up a hand to interrupt her. "You do not need to be sorry, Kaeleigh, I'm just not used to it." He paused, considering which of her many questions to answer. "I did not really *hear* your buzzing, but I could *feel* it. I am not sure, but I think I could hear something else... something under the static, almost like voices, but a kind of speech. I could not decipher it though." Daegan took a deep breath. "It sounded like something I, too, recently experienced." He closed his eyes once more and simply breathed. "I'll recover soon; I can already feel my body strengthening. I must have absorbed some of your weakened energy from the pain or maybe from giving my own energy. Like I said, it has never happened that way before." He raised his head and looked at her with a corner of his mouth turned up in a lazy smile that made those damn butterflies in her stomach jump around again. "No more questions?" Daegan asked sarcastically, looking surprised.

"Oh, I have plenty more," Kaeleigh bantered back, "but I didn't want *you* fainting from exhaustion before Finn got back to witness it."

"HA!" Daegan grunted out with a hint of laughter. "He'd like that, wouldn't he?"

Kaeleigh smiled. "Yes, he would... probably too much," she added. *This Daegan is playful. I like him.*

"My turn," Daegan said simply. When Kaeleigh looked up at him, confused, he added, "To ask the questions."

"Okay, fire away."

"Do *you* have any idea what that buzzing was?" he asked, a little more serious.

Kaeleigh shook her head, immediately wishing that she hadn't. Putting her hand to her head she groaned, "Should not have moved my head like that." She held her head as if she could stop the feeling just with her hand then looked up at Daegan and was surprised at the concern she saw in his eyes. *What was his question? Oh yeah... buzzing.* "Um, no I don't know what it was... although for some reason it felt familiar, but I don't know why. Back home I would get visions that were preceded by a fuzzy buzzing sound but nothing like that. Maybe it's similar?" She looked at Daegan without moving her head to find him frowning, deep in thought.

He noticed her and nodded. "It could be, perhaps more enhanced in Alandria." His words were indulgent, but his eyes were pondering.

"That made me feel crazy and sick with pain like I have never felt before." She rubbed her head. "That's messed up," she said gazing into the firelight.

"Okay. Next question." Daegan paused, checking that she was okay to go on. Kaeleigh nodded carefully and gestured *be my guest* with her hand. "Why are you here?" Kaeleigh looked at him, confused at his question. As she was about to say something, he cut her off. "Let me rephrase. Why did you come with me not knowing where you were going or what you might encounter, especially to a place that you do not understand—a realm outside of your own, with magic you should not even believe in?"

Kaeleigh gazed at him thoughtfully yet skeptically before she decided that she wanted to trust him with her answer. He waited patiently, encouraging her decision to trust him. "I have been looking for some answers to questions I have had about my life, who I am, who and maybe where my parents are... why they gave me up." Almost whispering the last part, she looked at the ground while trying to find the words to what she wanted to say.

"I have always felt different, like I don't fit in." She looked down at Chel, her best friend, lying asleep next to her on the ground. "Don't get me wrong, Chel and her family have taken me in and loved me like their own, but I'm missing a connection and have all these little holes in my heart that long to be filled." Taking a deep breath, Kaeleigh was surprised at her vulnerability with this *stranger*. She was sharing things she hadn't even fully expressed to Chel or Finn, but something in her made her want to keep talking to Daegan. "I don't know where else to look back home—which has never felt like *home*. Then all of a sudden you, a stranger, presented me with this completely wild and unbelievable alternative. So, of course, I jumped at it, thinking, why not? It couldn't offer me any less than what I know now." She laughed a little self-consciously and looked at Daegan.

Daegan looked a bit caught off guard, then narrowed his gaze at Kaeleigh. "That was very... honest of you." He looked confused and maybe shocked at Kaeleigh's frank vulnerability. "I noticed that you didn't say 'Why not? What could it hurt?' because it can hurt and it might hurt you, Kaeleigh," he said with a speck of torment flashing across his face.

Kaeleigh saw the look in his eyes. She recognized it. She was intimate with it. It was something that reverberated deep in a closed-off chasm of her heart that she dared not open for fear it might drown and suffocate her into oblivion. Her heart instantly hurt at the knowledge that he knew as deep a pain and loss as she did.

Just as she was about to say something, a rustling sound came from a patch of small trees and bushes beyond the boulder where Daegan was sitting. Finn jumped out from behind the bushes; well, more like tripped out. He stumbled and dropped the armload of wood he had been holding, which woke Chel up with a start. Everyone jumped up, which considering Kaeleigh and Daegan's current condition was more of a feat than it should have been had there been a real threat.

Finn placed his hands on his waist, breathing heavily. The scowl on his face, his eyebrows practically striking his eyes, accompanied by the rage of aggravation he let loose indicated his fury. The others stared between Finn and the tree line, waiting and watching with anxious anticipation. Finn stepped away from the bushes and studied the others, realizing the edge he put the others on. "Sorry... sorry, Chel, didn't mean to wake you." Finn's dusted himself off and glared back at the shrubbery. "I got tripped up in those stupid vines," he pointed back to where he broke through the tree line into the clearing.

As if on cue, the bushes rustled with movement. Two thin vines barnacled with thorns twisted and rotated like tentacles, breaking through branches. An overt gasp was issued from the girls. Finn, prepared with better footing, drew his knives from either of his sides and in one swift movement, sliced through each vine lobbing off the tail of it, leaving it to flop like a fish out of water until it stilled, defeated. He mumbled something incoherent as he went about his work, satisfied with what he had done, picking up the dropped pieces of wood. Unaware of the girls' eyes wide with shock and Daegan standing in front of them with his sword pointed out ready to strike, Finn continued adding the wood to the slowly dying fire.

Finn stopped and looked up at Kaeleigh with his intensely warm hazel eyes. He was more flustered than Kaeleigh had ever seen him, but all her nerves were on edge from his sudden appearance. She was still reeling with words she wanted to say to Daegan, adrenaline pumping from Finn's clumsiness, not sure if she should be getting ready to run or bracing for a fight, and concern over Finn's apparent unease about something she only wished she understood. He must have seen the confusion and fear in her eyes because he looked over at Daegan's eyes and flinched, seeing nothing but anger and the readiness to fight. Finn relaxed and slowed what he was doing.

"Everything is all right, Kaeleigh. There is no fight," Finn said, holding his hands up to diffuse the tension, more for Daegan than Kaeleigh. Daegan was recovering from having helped Kaeleigh and was caught with his guard down; an infuriation for a warrior with a charge to protect, a feeling he knew too well. He appreciated what Daegan had done for Kaeleigh and didn't want to start something for Kaeleigh's sake. Finn still didn't completely trust Daegan's motivations, but he would protect them—her—with the honor of a noble warrior and Finn understood that part of him.

Everyone stood facing the newly stoked fire, staring beyond it out into the woods. They had backed down, ensuring themselves while trying to calm the overriding adrenaline rush that, indeed, no fight was coming to them. After what seemed like forever, Chel grabbed Kaeleigh's arm and tugged her toward the opposite direction of where the boys stood in what looked to be another stare-down.

Daegan, not missing anything, but refusing to remove his stare from Finn, said, "Where do you think you two are going?"

Kaeleigh and Chel flinched at the anger in his voice, but then both regained their backbone. Chel jumped at the chance to counter Daegan. "*We* are going to find the little girls' room AND we are going *alone* AND perhaps we will look for some water while we are out!" Chel growled, her eyes big and saucer-like. Kaeleigh had never seen her friend so commanding before, but oddly it suited her so she backed her up with a nod and folded arms, daring the two overprotective male egos to try to stop them. The greater concern at hand broke the spell between the two warriors, and they shifted their penetrating stares to the girls.

"I don't think so!" Finn retorted. "Did you not just see me fighting those vines? It's dangerous out there." He pointed into the forest beyond.

"We saw, and we'll be careful," Kaeleigh came back.

"We won't go far, and you could always give us one of your knives," Chel added with a twinkle in her eyes.

"I will follow and get the water not far from you then," Finn stated.

Chel gasped. "Not while we are doing our business!"

Finn frowned, but Daegan assessed the look in Chel's eyes and, seeing something there he approved of, cocked an eyebrow and nodded. Finn stood there, shocked that Daegan had let them leave without one of them, privacy be damned.

Kaeleigh and Chel turned and huffed off laughing, walking quickly away from their camp before the guardians changed their minds.

"Give them a small head start," Daegan whispered to Finn, "she can handle a few seconds and we won't lose sight of them." *Her strengths are growing and perhaps I can get a read on Finn,* Daegan thought.

"Score one for Chel!" Kaeleigh giggled out with their small victory for a few minutes without *boys.*

Walking for not much more than a minute, they grew silent, both heavy with things they wanted to share with one another, but neither knowing how to begin. There is a point even in the deepest friendships when it becomes hard to share things if moments of lost or failed opportunities kept getting passed over. A rift begins to form and a bridge needs to be rebuilt, but sadly that was not this time.

Chel sighed and said in hushed tones, "You know they are following us, don't you?"

Kaeleigh nodded. "I knew they wouldn't let us get too far without them." She laughed with expected defeat. "It was nice for them to give us the illusion for a few minutes at least." Then she shrugged. Kaeleigh knew they could hear them too, or at least Daegan could. A few minutes later Chel pointed to small gathering of thick bushes that would work nicely for doing what needed to be done.

"Well, *anyone* following us better leave us be for a couple moments... for REAL," Chel playfully grumbled loudly enough for them to hear. They laughed, used the bushes, then headed back to intercept the guys on their way back.

Chapter Twenty-Three

It was too late when Kaeleigh and Chel realized that they may have "turned back" the wrong way. Surrounded by the darkness the canopy of the old forest provided, Kaeleigh could feel dawn quickly approaching. It tingled under her skin, even though it was still very dark. With only the light from the makeshift torch they had brought with them from the fire, they stumbled around, tripping on fallen twigs and branches in the dark.

Chills broke out all over Kaeleigh's body and ran from her arms up her neck and down her spine. A twig snapped behind and to their left, and both their heads swung in that direction. Kaeleigh jerked on Chel's arm, pulling her close to her side. They both froze where they stood, looking all about them. Chel's gaze landed on Kaeleigh, panic in her eyes. Kaeleigh held her index finger to her mouth. Without words, they simply listened. After a moment, each looked at the other, simultaneously mouthing "the guys," then relaxed and rolled their eyes.

"SNAP!" A louder snap from the opposite direction. Their head swiveled in that direction. Kaeleigh's heart began to race, a sheen of sweat escaped her brow. She squeezed Chel's arm harder. They looked around where they stood, seeing nothing outside of the limited light their torch provided. When Chel moved the torch back and forth too quickly for Kaeleigh to attempt at seeing anything, she grabbed it away from Chel. Another twig snapped in yet different direction from the last noise. The girls pivoted together toward it. Chel's eyes got big, then angry as she put her hands on her hips and brazenly began to stomp off in the direction of the last sound. Grabbing Chel and jerking her back against her, Kaeleigh hissed quietly, "What are you doing?"

Chel whispered back, "If this is their idea of a joke, it's not funny in the dark!" Her face tight with anger gave way to the true fear she felt.

Kaeleigh slowly shook her head. She cocked her head still listening for noises, any sign that something or someone drew near. The forest had gone silent, eerie with lack of sound from even the night insects. The forest made no other indication of life, as though everything around them froze when they did. After yet another noise, more subtle than the first and again in an entirely separate direction, Chel went white as a ghost and mouthed, "Not them?" knowing what the answer would be. Kaeleigh grabbed Chel's hand and whipped her behind her so their backs were together, each facing out.

Both girls stood back to back stunned in place staring out into the darkness, watching, waiting painfully, and listening intently... but nothing happened. They stood like that for several minutes before saying anything or moving a muscle. Kaeleigh went over in her head what they could do, if anything. *We have no weapons, and we are apparently alone. We know some self defense, but I have no idea how that fares to creatures of this realm.*

Kaeleigh whispered first. "Keep moving? Stay put? Or scream?"

"Um, keep moving?" Chel answered uncertainly, but Kaeleigh concurred.

Slowly, with arms linked, they kept walking in the direction they hoped was where the guys were. As much as they wanted time alone, Kaeleigh couldn't actually believe they really *let* them go off on their own—in a place they had never been, no less. The more she thought about it, the more pissed off she got; after all, they were supposed to be *protecting* her, and *Daegan* was supposed to be *guiding* her. Good luck with that, if she gets lost in the deep dark forest. Daegan's superiors wouldn't be happy that was for sure. He should be looking for her, if for no other reason than for his own self-preservation.

UGH! Since when had she *needed* anyone? When did she stop relying on herself? She took a deep breath, then looked over at her friend, who had selflessly accompanied her into the unknown and had always stood by her side. She would make sure they found their way out. They walked for several minutes without a sound from any direction.

"Do you think whatever was there is gone now?" Chel whispered.

"I dunno, Chel. I don't think so. I have that feeling you get when someone's watching you," Kaeleigh whispered back, squeezing Chel's arm. "We've got to be getting close to where the guys should be."

Chel nodded. "Is it me or does it seem to be getting darker? Isn't it close to dawn?"

Kaeleigh replied, "Yeah, it's getting darker. That's not right... I can *feel* dawn. Don't ask me how, but the sun is starting to rise. Stay close, Chel." *We should have screamed.*

Both Kaeleigh and Chel held their torches up, trying to see where they were going, but the fire only lent them a few feet of light in front of them at best. Kaeleigh's heart sped up and her palms began to sweat. Something wasn't right; that much was obvious. It didn't make sense they should be heading back toward the camp. They hadn't wandered off *that* far and they walked back directly in the direction that they had come from. Plus they both were pretty good with direction, especially Chel.

Surprisingly, Kaeleigh didn't hear the silent slithering across the ground until it was too close. She gripped Chel tighter. It all happened so fast, with hardly time to register what was happening. She couldn't hold on. Chel was ripped out of her grasp screaming. A rush of wind with an icy chill extinguished their torches, which had been thrown to the ground, leaving only darkness and the smell of burnt wood. The last thing she saw was Chel's horror-stricken face being sucked into a void of darkness. Then silence.

❊❊❊

Kaeleigh awakened out of a state of shock that felt like forever—but must have only been mere seconds—shaking, with a cold sweat drenching her head. There was a loud piercing noise that she could feel in her inner depths, making her chest heave until the moment she realized it was her screaming Chel's name over and over into the darkness. Anger like she had not known or had allowed herself to know flooded out from within her. Tingling shocks went through her body and—somehow—out from her fingertips. A fire sparked life on the end of her torch lying on the ground a few feet away from her. Surprised, but not allowing herself to think about it, she pulled herself up from the ground and grabbed the torch. She paused, willing herself to listen for any signs of movement, any signs at all as to which way her friend had been taken. Tears streamed down her face. She stood there, refused to believe or to even think of the possibility that her friend was lost to her, when she heard the faint sound of a struggle in the distance. *Yes!* Kaeleigh took off in the direction of the sound, not even caring what she might be running into other than the hope she might find Chel—alive.

A blinding light burst forth, piercing the darkness right in front of Kaeleigh as she skidded to a stop and held her arms up in front of her face. The light was accompanied by a strange static noise and a feeling of familiarity not unlike what she had felt before but without all the pain. Kaeleigh couldn't decipher at first what she only imagined to be whispering by several different voices. She cautiously began to lower her hands in an attempt to see something, but all she could do was squint, hoping the light wouldn't blind her. She didn't have time for anything but to find Chel. She felt defeat begin to overwhelm her, and then she heard her name whispered. Again trying to look into the light, she caught a squinted glimpse of something... a face. No body, just a face. A face without much definition that seemed to be altering and morphing into multiple faces all at the same time.

The voices spoke as one voice, again in whispered tones but louder this time. "Kaeleigh... Kaeleigh... time is short... you must listen... your friend needs you."

"Who are you? Can you help me find Chel? I need to find her! Please!" Kaeleigh shouted desperately at the face floating before her with tears streaming down her face.

The face flew right up in front of her. Kaeleigh jumped in surprise but did not back down. "Listen," the voices said again, "time and space have been suspended and altered in this place. You have what you need to bring her freedom, but beware as she is not the one sought after... It's a... They need... You need... in the end. Keep them close... to be set free..." The voice began buzzing and fading out like a radio station cutting in and out.

"Wait! What? Who needs to be set free? How do I get Chel? Wait..." Kaeleigh shouted at nothing as the face faded away and the light became darkness again as quickly as it had come. Looking around her, Kaeleigh realized she could see what was in front of her. *I can see!* It was still dark, but somehow she could see through the darkness like a veil.

Kaeleigh was shocked to see that not more than a yard in front of her was a rock face belonging to a shear cliff that stretched far above her, three stories at least. *Where did that come from?* It was partially concealed by an innumerable amount of crawling vines and branches. All behind her were thick groupings of trees, but these trees didn't have the same feel of the ones that she had just been surrounded with; these felt dark and creepy. Not only did they appear to form a barrier behind her, but they actually physically started to grow and weave together, fencing her in.

Trapped. Kaeleigh surveyed the area behind her: she had the cliff, positive she wouldn't be climbing; and next to her, a crevice of blackness nestled—hidden—into the side of the cliff. Panic welled up within Kaeleigh, surging through her body. *Of course there's a cave. The voices didn't say anything about a cave.* Her hands shook, her heart accelerated, and her breathing labored. She sighed. It didn't matter, she still would have come if it meant she had the slightest chance to help her best friend, her sister. Chel. *She has to be in the cave! Well, something has to be in the cave*, Kaeleigh thought, having already made up her mind.

Heading toward the cave, Kaeleigh spotted a sharp-pointed stick not too far away. She ran to grab it, thinking a weapon of any kind might come in handy. The same slithering sound she heard right before Chel was taken, grew louder behind her. Quickly, she spun around, stick pointed out reflexively. She couldn't believe her eyes.

The trees were knitting themselves together more tightly, causing them to move forward, herding Kaeleigh back toward the cliff wall behind her. Although she wasn't sure why she was surprised; after all, she *was* in a fantasy land where she didn't know what was possible or what the rules were. Before she had a chance to run into the cave, vines snaked out from behind the wall of trees that suddenly appeared to be quite impenetrable and pushed her forcibly against the cliff at her back. Kaeleigh struggled. The vines slithered around her ankles and wrists like snakes, anchoring her to the netting of vines and branches behind her against the cliff face. Still she struggled, and the vines slithered and snaked around her waist, securing her even tighter to the wall. She could hardly move, but still she writhed and wiggled in an effort to gain even an inch more.

Desperately trying to suppress the quickly rising panic, Kaeleigh searched frantically for something, *anything*, she could use to help her fight her way out. She *had* to get out. Chel was depending on her and she didn't know how much time she had to get to her. Flashes of the words from the Voices and from Daegan about being *the one* they had been waiting for and setting someone free were running like a reel in her head, then suddenly stopped. Kaeleigh remembered the pointy stick she had picked up; she was still tightly gripping it.

"I don't know who you all think I am, but I know I'm not going to let you hold me here," Kaeleigh ground out between her teeth. Then without thinking she released a shout that had been growing deep within her—the cry of a fighter, the cry of a lost warrior.

She fought with her body harder than she had ever fought before, all the while thinking of Chel and how desperately she needed to find her. Suddenly the vines gave just an inch or two, but it was enough for Kaeleigh to position her hand. She stabbed the vine holding her waist with the pointy end of the stick. The vine let out a screech and hiss before recoiling back into the wall and falling limp where she had pierced it. Growing hot in the unrelenting grip of her hand, the sharp stick seemed to absorb her strength and energy.

Again and again she stabbed at whatever vines she could reach until they had released her. She fell to the ground, scrambling away from the wall but not getting too close to the infantry of trees either. Panting and trying to catch her breath, she gripped her stick, pointing it out and all around her to ensure that the vines stayed slain where they lay on the ground. Though terrified and shaking, she felt strong and empowered.

As her breathing slowed, she realized that the stick she held felt heavier and smoother in her hands. She looked down at what was no longer a pointed piece of nature but a beautiful, shiny, ornate sword. Kaeleigh gasped in awe, completely confused, but not having time to consider it as rustling stirred the barrier of trees surrounding her. Grunts and hollers of satisfaction and victory were coming from behind or from somewhere within the web of vines and layers of branches that were woven tight. The impenetrable wall was slowly being brought to its destruction. Branches, leaves, and vines were being thrown in the air and trampled underfoot as metal slashed away and eviscerated the tangled web. As thankful as she was to see the wall being torn apart, she didn't know what was about to break through to where she waited, sword drawn out in front of her trembling slightly as her adrenaline wore off.

She was a mess; hair in knots, clothes disheveled, surface cuts, and what for sure would be bruises all over her body from the vines. But she would fight.

With a final "HA!" and vigorous hacks from swords, the last layer of the wall of trees fell. Bursting through came two fierce warriors of an unearthly kind. They took her breath away, bringing relief at the same time.

"Kaeleigh!" Finn shouted as he ran to her and gripped her in a tight hug. "You're okay! You are okay, right?"

Kaeleigh, more than a little relieved, hugged him back with tears running down her face. "Chel—they took Chel! You have to help me, we have to find her." Still holding onto Finn, she raised her eyes and looked back toward the wall, where Daegan was still standing, holding his sword and staring at her with a blind intensity in his eyes. He was angry. Infuriated that he would be angry at them, at her, for what happened, she pushed Finn away and marched over to Daegan, gesturing at him with the hilt end of her new sword.

"You are supposed to be protecting us! How could you let this happen? Why didn't you follow us? We *heard* you." She kept marching at him. "Chel's gone and you're angry at *me*? Where do you get off?"

Kaeleigh wanted to fight. She needed to take her fury out on someone, but he didn't even try to fight her back, which only made her more infuriated. In the background of her yelling, Finn was apologizing to her, trying to calm her down, trying to tell her that they had been "detained" by the evil vines and were being kept away. She either didn't hear him or didn't acknowledge what he was saying as she kept yelling at Daegan; there was strangely some satisfaction in being able to yell at him, to blame him... someone... when she was really so angry at herself for getting Chel kidnapped. *It's all my fault.*

Finally, Daegan interrupted her rant with one of his own. "YES! I am angry. You should not have gone off on your own in a strange—not to mention enchanted—place, especially a dark forest like this. You should know better. You should have stayed with me, but you just had to be independent and go off on your own." He sighed, running a hand down his exhausted face. "But mostly I am angry at myself. I let you go. We followed you, but I didn't hear the simultaneous attack, I couldn't fight them off fast enough to get to you." With his jaw clenched he inhaled through his nostrils, then he amended it with, "I couldn't get to you and Chel, before it was too late."

Daegan and Kaeleigh both paused, breathing deeply and staring at each other in the uncomfortable, intense moment they had created. Each with nothing more to say, yet the silence was heavy with the expectation of more that needed to be said.

Out of the silence, Finn brought the situation to an immediate change, his voice laced with worry and something sounding like anger. "Kaeleigh? How do we find Chel? Who took her?"

Abruptly, Kaeleigh turned to face Finn. When she did she saw a complexity in the emotions in his face that she had not seen before, and it gave her pause. She took wobbly steps toward him and tripped over the tip of her sword. Finn reached out to steady her as Daegan's audible gasp caused them both to quickly turn to see what he reacted to.

"Kaeleigh? Where did you get that sword?" Daegan said with suspicion, awe, reverence, even with fear.

"Oh, that," she said, looking over the impressive sword with detailed scroll work along the cross-guard. "I don't know," she started sheepishly. "I was fighting for my life, for Chel," Kaeleigh wanted to get moving on but was still shaken by her experience with the vines. "These vines attacked me and pinned me to the wall." Her eyes held back emotion and fear. "I was fighting them with this random stick I picked off the ground." Looking down at it she continued with more energy, "Suddenly, I started stabbing the vines with the stick, the stick became stronger, almost alive. I know it sounds crazy, but well, that's what happened." She took a deep breath. "When I looked down at it after the vines had retreated, I saw that it had transformed into a sword." Her eyes were glistening with excitement. "I mean, I was as surprised as the next person!"

When they both looked at her like she *was* crazy, she told them quickly about being blinded by light, and the Voices that tried to speak to her. Not willing to get too close, she pointed toward the wall, showing them proof of the lifeless vines strewn on the ground. Had they not had battled the vines themselves, she was sure that part of the story would be proof that she wasn't in fact nuts.

But looking back at the destroyed vines on the ground revealed more than what she remembered leaving there. She gasped. Where the vines had been growing amongst the cliff, now several small orchids bloomed, full of life. Oddly, when she turned back to the guys, she found the opposite of what she expected: Daegan pale and Finn suspiciously satisfied.

"What are *they* doing here?" She pointed a shaking finger back at the orchids.

"What do you mean?" Daegan asked.

"Those are *my* orchids! They've followed me around all my life." Kaeleigh spoke with a lump in her throat. Not knowing what they meant or where they came from, she was endeared to them just the same. And now here, of all places, they came to give her comfort. She wanted to take a moment to be comforted, to listen to the message they were relaying. *Things really would be okay.* But she knew they had to keep going.

Startling her out of her moment, Daegan whispered, strangely shocked but pointing to the stick-turned-sword. "Kaeleigh? Do you know what that is or what it could mean?"

Kaeleigh frowned at him. "It's a sword," she replied sarcastically, but without a reaction from him she continued, "As for *whose* it is or *where* it came from... I have no idea. How would I know? I barely know anything about this place." She then looked at Finn to gauge his reaction as he remained silently observing.

Daegan regaining his usual stoicism that Kaeleigh was beginning to believe to be a facade, squared his shoulders, and began to head toward the crevice in the wall. "I'll explain as we go. We must get to Chel. Quickly."

They couldn't have agreed more on anything. Daegan led their way into the dark cave while Finn brought up the rear, leaving Kaeleigh right in the middle of her two warriors. *At least I have a sword now too.*

CHAPTER TWENTY-FOUR

"**K**aeleigh, stay close. You never know what might be in the darkness," Finn cautioned as he held out one of the sticks that they had picked up to light. He didn't have to tell her twice.

Daegan had used magic to give flame to his own and to Kaeleigh's but when he started to light Finn's, he smiled wickedly at him and added, "No, you never know what might be in the darkness, do you, Finn?" Then he turned his back and kept walking into the dark cave, leaving Finn's torch unlit.

Kaeleigh turned to Finn and spoke loudly. "Well, that was just rude! Here, Finn, light yours off of mine. What was that all about anyway?" Finn shrugged without looking at Kaeleigh but stared blankly after Daegan ahead of them. *What does he know about me?* Finn wondered.

"Come on, we don't want to lose him... Well, actually, I do but not in here," Finn added with his familiar smirk and smile, pushing Kaeleigh on ahead of him.

Kaeleigh sighed. "Ugh, another dark, dank cave. I hate the dark. I hate caves, especially this one. It feels... dark."

Finn replied with a lighthearted, "Um, that's because it is dark."

"Nice," she said as she rolled her eyes at him. "No, I mean it actually *feels* dark... like evil dark. Can't you feel it?"

Both Daegan and Finn answered, "Yes."

But Daegan continued, "This is one of the caves at Vuldün. There have been whisperings of darkness—evil—here."

"I think it's more than just a rumor," Kaeleigh said as she held herself and tried to look around.

As they walked, the light from their torches bounced off the compacted dirt walls. Above them dangled tangled messes of roots that had broken through their earth's boundary. A musty smell attempted to choke Kaeleigh, and she tried to breathe as little of the air as possible. She brought the front of her shirt up over her mouth in attempt to squelch the noxious odor. Where the light hit on the tunnel around them, it sent creatures scurrying back into the darkness behind them. Kaeleigh tried to shake off the chills that kept running up and down her spine. The creepy-crawlies did not help.

"Daegan?" Kaeleigh asked quietly. She wasn't sure if it was okay to be talking or not, but she needed a distraction as well as answers.

"What, Kaeleigh?" he replied. She couldn't help it, she smiled when he said her name. It made her feel wrapped in warmth even in this dark cold place. For the briefest moment she was grateful that it was more dark than light. She felt safe with him—well, with both Daegan and Finn—there with her. In her heart, Kaeleigh knew that she would have braved this darkness to find Chel on her own, but she was extremely grateful she didn't have to now.

"Who do you think took Chel?" Kaeleigh asked, trying to get him talking again.

A long silence left Kaeleigh despairing the answer was far worse than she could imagine. Daegan sighed, then answered, "There are evils in this land. You must understand, most are not heard from much. Recently, a shift in the stars occurred, and all things evil and dark began stirring in different parts of Alandria. Something is happening, but we do not yet know what. The change in the stars was caused by a rift in the earth magic that protects our realm."

While Daegan paused, Kaeleigh interjected impatiently, "But what does that have to with Chel? And *who* are they?"

"Many different forms come out of darkness. But who I think took Chel, and is holding her, is someone who works for or is a part of the Droch-Shúil." Daegan stopped talking when Finn gasped and dropped his torch.

Kaeleigh spun around. "Finn?" she asked, concerned.

"I'm here, Kaeleigh. Just dropped my torch."

"Who or what is this Droch-Shúil?" After making sure Finn had his torch, she looked at Finn. "Do *you* know what it is?"

Finn paused. "I was shocked to hear that name. It's a name I haven't heard in quite some time." Numbly, Finn motioned for them to continue moving. He looked to Daegan expectantly, as if to say that because he hadn't been here in quite some time, Daegan should take the lead.

"Daegan, what do they want with her?" Kaeleigh asked, wanting Daegan's answer more than Finn's secret knowledge.

Daegan was still staring back at Finn. *What is this guy about?* Outwardly, he wouldn't let Finn in on his thoughts, so he shrugged his shoulders and simply said, "I do not know." He kept walking and urging the others to keep up. He paused and looked back, impressing upon them the gravity of the situation. "It is possible we are walking into a trap. We must be prepared for anything." Daegan turned and continued walking cautiously forward. "The Droch-Shúil is an ancient entity of darkness that is a host for souls that went bad—thus the name for the unforgiven dead. Some even say it is a kind of collective demon; the host itself being an elusive creature made up of darkness, and its extensions made up of followers." Eerie silence weighed heavily upon them for the next several minutes while Kaeleigh processed Daegan's information.

Dun dun dun, Kaeleigh's inner monologue couldn't help but insert in response to her already frayed sanity.

"They usually employ others to do their dirty work as they reside in another realm for the exiled. Their venom is poison; you do not want to get bit or scratched by one of them," Finn said quietly.

Kaeleigh looked back at Finn, confused. He replied in answer to her silent question, "I've read some ancient histories of Celtic myths and legends; it is similar to a creature they refer to. I've heard about the Droch-Shúil before, but be warned here myths are also real." Finn's voice and tone belied truth, but something in the color of his aura caused red flags for Kaeleigh.

"It is true," Daegan jumped in. "The Droch-Shúil have been around forever, and they are known to many different times and places as different things. The souls that get taken to the realm of Exhile are consumed into the desolate land. But if they are enslaved by the demon hosts before that occurs, they become part of the Droch-Shúil." Daegan looked back at them briefly as he walked, continuing his education surrounding the evil entity. "The lost souls and the souls of the damned are taken to Exhile by the Ferriers—a race of beings whose sole purpose is that. But it is rumored that some Ferriers have chosen a side and become part of the darkness." Chills ran up Kaeleigh's spine and she shuddered. Finn placed his hand on her shoulder.

Daegan went on, "The concerning part is why now and why here are they choosing to focus their efforts?" Though he spoke out loud it was clear he was talking mostly to himself, as he knew an answer wasn't to be found among them. "We need to seek counsel after we have found Chel, assuming she is still alive," Daegan added almost heartlessly.

Kaeleigh inhaled at his bluntness. "She most certainly will be alive! You could try to be a little sensitive," she stated shakily. "I can't lose her. I won't lose her," Kaeleigh whispered to herself.

Finn's hand found her shoulder again and squeezed it. "We'll find her in time," he said, trying to reassure her. Not saying anything else, she reached up and squeezed his hand in return.

Daegan lowered his head and stopped. He turned and looked Kaeleigh straight in the eye with awkward, but genuine humbleness. "I am sorry, do forgive me."

Taken aback by his sudden vulnerability toward her, she nodded in acceptance.

"Listen," Daegan cautioned. They all stopped and listened intently.

"It's the slithering. We must be getting close," Kaeleigh whispered, knowing he could hear her.

"That—or it's getting closer to us... Have your swords ready," Daegan said as he drew his weapon out in front of him. "Kaeleigh, can you wield that weapon?"

She glared then smirked. "Well enough," she replied, remembering how she could feel something within her directing her movements outside of the cave. It gave her strength.

Suddenly, slithering noises seemed to be on all sides of them in the dark tunnel. The same snakelike vines that were outside the cave were now burrowing their way out of the walls, flailing about as they broke from the dirt seeking purchase on their victims. Kaeleigh sucked her screech in, fear gripping her to the core as one grabbed at her ankle and then again at her arms. All three of them sliced and hacked away at any that got close to them as they kept trying to push forward through the tunnel. The walls began to shake as vines kept breaking through. Dirt was falling in their hair and their eyes. They had to get to Chel at all costs.

This would definitely slow them down, but they were determined and continued on, hoping it wasn't much further.

In a cavern, at the end of the tunnel not far from where Daegan, Finn, and Kaeleigh battled the unrelenting vines, Chel was chained to the only part of the wall that had stone. Not only was she chained by the black metal shackled about her wrists and ankles, but she was also held captive by thick, thorny vines jutting out from holes in the stone and wrapped around her torso. Weak from having struggled with the vines and those vile creatures, she let the vines hold her weight as she tried to regain some strength.

On the ground and on her skin were trails of dried blood where the thorns had originally pricked her flesh, joined by fresh blood tracks from wounds that kept reopening when she moved and kept her weak. Her flesh would heal then start the process over again each time she wiggled too much. *Best not to move, Chel*, she chided herself. Welts and bruises had formed in multiple places, but overall she had not been injured too badly, considering she had been kidnapped. How long she had been there—days? hours?—she had no point of reference.

Chel thought that perhaps one of her wrists had broken when they tried to wrench her into the black cuffs that burned her skin, but she couldn't feel it anymore. She was, however, pretty sure that the thorns had some kind of poison or drug in them as she felt strangely delirious when she was coherent. Other times, she would wake up groggy, not knowing where she was, how long she had been there, or how she had even gotten there. A couple times she opened her eyes to see a large, ugly, beastly face inches away simply staring at her. She would scream until she passed out again. They never said anything to her. Trying to figure out why she was here, she would yell and scream at them hoping for something—anything—until she finally realized it was a futile attempt.

In a rare moment of clarity, she tried to listen to her captors. They must have thought she was unconscious because they were mumbling amongst themselves not only in a foreign tongue but also without words. Chel thought that they must have been some kind of animal, or at least part animal, as she was able to pick up their thoughts or mental images with her newfound gift. Unfortunately, she didn't seem to be able to control it and it only seemed to work when they were communicating, which was hardly ever. What she did picked up, though, was disturbing, evil, and dark. It included a girl that they were supposed to capture, and at first Chel figured they'd accomplished that part of the plan. The image was blurry, but right before they stopped "talking," she saw the image. Hanging her head, she realized this was a trap, and she was the bait. She didn't know why, but she knew who they wanted.

CHAPTER TWENTY-FIVE

Daegan, quickly scanning the two-story-high cavern filled with stalagmites and crystals as he slashed through his last vine obstacles, spotted Chel chained to the back stone wall. She struggled profusely against the vines when she saw him enter the cavern. He saw a weak but very much alive girl, eyes big with fear but also determination. Hope and relief shone in her eyes, quickly squelched by naked terror as she spotted Kaeleigh. "Kae... no... it's..." Chel's attempts at whispering were hampered by her weakened, delirious state. The word "trap" was discernable just as she slipped into complete unconsciousness. *Exactly what I thought* Daegan reflected silently. This was going to be improbable, maybe impossible to emerge from whole.

Daegan had no sooner let his thoughts settle when Kaeleigh's light feet began moving in a run toward Chel. "No Kaeleigh." Daegan stopped her, holding her hands tightly in his and shoving her without hurting her behind himself. "This is a trap, we have to approach carefully."

Struggling, she frustratingly ground out through her teeth, "It's Chel!"

"It is a trap," he reiterated.

"I don't care! I have to get her. Make sure she's okay," Kaeleigh choked out, swallowing the despair that threatened to take over as she still struggled with Daegan. Finn came up beside her and grabbed her arm. She relaxed, glad to have him on her side, just to be held back again.

"He's right on this one. Just wait and listen," Finn whispered.

Kaeleigh gasped in horror.

"We will get her," Finn pushed out frustrated.

Outraged that Finn was siding with Daegan, she shrugged them both off, squared her shoulders, and started scanning the cave for would-be attackers.

"She's alive. She warned me about the trap before she passed out," Daegan said, then paused briefly before saying, "I can feel them in here."

"What are they waiting for?" Finn mused.

Daegan replied, looking around the room, mentally strategizing, "They are waiting for us to make a move."

Swords drawn and eyes constantly scanning the room, they waited. Impatiently, Kaeleigh mumbled, "Then let's make one."

"How many, can you tell?" Finn asked.

"Seven," both Daegan and Kaeleigh answered to everyone's surprise, even herself. "I don't know, it just came out," Kaeleigh said in response to their questioning expressions.

"It must be your instincts. Don't ever doubt your instincts, Kaeleigh. Trust yourself," Daegan instructed.

"Okay, Obi Wan," Kaeleigh said. Although the sarcasm was lost on Daegan, Finn snorted.

"Now can we take 'em so we can get Chel and get out of here?" she said, anxiety getting the best of her while she watched her best friend hanging unconscious, trapped by those vines injecting God knows what kind of evil into her system.

Daegan stared deeply into her soul, seeking an answer to an unasked question. A spark glinted in his eyes and a confident smirk emerged. He nodded between himself and Finn, "*We* can 'take them,'" he said, using air quotes, which surprised Kaeleigh more than anything. "*You* go to Chel." Kaeleigh nodded ready for action. "Cut the vines around her but don't get too close. They will be ready to attack quickly, so strike as many as you can at one time. Wait for us to cut the black chains—they hold an evil all their own."

Kaeleigh nodded with understanding and smiled. She was actually going to be able to free her friend. Adrenaline coursed through her veins; she felt confident she could take on the evil bastards that had tried to take her friend away.

Finn grabbed her hand and gave it a quick squeeze. Kaeleigh looked into his eyes. They had been friends long enough, he didn't need to say anything for her to know he was concerned. "I'll be careful, Finn, don't worry, but I have to get Chel and you have to fight them off so I can." He nodded reluctantly, but filled with purpose as he turned away to check his knives and other weapons he had been hiding, including some kind of Chinese throwing star or something resembling one.

Kaeleigh slowly inhaled a calming breath, focusing on the task at hand. She looked down for strength before running straight into danger. She would come through for Chel. She had to.

As they stood side by side getting ready to engage whatever creatures lurked in the darkness, Kaeleigh, on the far end next to Daegan, took several deep breaths and confidently told her warriors, "Take 'em down, boys! Chel needs us."

Quirking his lips, Daegan reached to the side and gripped her forearm, then seriously added, "Remember, this is a trap. We do not know what or *who* they want so watch your back and we *will* get to you as soon as we can." As he looked at her with an undefined expression, she suddenly felt awkward and broke his stare. She looked toward Chel and nodded. *Focus. Chel.*

Finn and Daegan both took their fighting stances and crept forward, hoping to draw out the creatures in order for Kaeleigh to sneak to where Chel was bound. Kaeleigh briefly watched Finn, still struck by the warrior side to him that she was getting to know. He sharpened his knives one against the other in a taunting fashion, trying to draw something out from the dark shadows of the cave. He had always been moody and a bit mysterious, but something about this new fierceness was exciting. He seemed more alive. Finn moved with skill and experience, and she got the feeling that this was not as "new" of a side to him as she would like to think.

Distracted by her thought, she almost missed the first creature jumping out from the shadows, landing in front of Daegan with a terrifying hiss. Kaeleigh swallowed a scream, holding her hand over her mouth as she quickly regained her focus not wanting to be a distraction. Daegan's sword met that of the creature's with a loud strike of metals. First the one, then two more slinked out of the shadows. Dark-brownish cloaks billowed behind and below them, making it look as if they floated on clouds of darkness. Red eyes blazed with the fires of hell, steam snorted out from where a nose should be, and short but sharp crooked horns jutted out the tops of their heads. She couldn't tell what the creatures truly looked like; although, despite being hunched forward, they stood taller and wider than an average person. And the smell! A god-awful stench—like decay and death—wafted to Kaeleigh's nose as they darted about the cavern, their robes smacking upon the rocks and flapping in the wind as they moved. Blackened daggers extended from their robes, held by clawed hands, clanging with each strike.

Both Finn and Daegan were each fully engaged in fighting off clone upon clone as they continued darting out from where they hid. Six of seven creatures were now in the fight, although it looked as if two had just been taken care of, already disintegrating as they hit the ground. Kaeleigh started moving toward Chel as soundlessly as she possibly could, running from one stalagmite to another, hiding in the shadows, trying to stay under the radar of the creatures engaged in the fight. *Almost there.* One more stalagmite away until she reached the open space leading to Chel. Taking a deep breath and a quick gaze around her to make sure she was still in the clear, she rushed out from behind the growth that was the last obstacle between her and her friend, making a thirty-foot dash across the open cave flooring.

Kaeleigh! Behind you! Daegan's voice shouted not out loud but in her mind. Instinctively, Kaeleigh turned on a dime, thrusting her sword up and away at the same time, sinking it right into the chest of the seventh dark creature that had yet to expose itself. She heard a high-pitched wailing, and the creature imploded on itself into a crumpled heap on the ground. When she pulled her sword from the beast, a black, oozing substance seeped out and into a crack in the dirt floor as the rest of the creature began to disintegrate. Panting and scooting away from the smoking pile of ash, she shot a quick glance to where Daegan was fighting and briefly caught his eye. Quickly she ran the rest of the way to Chel.

Kaeleigh quickly assessed Chel, *Okay breathing, shallow but breathing.* She could see vines binding Chel in place. They were twice or three times as thick as the ones that Kaeleigh had freed herself from earlier. She wavered a moment. Maybe she wouldn't be strong enough to reduce these vines. Maybe she should let the warriors help. *Warriors? When did I start using that word?* So much changing and so quickly, she hardly had time to reflect on anything.

A flash of light and a faint buzzing behind her eyes shocked her out of whatever effect being close to those vines had on her. Her mind had been heavy in a fog of confusion and doubt. Unsure why or how, but grateful for the light to shake her out of it. *That wasn't me. Screw that! Chel needs me,* Kaeleigh thought, infused with new strength and clarity she made her resolve to get her friend out.

"Chel. Chel!" Kaeleigh whispered, trying to wake her. "We're here. I'm going to get you out of here, hold on!" Kaeleigh raised her sword, gripping the hilt tighter than she had before, and brought it down with a force great enough to slice straight through the many layers of vines at one side of Chel's torso. These vines let out a high-pitched wail as they lost their grip on their prey. Where the thorns still stuck into Chel, Kaeleigh had to pry those vines off and out of her friend's body. She winced every time one tore at Chel's body as its grip was released and her blood freely followed it out. When she finished pulling away the final vines, Chel, though still unconscious, released an audible sigh of relief.

Chel's body swung away from the wall, but not far as the black chains still held her wrists in place over her head. Kaeleigh dropped her sword and rushed to her, frantically assessing Chel, trying to get her to wake up. Chel moaned and fluttered her eyes but that was about all she managed. Kaeleigh kept whispering reassuring words to Chel, letting her know they were there and were going to free her.

Too late, Kaeleigh realized that she left her sword out of reach just as one of the creatures, who had slipped out of the fray with her warriors, was silently almost upon them. Not having the time or distance to reach her sword and not knowing what else to do, she jumped in front of Chel protectively and shouted "STOP!" with her palm out in the creature's face.

Confused and startled for the briefest second, the black creature did indeed stop. But only for a moment, and then it continued moving toward her and Chel in that creepy floating way that they moved. It was only feet away and seemed to get bigger as it straightened from its hunched stature, preparing to unleash whatever kind of evil it had at Kaeleigh.

It didn't exactly have solid arms but more like wisps of smoke that snaked out from its body while at the same time unveiling a black and red sword held by very tangible claws, hidden under its cloak. If there was ever an "evil-looking" weapon, his was it. Darkness literally radiated from it. Great terror and anger simultaneously welled up within Kaeleigh as she refused to let this creature of the dark have her friend. Refusing to give in to the fear and close her eyes, she stared this evil in the eyes and screamed "NO!" as it was about to bear down on her with its sword raised high above his head, ready to cleave her in two.

Instead, a blindingly white sword tip speared through the heart of the creature from behind, stopping mere inches away from her own heart. The creature stopped dead in his tracks, literally, but before he fell to his death, becoming ashes and fleeing once more into the ground from whence it came, Kaeleigh saw her reflection in its eyes. Eyes that once had fire in them now showed a reflective onyx black. But what she saw was not how she stood now, but rather falling to her own death, pierced through by another's sword. Then it was gone; the reflection and then the creature. Standing where the creature once stood was Daegan. Fierce, intense Daegan.

He looked at her with a pained expression. "I thought it—" But before he was able to finish, shock hit Kaeleigh fast, knocking her off her feet as she began to fall to the ground. Daegan caught her and seemed to just hold her in an awkward embrace for a brief moment while he righted her to her feet.

She looked up at him. "I did too. It would have without you. Thank you."

Finn rushed to her side. "Are you okay?" Once he was satisfied that she was, he yelled at her, "Are you crazy? What were you doing? It would have killed you! They wanted *you*! If they were going to kill Chel they would have already done it."

Kaeleigh flinched. Understanding his reaction was because he cared, she reached out and touched him on the arm. "I'm okay, Finn." Quickly, Kaeleigh turned from understanding to an almost all out panic, "Chel. We have to help Chel!"

Finn grabbed her and pulled her to him in a crushing embrace, kissed her on the head, then let her go, making sure she was steady before releasing her completely. She grabbed his arm and pulled him over to Chel. Daegan stiffened, closing off any vulnerability she had just witnessed, and began to inspect the black chain.

"Daegan, what kind of chain is this? How do we get her out?" Kaeleigh asked him.

He studied the chains for a moment. "Stand back." He raised his sword and swung up above Chel's head—which wasn't too hard as she was slumped over—hitting the chain dead on, expecting it to break. Except it didn't. Daegan's sword actually bounced off of it, not affecting the black chain at all.

"Well, I did not expect that," Daegan said, frowning. He then looked from Kaeleigh to her sword that was still on the ground and then back to her. "Kaeleigh, give it a try," he said as he nodded toward her weapon.

Kaeleigh reached for her sword, still shaking from the shock of her near death experience only moments ago and not understanding how Daegan and Finn could remain so calm after such an intense fight, like flipping a switch on and off.

Finn jumped to her side. "No, Daegan. She doesn't have the strength for it, especially if you can't do it."

Sighing, Daegan shrugged his shoulders. "Then Finn, you try it using Kaeleigh's sword. Let's see what happens."

Kaeleigh interrupted. "Give it to me, Finn, I'll do it. We don't have time." But Finn was already raising her sword to the chains and following through, only to reach the same end as Daegan.

"Her sword didn't work either. We'll have to figure out some other way," Finn said as he looked around. He then began to study the chains where they latched onto Chel at her wrists and ankles and then again where they attached above her head and at the base of the stone wall, trying to find a weak spot.

"Kaeleigh..." Chel whispered as she began to gain a bit of lucidity. Both Daegan and Finn looked to Chel just as Kaeleigh gripped her sword in both hands and raised it above her head with her eyes closed, steadying her breath.

Kaeleigh visualized herself with strength enough to slice through the darkness of the black chain and the chains breaking, bending to the will of her blade. As she did her sword began to softly illuminate with a pure white light. She felt the warmth of it flowing from her sword into her body. She felt strong.

Opening her eyes as she didn't want to miss and hit Chel, she let out a fierce cry, bringing her sword down onto the black chain. It sliced through the chain effortlessly like cutting through water. Daegan caught Chel just as she was cut loose from the chains so she wouldn't hit the ground. Kaeleigh cut each of the chains that held Chel's legs too then very carefully cut the cuffs off that were around her wrists without touching Chel's skin. Once Chel was free, Kaeleigh dropped her sword and collapsed.

An almost invisible black smoke began to hiss out of the black chains that had fallen to the ground. Finn sensed it, cautioning Daegan, "We can't fight this one, especially not with these two."

Daegan agreed, looking down at both girls. "We need to get out of here."

Finn bristled as Daegan reached for Kaeleigh, but he was closest and the most important thing at the moment was to get out. He picked up Chel carefully, not sure of her injuries and trying not to jostle her.

Daegan followed suit and picked Kaeleigh up, cradling her to his chest. He didn't have time to acknowledge the warmth of her body against his or how fragile and innocent she looked being held in his arms. He had vowed to protect her and he would.

They both moved quickly, more than humanly possible even with their new burdens. They had to get to the opening that led back to the tunnel. Daegan kept looking back over his shoulder at the rising black smoke that seemed to still be rising and forming some kind of shape. A driving need to get out into the light, or at least as much light as the old forest would give them, pushed him to go beyond what he thought his limits were.

Reaching the end of the tunnel, Daegan could almost *feel* the light. It was there, waiting for them, offering safety in its embrace. They just had to make it a bit further. Kaeleigh began to stir in his arms, but he just hushed her with a low calming tone, knowing she would put up a fight. They didn't have time for that right now. Daegan focused his mind and yelled for Finn to keep up. Finn was just fine, but Daegan needed something to say.

The entrance of the cave rose up before them—the exit to their immediate freedom. He and Kaeleigh made it through just as the black mist began to solidify behind them and threatened to block Finn and Chel from the exit. Daegan growled in frustration. They had made it this far and after everything, he was not about to leave Finn and Chel behind like this—even though it provided the perfect opportunity for him to "lose" them. Kaeleigh would never forgive him. Daegan wasn't sure why it suddenly mattered to him, but it did.

"Finn, RUN! Jump through it before it solidifies, or you will never get out," Daegan yelled as he set Kaeleigh down in a small patch of sunlight he spotted. Running back, he grabbed Finn's arm to assist in pulling them through the partially solidified black mist. It was like pulling something through a thick cobweb. He used his other hand to cut through the darkness, aiding in their release. In a matter of seconds, they tumbled through, barely clearing the entrance before the *thing* solidified.

Breathing heavily, Daegan grabbed Kaeleigh, shouting at Finn to keep running. They had to get farther away. He looked back just as snakelike tendrils—or tentacles—began to grow out of the solid wall of black that suddenly had red eyes of fire. He didn't know if this was a messenger of the Droch-Shúil, or an actual part of it. With shivers of unease, he thought perhaps the latter. A hissing whisper of words began to flow out of the creature of darkness, audibly carried on a visible vapor of evil.

"Run, but we will find her; there will be no escape. The Orchids will be destroyed." The voice faded the further away they got.

They ran until Daegan was certain it was not still reaching them. But to be safe he ran to where he knew the nearest clearing was, where there would be sunlight enough to keep out the darkness that pursued them. The darkness that pursued *her*. She was the one—the Sol-lumieth—and now he knew it without doubt.

Chapter Twenty-Six

Finally having settled in yet another small clearing, the entrance to which had been sheltered from the rest of the forest by some overgrown thorn bushes and worn down with time, they slept.

Sometime later, Kaeleigh woke up feeling somewhat refreshed. Seeing Chel asleep next to her looking much better than when she was bound in that cave, she took a deep breath of relief. Slowly, gently, not wanting to wake her, she reached over and put her hand on Chel's arm. She needed to make sure that she really was all right. Her eyes widened as she realized they were also alone, once again. No Finn and no Daegan. After everything they had just gone through, Kaeleigh couldn't believe they would leave them alone again. They had to be nearby. Desperately, she wanted to wake Chel. She looked at wounds that were almost healed—much further along than she would have expected. She needed to let Chel's body heal before they moved.

Kaeleigh got up and dusted herself off. She still felt weak after everything that had happened the night before and hoped they would find some food soon. Looking down at where she had been lying, she saw her sword placed in some kind of scabbard that Daegan must have put there for her. She strapped it around her waist, feeling more confident having it on her person as she walked.

At the edge of the clearing, she sought to get her bearings. Since being in the forest, her instincts had intensified. She felt a lot of things changing inside her; things she couldn't even describe. Her thoughts, her emotions, her vision and hearing—it all seemed to be intensifying out of her control. She wasn't sure how much longer she would be able to contain it. Lately, she felt as if she might explode from within, but oddly she wasn't afraid of it and consequently it felt more right than anything she had ever felt before.

"There is an energy radiating from you now. I can see it—I've been watching it seep out, but the barrier holding it back is about to let loose. I have never seen it work like that before. You'll need to learn how to suppress it," a voice spoke from the shadows within the trees just beside her.

Kaeleigh walked fearlessly a few steps closer. "And why would I *want* to do that?" she retorted, knowing the voice to whom she spoke.

"It makes you an easy mark. *You* are being hunted, you know," Daegan replied nonchalantly. He didn't show any sign of getting up to join her. "They weren't after Chel in that cave, it was a trap set for *you*," he continued. Then, standing up but not moving forward, he said with extreme intensity, "Who *are* you? Who are you really and what have you to do with Alandria? This is something you *need* to know." It was almost accusatory.

Kaeleigh stood tensely, offended at his inquisition. After all, *he* was the one who had sought *her* out and brought her here! Still, she was trying to answer the same question for herself. On a deep sigh she said quietly, "I don't know. I mean...   I'm just *me*. I don't know what it is, but I feel a connection to this place. I don't understand it yet, but I *will* figure it out. It feels heavy and important."

Suddenly Daegan was in her face, staring intently into her eyes, his hands gripping her upper arms. "Kaeleigh, it IS important. This isn't a game. They *will* kill you, and I need to know why. I need to know *why* they are hunting you and *if* I should keep protecting you, *if* I should put *my* life on the line before we get back to those who've sent me," he said desperately as they were so close they were almost touching. Heat from his body was radiating away from him, almost seductively surrounding her. Breathing deeply, heartbeat accelerating, he let his eyes wander slowly from hers, exploring her face landing on her lips, then quickly back to her eyes. He released her arms.

Kaeleigh blinked, breaking the spell that kept her lost in the deep dark abyss Daegan had for eyes. She took a step back, releasing her body from the magnetic pull of his own, allowing her brain to think. Kaeleigh didn't want to think when she stood so close to him.

"I know I am here for a reason, and I can't choose for you, but you gave an oath to be our guide and protection until we were presented to those who sent you. I will hold you to your word. Nothing more. I did not and will not ask you to give your life for mine. After we reach our destination, you will no longer need to risk your life on my account or that of my friends. I'm grateful for your service, Daegan, especially back in the cave for my life and for Chel." Kaeleigh took a deep breath, suddenly angry but trying not to let Daegan see her slowly losing it. She had been so good for so long at controlling her emotions, but with wave after wave of fighting, life and death encounters, she was unable to keep them at bay, and this angered her.

Daegan watching her intently, and without expression, nodded. "Very good. You just dampened your energy flow, even though you were angry," he replied, as if everything she just had said was gibberish.

Ugh! Suddenly feeling extremely patronized, Kaeleigh took another step backwards and started to turn away from Daegan.

He reached out to grab her arm but she jerked it to her side before he had the chance. "Kaeleigh..." Daegan sighed with surprised regret at having lost his brief connection with her and took a step toward her.

"If it's not too much *trouble*, could you keep an eye on Chel until she wakes up and could you tell me where Finn is please?" Kaeleigh asked politely, covering up the anger that she was using to suppress the hurt that she was unexpectedly feeling.

Daegan, realizing she was shutting off from him, did the same. The last thing he needed was to make this more than a business transaction between him and Maleina. "Finn could not sleep. He had... things on his mind, I think you would say. You will find him straight that way, not far. He asked me to keep you here, but I do not care what he wishes. There are things you should know."

Frowning, Kaeleigh began to head in the direction Daegan pointed. Then she stopped and looked at Chel and, turning back to Daegan, she asked, "And Chel?"

Daegan nodded then said, "Of course. She will be safe with me."

Kaeleigh nodded and headed in the direction where Finn was mysteriously doing whatever Finn was doing. *Maybe he will finally tell me what is going on.*

He watched her go, taking a deep breath and wondering how she seemed to affect him so. He thought about how he had held her as he ran with her from the cave. When he saw that creature about to end her life, he couldn't breathe. His reaction had been instantaneous. It wasn't just to protect her as he had promised or to see what she could possible do for his realm; he wanted to keep watching her... to be near her. When he had brought her into this clearing, to his surprise, in her partially conscious state, she had actually seemed to try to get closer to him. Not quite sure what to make of that, he tried to ignore it. She probably thought it was Finn; they were close. Without meaning to, he had smelled her hair as wisps of it flew into his face. Vanilla and cinnamon mixed with the natural scent that seemed to be femininity infused with scents of the forest. Intoxicating. He found he could get lost in it, but he wouldn't.

❋❋❋

Kaeleigh didn't have to walk through the forest far before she heard a small bubbling creek and followed the sound toward the base of a small decline. This part of the forest felt different than what they had walked through already. It felt lighter, airier, younger even as the trees were spaced further apart, spattered with newer growth here and there. It was even playful as the trees swayed with the wind. The sound of the creek slowly trickling over rocks was a welcome sound. Peaceful. She hadn't realized that she was thirsty until now and headed to refresh herself and clean up a bit. Now that she thought about it, the rest of them could use some cleaning up too. She made a note to bring them down here before they kept moving.

❋❋❋

Finn was sitting at the base of a large oak tree right on the edge of the water, his back facing the clearing behind him. He felt like his skin was crawling and he wanted to do nothing else than scratch it raw, but he ignored it. He had been ignoring it since he got into Alandria, but it suddenly grew worse with their present location. This was a place of redemption, yes, but also of his shame. Finn became vividly locked in the regret and memory of another time as if it had happened yesterday...

From the center of the circle, Finn could see the Elders cloaked in their ceremonial cloaks surrounding him. The white hooded one had released his bindings with a simple touch of his hand. Finn could feel the magic releasing his hands but also holding him captive where he stood on the boulder. He held out his left hand, palm up, waiting for the sting of sliced flesh. Closing his eyes, he could smell the coppery scent of his own blood before registering the pain. He refused to flinch or utter a sound. He wouldn't dare. He deserved this, and more. This was the commencing of his punishment...

"The blood spilled here tonight is not only an offering, but represents what will happen to the one who breaks the vow. The boulder is the strength of the bond created and serves as silent witness. The earth absorbs the secrets of the vows; it is ever present and will execute punishment as it deems necessary, even if all others are unaware...

"Your crime of murder upon the Ferrishyn... You have been spared and commissioned with the guardianship and protection of a blessed child. Let it be known..." As the Elder paused, Finn hung his head and let the Elder grip his forearm. Looking him straight on, the Elder waved a hand over the space on his forearm, placing a magical brand that could never be removed. Head already hung with shame, Finn dropped his shoulders, his final stand of pride stripped, wishing for death instead. "You are hereby banished!" The words would forever echo in his mind.

He had vowed then to protect Kaeleigh with his life or with his death, and this would be no exception. Alandria was no longer his home, but she was. He would do what he had to, to keep her safe.

She gasped when she saw him. "Finn!" she shouted. "What are you doing?" Kaeleigh kneeled beside him and grabbed his hand, which had a white-knuckled grip on one of his knives, and pulled him away from his other arm, on which he seemed to be CARVING.

He looked up at her with both anger, confusion, and a sad, faraway look that she had seen only a couple times before when he didn't know she was watching him. Finn jerked his hand away from her and scooted back to where he could stand. He looked like a frightened cat about to bolt, but he didn't. He didn't say anything. He just stared at the water.

"Finn?" She paused, trying to sound weak and nonthreatening, the way you would with a scared animal that you were trying to calm. "Finn, what's wrong? Why are you doing that to your arm?" she said, unable to take her eyes off of the rivulets of blood flowing from the gash in his forearm and streaming down to his fingertips then onto the grass below him. Still no answer from Finn. Furious and scared that one of her best friends was hurting himself and that it might be her fault, she lashed out at him. "FINNLAN! Answer me... What the hell are you doing to yourself?"

Angry that he felt *compelled* to answer her, here of all places, he shoved his bleeding arm out at her. Nodding at his arm, he spoke quietly but full of anger. "You don't want to know what *this* is. There are things about me that *you*, of all people, don't want to know about. You think you do, but you don't. If you really did, you would have seen and asked questions long before now. You've explained away a lot over the last years. You are supposed to, though, it's your brain's defense."

Completely caught off guard, Kaeleigh sat down, trying to make sense of what Finn just said. Still worried about the condition of his arm, she kept looking up at it. Sighing, Finn covered his bleeding arm with his opposite hand to staunch the blood flow then sat down beside her.

"Kaeleigh, there are things that I *can't* tell you about myself." Seeing her angry expression and that she was about to say something, he cut her off with further explanation. "I mean there are things to which I am *bound* not to explain to you. Things that you need to figure out for yourself." He sighed. "I didn't want you exposed to... there are those who would try to find you, maybe even hurt you... I wanted to protect you from..." Finn hung his head in defeat. "I'm sorry, I know you're confused, but I am not *able* to say anything more. I'm sorry for what truths you may find."

Kaeleigh blinked several times in silent confusion, trying to process what her friend of the last several years had just said—well, not said, really. While she was thinking, she started to tear a piece of fabric from her shirt to bind his arm, but he grabbed her hand to stop her. Looking from his bloodstained hand on her arm to where the hand should be holding his own arm together, her eyes widened in disbelief. "Your... your arm..." Kaeleigh stammered, pointing at his arm that just moments before was a self-inflicted open gash, but now was smoothly knitted together skin with only traces of stained blood.

Looking up at the sky, Finn spoke through a single wet, sparkling tear running down the side of his face. "There are things about my past that I would change if I could, things I try to get away from," he said soberly as he gazed at his arm. She followed his gaze. If she didn't stare directly at it, she could see a flicker of an extremely intricate circular shape, which looked like some kind of a seal with black and purple shades within it. It was floral, almost feminine, but not quite. Every time she tried to focus on it, it would disappear. Revelation struck her like a lightning bolt.

"You're from here, aren't you?" she probed.

Pause. No response. "Please give me something, Finn," she said quietly.

He looked blankly out at the water. "I am an Elf, a servant to the throne of Adettlyn, and I have been your guardian."

"All this time? Did you not think you could trust me with your secret? That I would still be your friend?" Kaeleigh was shocked and hurt.

Finn didn't move. He didn't say anything. Numbness began taking over his mind and his body. The one person who had truly ever befriended him; the one person he had guided, guarded, and protected with his life; the one person he had lo... He was broken. "Kaeleigh..." Finn started but didn't even know what else to say or what more he actually could say. "I wanted to. I even tried a few times, but it was so far from anything you could've comprehended that you wouldn't have believed me if I had," Finn said sadly. "So much time had passed, then it became easier not to even try, not knowing what to reveal and what I couldn't." He breathed deep. "I have never deserved your friendship and I don't now. I understand if you can't accept me for who I am."

"You LIED to me for years," Kaeleigh said, now pacing back and forth in agitation. "I trusted you. Was any of it real? Was any of it true?"

Finn interrupted her tirade. "Of course it was true. Our friendship was real...I am real. You're just missing the back story." Finn stood up, his face a blank canvas, masking his emotion. "How can you be okay with who *he* is, but not me?" he said with disgust as he pointed up the hill back where Daegan was.

Abruptly stopping from the path, she was beginning to wear in the grass, she slowly turned to face Finn. "It's not *what* you are, Finn. I don't even know who or *what* I am at the moment. It's that you had all this time with me living this *lie*, making me believe you were someone else... or at least holding back part of you from me. Do I know the real you at all?" Kaeleigh now sounded more sad than angry.

Before Finn had the opportunity to respond, Chel slowly came down the hill, looking haggard but mostly recovered. "There you are," Chel said, a bit winded as she approached her friends by the creek. She quickly sensed the tension she had just interrupted. Pausing once she reached them, and looking back and forth between the two of them she asked, "Is everything okay?"

Kaeleigh embraced Chel in a bear hug. "I'm so glad you are all right, I was so worried about you." Kaeleigh assessed her friend, making sure that she was indeed recovered. Satisfied, she smiled at Chel and hugged her again.

Chel, clearly uncomfortable with all the attention and affection, shrugged her off. "Yeah, yeah, no biggie. I'm alive, just a little weak still." Suddenly serious, she looked Kaeleigh in the eyes. "Thanks to you, and to Finn and Daegan." She nodded at Finn with affection. Needing to move on, she went back to the tension at hand as Daegan slowly made his way down to join them, clearly still keeping his distance and not wanting to be a part of this discussion. "Now, what in Hades is going on down here?" Chel asked.

Kaeleigh pointed directly at Finn. "Did you know he is one of *them*!" Then pointed at Daegan.

Chel took a long look at each of them then sighed. "To be honest, I had a pretty good idea." Kaeleigh gave Chel a perplexed look.

"I'm not the only one with secrets, am I, Chel?" Finn said somewhat cruelly to take the focus off him.

Chel glared at him, but Kaeleigh turned to Chel. "Please can we finally talk about this now? I have tried to be patient, but there is so much going on, and I really need you both."

Chel sighed and gave in, "The world you have known is not all that it has appeared to be. I *tried* to tell you, back at The Station. I tried to share what was going on with me, but you were a little too consumed by your 'stalker' to notice what was happening," she said, nodding at Daegan, who shot his hands out in front of him in a mock pose of surrender.

"Yes, you did try to tell me, Chel. I'm sorry, I wasn't a very good listener or a good friend when you needed me to be there for you." Kaeleigh gave her friend a small smile. "Please tell me what you can, what is going on with you?"

"I can't tell you how much I want to tell you absolutely everything," Chel bounced on her toes. "It will take more time than we have right now, and some of the history part is my parents' story to tell. But," Chel leaned in conspiratorially, "but I've decided that what affects me as an individual is my choice to share." She beamed with the revelation she came to on her own. Kaeleigh leaned in, anticipation brimming in her eyes.

"We cannot stay here. You've created enough noise to alert the entire forest of your location. Clean up in the creek quickly, then we need to move on," he said, seemingly not affected by any of the rest of them and their issues.

They all sighed, deflated that they were finally getting to communicate things that had been pent up, sealed tightly away for too long only to get cut off. However, the new hope in each of their eyes spoke volumes to the possibility they could repair what had been broken and hurt in their friendships.

"He's right. We can talk this out later," Kaeleigh agreed, looping each of her arms through one of Finn's and Chel's, uniting them together despite the chasm of honesty they still needed to cross. Then she stormed over to Daegan and pointed directly up in his face and shouted at him in a whisper. "You... you knew about both of them, didn't you?"

Daegan looked at her. "It wasn't mine to share, but you did need to find out eventually. Deal with it and move on." Daegan pushed off of the tree that he was leaning against and held his hand to his left upper arm, wincing.

Kaeleigh was completely put off by his abruptness, but softened the tiniest bit when she saw the gash in his arm that he was trying to cover. Stiffly, she said, "You're hurt. You better clean it up before it gets infected." In an unusual show of submission, he nodded and started to head to the river. But before he was able to get far she said, "It's your turn... What are you? Are you an Elf like Finn?"

"No." He barked out a laugh. He looked away, then turning his gaze back to Kaeleigh, he answered with pride, "I am a Ferrishyn, one of the Faerie warriors from Feraánmar."

Taking it all in, she asked, "Is that why you and Finn don't get along?"

"Perhaps," he said vaguely with a knowing look.

She frowned curiously, then softened. "It's obvious you take great pride in who you are."

"I do."

"You must know I have no idea what you're talking about, right?"

He nodded with a smile. "I do."

Ugh! Man of many words, Kaeleigh thought with a roll of her eyes and a hint of a grin.

Then suddenly insecure, she dropped her head. With a defeated whisper, she asked no one in particular, although she knew he could hear her, "What am I?" His face pinched, he simply shook his head, not knowing what to answer.

After he washed his wound, she ripped the rest of the torn piece from her shirt that she had started for Finn. She reached out to him, but he jerked away. "You need to stop the bleeding," Kaeleigh said impatiently. Then she added out of curiosity after a quick revelation, "Why aren't you healing? Don't you heal quickly, like Finn just did?"

"Normally, yes. This," he said, nodding down at the scrapes, "is from the dark creatures in the cave and they have been infected with the poisons from the Droch-Shúil. It will heal, just slowly and more painfully."

Kaeleigh gasped as he took his hand away to reveal purple/black veins stretching out from where the wound was deepest. He saw the concern in her eyes and fought against it. "It will need more than just being bound," Daegan replied with anger.

Kaeleigh flinched, but shot back at him, "Then what do you need? I'm going to help you whether you like it or not. Deal with it and move on." She threw back the words he had used with her just moments before. He smirked and nodded.

Finn came up behind them. "He needs the salve of a scarlet bush. Normally, it would need to be boiled down, but he doesn't have time for that. The juices directly in the wound should work." He looked at Kaeleigh. "I saw some not too far back in the forest. I'll get some." Finn must have felt the need not to hold back anymore on who he was because he moved inhumanly fast to fetch the plant, returning only moments later.

Kaeleigh gasped in shock at seeing Finn like that... so *other*. It fit him. She was not only understanding him for who he was for the first time, but also seeing a blending of who she knew him to be before. Still, she wasn't ready to go there with him yet. Sincerely, she said, "Thank you, Finn." Then she turned to Daegan for instruction. Again, it was Finn who answered, seeing that Daegan was suddenly weakened by the poison.

"We have to move fast. Break open the bud and smear it on the fabric, then squeeze the juices directly into the deepest part of the wound." Finn paused, frowning. "On second thought, smash up a flower and put it directly inside the wound, then bind it with the salve too."

"You want me to leave the flower *inside* him?" she asked nervously.

"Yes, his quick healing abilities will absorb the flower into his bloodstream."

Kaeleigh nodded and quickly did as he said. She rolled up the rest of his sleeve to have better access and noticed the tattoo he had higher up on the bicep of his arm, just below his shoulder. She could feel both Finn and Chel beside her watching and waiting to see what would happen. Looking briefly at his tattoo, she thought she saw it move but didn't have the time to think twice about it, considering she was suddenly afraid for his arm—maybe even his life.

However, beside her Chel made a barely audible short intake of breath when she saw it, getting closer and frowning as she studied it. Chel was obviously making Daegan uncomfortable, as he watched her look from the tattoo back to his eyes, appearing to see something that the rest of them didn't. Daegan shook his head, whether it was in response to Chel's sudden curiosity or to Kaeleigh's needling with his arm, Kaeleigh wasn't sure, but she didn't have time to figure it out now. She added it to the other things she needed to talk about later, whenever that would be. Chel had always had an affinity for artistic symbols and tattoos. Perhaps she saw something unique or some odd symbolism she was interested in. Maybe she knew what it meant.

Everyone, including Daegan, who seemed to be quickly regaining color to his face and strength to his demeanor, took a deep breath and sat back after Kaeleigh finished tying off the binding around his arm.

After a couple of minutes, Kaeleigh looked up, to be pierced by the intensity of dark chocolate orbs locked on her. Pieces of his hair were sticking to his sweat-sheened forehead in a way that made her want to brush it away from his face, but the way he was staring and the uncertainty and intrigue she saw in his eyes made her uncomfortable enough to break the connection and look to her friends. He stared a second longer then shifted his gaze out to the creek.

❋❋❋

Standing up tall, albeit a bit shakily, Daegan made his way away from the little group that had surrounded him. He needed space. Invisible walls of doubt were creeping up around him, pressing in on him, causing him sensations of claustrophobia. Stumbling down to the creek, he ignored all the shouts asking where he was going, if he needed help (him *need* help, ha!), he was too weak still (*they* didn't know the meaning of *weak*). He needed to focus, to clean off the poison, to clear his head of anything but the mission he was on, to breathe. This was all too much. He needed it to be over. After his visit with the Elder, he had made a plan. The ending of it had still been vague as he waited to see if this "new power" was to be anything like what the prophecy foretold. He hadn't thought she would be, but now he wasn't so sure. He hated the struggle this situation—this *girl*—created in him.

Cleaning himself off and taking deep breaths, he could feel himself coming back to his usual "friendliness." His arm was hurting, pulsating actually; not the open wound that was now healing already, but his upper arm where his marking was. It had bothered him a couple times before now, often followed by something destructive. His head hurt, his eyes felt pinched, and his vision went black for a moment then returned. Perhaps this time it had something to do with the poison that had just invaded his system. It could have somehow triggered an irritation. He had his suspicions back before they had put it on his arm, but now he wondered if he wasn't correct. His "aunt" Maleina had been so *supportive* of him getting it, *too* supportive—almost forceful about it.

He usually didn't go along with the things that she asked of him. Daegan always made sure it looked like he did, but unfortunately sometimes even *he* carried out her heinous orders. A few times he hadn't even realized until the task had been "finished" that he himself had carried it out. It was usually when he felt the most resistant to Maleina's command that odd and sometimes horrific things would happen. Every time something odd occurred, looking back, it had been accompanied with a pulsing ache in his arm where his mark was and a dull headache.

Flashbacks of specific times he tried to disobey ran across his vision. The time she had tried to convince him that a particular old man was a threat to "her people" and needed to be "dealt" with. The time a family was trying to flee to another part of Alandria out of fear for the futures of their mixed-race—or Twined—daughter. That one was the worst. He had tried so hard to hide them from her sight, to get them out of town himself before she suspected anything, but she had found them. It being the one most carved into his memory, the one he would never be free of... little Katéri.

He had run into the still-burning house to see if anyone was alive, but when he went into the bedroom, all he saw was the unmoving hand of the youngest daughter lying peeking out from under a burning pile of fallen beams. She was part shifter and hadn't even had the chance to experience her first shift. He had liked her. Clutched in her hand was the smooth round piece of obsidian he had given her to play with. He grabbed it quickly and fled the house, turning his back on those he had failed to save and the piece of his heart that had tried to care.

Suddenly snapping out of the fog that had taken over his brain, Daegan absently rubbed at his arm while trying to get a grip on his suddenly wild emotions. Without realizing it he had slid his hand down to his forearm, where Kaeleigh had bandaged his wound. She hadn't done too bad of a job; he could tell it was already healing. He felt shocked and furious at how he had allowed himself to get injured and how that poison had affected him so, as if he was some kind of weak mortal. *My emotions are out of control. I must focus. I have a duty to complete*, he reminded himself with deep breaths.

Looking up, he could see Kaeleigh and the others now, anxiously waiting to get moving. He didn't understand her and didn't know what she was or what part she had to play, but he was beginning to wonder if there might be some accuracy to the ancient prophecy. There was definitely something about her. She was stronger than he thought she would be. All this new information and yet, still not any of the answers she was looking for. Her friends had had their own secrets and demons that they had kept hidden from her, whatever their reasons, but she was trying not to let her minuscule world crumble around her.

No! He would not think of her. He would not try to figure her out. He could not care; he had a job to do and, despite what the Elder Arileas had asked of him, he was going to deliver her. She didn't have any idea what she was being delivered into, although neither did he, and he didn't like the feeling he was getting about what his "aunt," the Paladin, might be up to.

"Daegan?" Kaeleigh suddenly said from the edge of the stream right in front of him. He looked up at her, clearly caught off guard at her sudden approach. "If you are all right, shouldn't we get going before it gets dark? You had mentioned making it to a safe resting spot by tonight."

Shaking off all emotion, Daegan replied, "Yes, I'm ready. We have a ways yet to cover before nightfall." He began to stalk past her, but stopped for the briefest moment, unable not to acknowledge her. "I appreciate what you did for me," he whispered for her ears only as he gently patted his wounded arm where she had bandaged it. It was so fast and subtle that Finn, who was helping Chel up from off the ground under the tree several feet away, didn't even notice. Within the blink of an eye, Daegan was closed off, unreadable, and unapproachable, walking off and expecting everyone to follow him, which of course they did.

Chapter Twenty-Seven

After several hours of walking in awkward silence, they stopped at what seemed to be the edge of the forest. Literally. Rows of the ancient giants towered both to the right and to the left as far as anyone could see, but in front of them was apparently the last row. Slowly walking closer to the edge, Kaeleigh moved ahead of everyone else, curious about what could be beyond the trees. From where the rest of them apprehensively stood, all that could be seen was a foggy mist slowly moving up toward the sky, but nothing could be seen beyond or through the mist.

"There it is," Daegan said, staring out at the mist in front of them.

Kaeleigh, startled at the sound of his voice—or anyone's for that matter, as no one had spoken for hours—turned to him. "What is *it?*"

"You will see as we move past the trees, a bridge that will carry us across to the other side and out of the forest," Daegan said as he pointed into the fog.

Kaeleigh spared a glance at Finn, who stood staring intensely out into the misty abyss. As he caught her gaze, he sighed and lowered his eyes in deference to her decision but still clenched his fists at his sides. Initially angered, but softening when she felt a flare of electric flutters stir in her chest, she took a deep breath then asked him, "Finn? Thoughts?" She needed her friend and hoped he would accept her meager olive branch.

Surprised, Finn raised questioning eyes with the slightest hint of hope to her. "You're asking me what I think?" Then much softer he added, "I thought you hated me."

"Finn, I don't hate you. I could never hate you. I'm confused and hurt, even a bit angry. I mean I'm having to figure out what things you've told me were lies and what were truths, but aside from all of that, I know you have been there for me. So yes, I am asking what you are thinking. You have been here before?"

Finn slowly nodded then took a deep breath. "Daegan is correct. The bridge will lead us away from the dense part of the forest and eventually toward the heart of Alandria." He paused and glanced over to where Daegan was watching their interchange with amusement, which only angered Finn, making him continue more confidently, "What you must know, however, is that the mist has magical properties to *reveal.* When you cross the bridge, the mist will cloak you and strip all magic used in glamouring. It will leave you defenseless, even if for the briefest moments... and... I must ask you not to cross it." *She won't listen, but might as well try.* Then to Daegan, "Another way exists. Why did you bring her this way?"

Daegan shrugged his shoulder and offered a sly smile, "I was curious. I thought you all might be as well."

Kaeleigh spared a curious frown toward Daegan. Considering what Finn said and knowing that it would be revealing not only to her, but also to him and to Chel, she glanced at Daegan, who wore an impatient yet expectant smirk on his face. Kaeleigh glanced back at Chel, who nodded in approval. Even though it would expose her secret, she seemed almost relieved and excited at the mystery. Glancing at Finn, who oddly seemed resigned, she said, "I am sorry, Finn, but I have to know for myself. You and Chel don't have to come. I wouldn't ask that of you."

"I know." He sighed and ran his fingers through his messed-up hair. "But I had to warn you. And there is no way in hell, or in our case, reincarnated purgatory—if that's what it comes down to—that I would not go with you!" Finn said sternly.

"After all this, you think we'd miss out on something that could give us answers? You've been waiting for this too long, and I want some answers too," Chel interjected with emotion, to which Kaeleigh just smiled.

Daegan shoved off of the large tree that he was leaning against, looking bored. "Then let us keep moving." He headed through the final stance of trees and *disappeared* into the mist. The others scrambled after him trying to not lose him inside the mist, but he took off too fast.

Finn, Chel, and Kaeleigh paused closely together once inside the mist, hoping for their eyes to adjust. "Daegan?" Kaeleigh called out, irritated by his lack of concern.

Finn interjected, "Stay close, I can get us to the bridge."

Unexpectedly and not sure why she could sense him, Kaeleigh felt Daegan's presence close and getting closer. Confused and irritated by whatever game he was playing, she blindly reached out and let her senses take control. At the exact moment he was about to pass by her, she reached out and grabbed his forearm, her accuracy surprising both of them. As soon as contact was made, Kaeleigh was given sight to see through the fog. Daegan reacted with a raised eyebrow and a smirk. "You are learning quickly," he whispered.

Kaeleigh glared at him. "Trying to lose us? Or are you testing me?"

Daegan simply shrugged, *I am trying to see what you are capable of and teach you to use your instincts without reacting with emotion first.* Then he added out loud, "Seems that if you all hold on to each other, Kaeleigh should be able to pass my sight onto you. She seems to be acting as a conduit." Then silently he added playfully, knowing that only Kaeleigh would hear him, "Better hold on tight."

Kaeleigh responded by digging her nails into his forearm. She felt him resist reacting to her childish demonstration, but he flinched almost imperceptibly, which satisfied her and prompted her to release her grip. The instant she did, he pulled out of her grip, leaving them all blindly groping for their way in the mist. Shouts of "Hey!" and "What's going on?" were weighed down under the dense precipitation. Before they could all freak out on him, Daegan grabbed Kaeleigh's hand and gripped it tightly, giving them sight and sending small pricks of electricity shooting through her arm, but the smug look of arrogance and dominance he shot at her sent combating pricks of irritation. *Amazing how fast he can spin my emotions! What is he playing at?* Unwilling to react to him, Kaeleigh reined in her anger and simply smiled sweetly back at him, willing him to feel her deep-down frustration with him.

Daegan's eyes lit up with approval when she realized that she had done exactly what he wanted her to do. *Ugh!* He was teaching her to temper her emotions, and it only pissed her off more that she had given in to what he wanted... that he had figured out a way to push her buttons, so to speak. To spite him, she let out a single flare of irritated emotion and then pulled it back inside her. She knew he got the message when he paused briefly to look back in her direction, his eyebrow quirked. Then squeezing her hand more tightly, he unknowingly sent those same odd pricks of electricity into her hand. The only word she could think to describe what that one little squeeze made her feel: *giddy*. She felt a little silly but let a smile escape despite knowing he was watching.

Then suddenly, there was a buzzing. She gripped Daegan's hand hard. Images began skimming across her vision from her dreams and flashes.

A faceless stranger holding her hand. Foggy mist. More images. *Various races of beings.* Buzzing. *Cliffs. A battle.* Other images: *Wedding. Orchids. Again his hand. A ring.* Feelings of peace and calm electricity.

Just as fast as they came, they were gone as though they hadn't happened—except for Daegan peering back at her with confusion in his eyes as if he had just been a bystander to everything she had just seen. Realizing Daegan was gripping her hand harder than needed, she looked down at her small feminine hand inside his tough masculine hand. She noticed something: a ring on his finger that looked exactly like the one on the hand of the stranger in her dreams. *How have I not noticed this before?* Eyes wide, she looked at him. "It was you?!" she said both as a question and a declaration.

Daegan looked back at her, completely confused and even a bit rattled, his face pale and chalky. Shaking his head, he replied, "I don't know what you are talking about, but those images... where did you... how did you..." Frustrated, he took a deep breath to concentrate. "Those were *my* personal dreams. I do not understand. How did you do that?"

"How did *I* do that?" Kaeleigh shot back, confused. "First of all, how did *you* do that? Those were from *my* visions AND how did you see what I just saw?" When he didn't respond she continued, "How is it that you were in them? That was before I had ever seen you."

Before he could shrug it off and shut himself off from her completely, Chel and Finn interrupted, "What is going on with you two?" and "Care to fill us in back here?" respectively as they both moved up beside Kaeleigh, each careful not to let go of each other so they could still see.

At the same time that Kaeleigh said "Yes," Daegan not surprisingly said "No" to Finn's question. Kaeleigh turned toward them. "Did either one of you see the vision or whatever it was that I just had?" Both looked at each other then shook their heads.

Daegan sighed impertinently, directing Kaeleigh's attention back to the issue at hand. She rolled her eyes and focused back on Daegan. *What a buzzkill!*

"I don't know why I saw what you saw. It must have been our physical connection," he said, looking down at their hands still clasped together and suddenly feeling very awkward at their forced connection to be able to see each other. He pulled away from her and left them without sight, not caring. He needed to regain his composure. Continuing, he said, "That couldn't have been me in your dreams. And if it was, then why? I didn't recognize the scenes that flashed as anywhere that I had been before or if they were even of any importance." Daegan paused, and no one said anything for a minute that seemed to last an eternity. "Let's analyze this later. We must get across the bridge by dark, which is not far off." With that, he grabbed Kaeleigh's wrist, this time careful not to touch more skin than needed for their connection to sight.

The bridge turned out to be closer than she thought it should have been, but then again all seemed lost and far off in the dense mist.

Chapter Twenty-Eight

As they approached the river, they were finally able to see on their own and broke their physical connections. Kaeleigh felt both relief and for some reason... loss. Human touch, warmth and love from people she felt at home, offered her a sense of security and courage when facing the unknown. She wasn't quite so alone.

At the transition where land met water just under the bridge, stood a cliff with a thirty-foot drop into raging rapids that crashed on and around large jagged rocks. Kaeleigh, suddenly feeling her stomach drop out from under her as a wave of acrophobia hit her in the gut, took several steps back. She had never been good with heights. Today was no exception.

Finn stepped back beside Kaeleigh as they both looked out at the great expanse from a slight distance. "Ready to cross over into the great unknown?" he said with a wink and partial smile. She couldn't help but smile back at him. That had been one of their jokes they would say to each other when they watched cheesy sci-fi movies. It referred to the times when the hero or the heroine would cross some barrier between time and space into what should be their greatest moment ever, but oftentimes was their greatest mistake. They would comment that had the character just been content with their normal lives, then what's-his/her-name would not have died. After the movie was over, one of them would ask the question and the other would reply... "Ready as I'll ever be!" just as Kaeleigh did.

But before she moved, a sober moment passed between them. "I'm sorry I couldn't tell you the truth, Kaeleigh. So many times I wanted to just forego rules and timing and just spill it all out." Finn stopped. "Even now there are some things that I can't tell you yet," here he paused, "but know that I was always there to protect and guide you." Then winking at her in that Finn way, he added, "Not that you ever really needed it."

To her surprise, Kaeleigh had softened. Rather than hearing herself in an outburst of anger and questions, she realized that she was content to just let things play out. After all, Finn *had* always been there. "I'm sorry too, Finn. You have always been there, and I will just have to trust in that... in *you*... right now."

Not too far away, Chel was lying on her stomach, attempting a closer and "safer" view over the edge of the cliff, and lost in a trance gazing at the rapids below. As she saw Finn holding Kaeleigh's hand, guiding her to the bridge and following Daegan, she jumped up to get on the other side of Kaeleigh. She wrapped her arm in Kaeleigh's, but not without giving her a quick squeeze and a smile. Chel couldn't help it, she was excited to see what, if anything, would happen to Kaeleigh as they crossed over the bridge. Suddenly, the thought occurred to her that the river might reveal more to them all than just Kaeleigh's unknowns. This made her jerk back and pause apprehensively.

Daegan sighed impatiently, "What is it this time? We really must get across the bridge and to shelter before nightfall."

Kaeleigh glared at him and gave him the universal "one minute" hand signal. Approaching Chel, she sensed her nervousness and quietly said, "We are in this together, no matter what. It'll be okay. I'm scared too." Knowing that would do the trick, Kaeleigh took a step back.

Chel stood up straight and looked at Kaeleigh defiantly. "I am not scared! I just didn't want you to be outshone by the wondrousness of me that is about to be revealed," Chel grabbed Kaeleigh's hand, squeezed it, and pulled her toward the bridge along with her.

Daegan mouth twitched almost imperceptibly and a spark lit his eyes as they came up alongside him. Kaeleigh tried to hide the slight blush reddening her cheeks. *Why does getting his approval give me unsolicited little warm fuzzies?* She let her eyes wander over the waterfall, as quickly squashed the unexpected feelings down as she didn't want him to sense them. She also didn't want to *want* his approval or care what he thought about her... but she was starting to.

Looking out over the bridge and then back at everyone else, Daegan said, "It is a very narrow bridge, but it is safe. That being said, we can only go across one at a time. I will go first to ensure safety on the other side, girls will follow, and Finn, you will bring up the rear." Finn nodded as if expecting and approving Daegan's direction. As Daegan began to head across the bridge, Kaeleigh reached out and grabbed his arm, but almost as quickly released it. "What happens once we are on the bridge? Do we need to do anything?" she asked him, then bit her bottom lip nervously.

Daegan, irritated, stared at her for a moment too long before he seemed to remember she had asked him something. "Once in the middle of the bridge, wait for and watch for the mist to perform its magic." He lumbered on to the bridge. "You will see..." but that was all she could hear before he was in the middle of the bridge.

That was awkward Kaeleigh thought.

From the edge of the overpass, where everyone else stood waiting, they could see what was happening in the middle of the bridge. Kaeleigh's anticipation was as high as her anxiety. The idea of everyone being able to see *her* before she was really able to see for herself who or what she was raised a panic within her. She had always been so private about her life and her feelings. Despite the fact that these people standing with her had been her family, she wished she was doing this alone in a dark closet or something. Fearing the unknown, whether she was truly from this place, whether she was a Faerie or an Elf or some other race she was unaware of, left her vulnerable and insecure. But the greatest unknown that haunted her mind... *What if I'm not anything?*

Caught up in her own mental ramblings, she jolted back to reality as the mist began to swirl around Daegan and then cleared—revealing the real Daegan. Magic indeed! The way he looked was not unlike the appearance she had grown accustomed to, simply more and *other*. She had heard Daegan refer to a glamour before, the magic used to disguise your appearance or make slight alterations. He had been glamoured to not stand out in the mortal realm; because seeing him now, she realized, he definitely would have stood out more than he already did.

The features of his face were mostly the same, just more prominent, but with the same intense and piercing gaze that he already had—a gaze that suddenly found Kaeleigh's eyes through the mist as if he felt her scrutinizing every inch of him. His skin was a bit darker, richer, surrounded by dark hair reaching and falling into his face in an even longer and shaggier way. That dramatic hair was intensely darker, almost a midnight black with blue hues filtering through. Slightly pointed tips that must have become an addition to his ears jutted up through strands of his black hair. Still tall, dark, and brooding, he was even taller than he had been at what she would have estimated to be something like six feet. Now he was perhaps a few inches more. He was still lean and muscular, but with more bulk to his build. He was warrior and then some!

Suddenly feeling self-conscious, she felt a blush creep up her neck and into her face, but no matter how she tried, she couldn't take her eyes off of him—or, of course, the magic misting around his strong... ahem. *OMG quit looking!* As he turned to continue walking forward, he looked back at her and beckoned her with his hand to follow after him but with his eyes, he dared her to.

Kaeleigh took a deep breath, but just before she stepped onto the bridge, she watched him walk to the other end of the bridge, noticing a dark marking on his opposite arm from the one she had bandaged. It was a marking on the inside of his forearm, simple yet tribal. From the distance she was seeing it, it was circular with markings making up the inside much like a shield. It hadn't been there before or she was sure she would have noticed it. She wasn't sure why, but for some reason she couldn't take her eyes off of it. She found herself holding onto her wrist where she had covered up the marking that had burned its way onto her own wrist not that long ago. His was the same bluish-green color.

Absent-mindedly, she unwrapped the fabric bracelets that she had tied onto her wrists and looked down at her marking, wondering what it meant and where it came from. Kaeleigh had always wanted a tattoo, she had just hoped to have a say in design and placement. Closing her eyes, she hoped that she was about to find out. She took her first step onto the bridge, just to be yanked back by Finn.

"When did you get that marking? Did *he* do that to you?" Finn asked, pointing across the river at Daegan.

"Hey!" she yelled, confused, and jerked her arm out of his grasp. "What? No, are you kidding? He didn't do anything to me. It just appeared a few days before we got here... more like it burned its way onto me."

Finn stood there staring at her wrist, even more confused. "I don't understand, it shouldn't look like that," he mumbled out loud.

"What?" Kaeleigh said, her eyes wide. "Do you know what it is?" Daegan had seemed confused by the mark on her wrist when he saw it too.

"Wait! What do you mean, 'it shouldn't look like that'?" At his tight-lipped expression she rolled her eyes. "Ugh, another secret, huh?" Kaeleigh said, clearly frustrated. "You know what? Never mind, I'm going across now."

"Wait. Please, Kaeleigh. Let Chel go first, I'll try and explain what I can," Finn said. Kaeleigh looked to Chel, who just shrugged, not caring in which order she went, so Kaeleigh nodded for Chel to go ahead of her.

Finn started to explain something about how markings in Alandria were given when you are born, but usually didn't appear until after 'the stage of becoming,' which had something essentially to do with puberty and the coming of an age of independence. However, Kaeleigh had missed most of what Finn was saying—although important—she didn't want to miss anything as Chel crossed over to the other side. She put her hand on his arm and wordlessly pointed to Chel in the middle of the bridge being caught up in the foggy mist swirling about her and then quickly dissipating as it revealed... Chel. The Chel she had always been, but vibrantly much more! She wore confidence on a new level; stronger and in control.

Kaeleigh and Finn both stood gawking at their friend as she transformed into someone, aside from the physical changes, that Kaeleigh always knew was deep inside Chel. They were both smiling and Kaeleigh felt her heart bubbling with joy for her friend, her sister. Just as Chel was taking steps to head toward the other end of the bridge, her image faltered.

"What's happening?" Kaeleigh asked as she gripped Finn's arm.

"It's not done... the *revealing*."

Kaeleigh couldn't tell if Finn was worried or just fascinated with the process. Maybe both. Chel's physical appearance wasn't actually changing, but her image was suddenly like a holographic picture where one second she was Chel and the next she was... something else entirely. Her image flipped back and forth, rapidly changing between Chel and a beautiful black wolf with white and gold mixed in.

Both Kaeleigh and Finn gasped in amazement as they watched. "She's a shifter!" Finn whispered in awe. "I mean I knew that, but I didn't know for sure what she would become... Amazing." Finn continued talking while Kaeleigh watched also in amazement. "Her parents are too. She should be able to shift into several forms once she learns how, but this wolf must be her primary form."

They could see Chel watching her own image change back and forth, at first fearful and then awed with acceptance of her own transformation of who she really was, or at least who she could be. She walked off the bridge to where Daegan was standing, nodded at him, and smiled. Kaeleigh wished she was there to share this moment with her friend.

Daegan looked back across the river and gave a deep nod to Kaeleigh, gesturing it was her turn on the bridge. She looked to Finn as he walked her to the edge. "Your turn," he said expectantly with a smile. His eyes lit up with anticipation. *Home. This is what coming home feels like.* Finn's heart leapt. He hadn't been back in so long and to share this moment with Kaeleigh was a reward in itself, though marring the pure joy of the moment was the anxiety that while her guardian, he was still banished and should not be here.

Kaeleigh walked cautiously—one foot in front of the other—toward the center of the bridge. Slight tremors of nervousness raced throughout her body, her heart pumping adrenaline of expectation. Almost to the center, Kaeleigh paused, her breath caught in her throat, her thoughts and emotions suddenly out of control.

What if nothing happens? Maybe I don't belong here... Oh my god! What if I DO belong here?

Kaeleigh's chest began to constrict; she felt like she was hyperventilating. Paralyzed where she stood, she stared out at the ominous center of the bridge. It taunted her, dared her to take that next step; see that she would never be anything other than an orphaned girl trying to make it on her own. She looked back at Finn, who looked intently concerned but didn't come any closer.

"I'm sorry, Kaeleigh," Finn said remorsefully. "I can't go across with you, you have to go alone."

Kaeleigh looked back to the bridge. She had to face this. It seemed ironic to feel so paralyzed when all she had wanted for so many years was to know who she was and where she belonged. The reality of what she wanted seemed so much heavier than the dream of wanting to know.

"Kaeleigh." Daegan's voice, quiet but confident, broke through her fog of doubt. "Kaeleigh, the first step is the hardest, you can do this... you *need* to do this. Walk to the center, find out who you are."

Kaeleigh took a deep breath, realizing that she now felt free from the doubt that was paralyzing her. She glanced across the river at Daegan to see that he seemed to be in an intense discussion with Chel. He couldn't have just spoken to her. How did she hear him then? Was he in her mind? She shook her head to clear it, stood tall and proud, and marched to the center of the bridge.

Before she even realized she was in the center of the bridge, the mist rose up from the river and swirled vigorously around her, starting at her feet encircling her up to her head. It tickled as it quickly kissed her skin as it read who she was, who this girl crossing over was. She felt giddy and light, as if she could fly. Just as she thought it, she was lifted from the ground by nothing more than the swirling mist. Holding her arms out palms up, she tilted her head back, abandoning herself to the mist. After all, she had come this far, and she was not about to miss out on all that she could experience. Looking up, she could see sparkling rays of light... and orchids. Orchids began falling from where she couldn't see, but they caressed her skin as they fell to the ground and encouraged her soul. The mist was moving faster and faster, becoming a tornado of fog. She could *feel* the magic. It was *alive*. Her body was tingling all over with small electric pricks. It was all-encompassing.

The breeze began to swirl around her face and caught her off guard, leaving her feeling tight, claustrophobic, and trapped. Pierced with fear, her pulse began to race. This hadn't happen with the others; no one told her this *could* happen. Kaeleigh closed her eyes and took deep breaths, trying to calm herself. Breathing through her nose wasn't enough. She opened her mouth, inhaling the mist and swallowing it deep inside her when she did. She struggled and choked, but was instantly filled with peace when she imagined Daegan touching her hand and remembered the feeling of peace he had given her in their dreams.

As she relaxed, she felt magic weaving within her and around her on the outside. She could literally feel it tugging at what must have been her glamour. The tugging became more insistent. There were sparks flying around her mixed in with the fog. Then a burning sensation started in the soles of her feet and slowly moved up her legs. It was the most intense pain she had ever felt. There was screaming, but she couldn't see anything outside of the fog mummifying her. The fire that was her legs spread up through her torso and into her head. It burned so hot, she couldn't take it anymore. Kaeleigh felt her body giving out. Irrationally, she thought perhaps it was what drowning might feel like minus the flesh being torn from her limbs. There it was again... more screaming. And then silence.

Chapter Twenty-Nine

K aeleigh's eyes fluttered open. *I'm dead, aren't I? Lovely.* No, she could feel the hard, cold, and moist planks of the bridge underneath her. She could feel her lungs filling and releasing air. Her heart was beating, albeit a bit slower. She was slumped partially on her side and her stomach. *Am I hurt?* Clutching her head, Kaeleigh couldn't remember what had happened. Slowly she lifted her head. *Why is everyone yelling?* Suddenly her attention was snapped back to the present, flooding her mind with what had happened and where she was.

Gasping, she looked back behind her. Finn was standing on the edge of the cliff looking utterly dumbfounded, jaw agape, when seconds before he had been yelling something. Everything seemed to be moving in slow motion and muted. *Did I lose my hearing?* She looked to the opposite end of the bridge. Chel was off to the side of the bridge, pacing with her hands clasped and held up in front of her mouth. Kaeleigh cocked her head, trying to understand Chel's reaction as she had tears in her eyes. Confused, her gaze moved to Daegan where he stood at the edge of the bridge, fully tense, flexing and releasing his hands over and over like he was getting ready to rush the bridge. Yet her nerves continued to rise within her. Then he saw her looking at him. His eyes grew large for a second, as if surprised, and then returned to normal. He seemed to relax the tiniest bit when she began to stand up.

Kaeleigh felt like all the life had been drained out of her and was slowly seeping back in to every little inch of her body. Getting up, she faltered and fell back to the ground like a newborn foal. Slightly embarrassed that everyone was watching her, she looked at her feet trying to find their way. Out from under her eyelashes, she saw Daegan muttering something but again couldn't seem to hear anything; she felt like her ears were filled with gauze. He looked angry. Suddenly there was an audible crack, then Daegan was stalking toward her on the bridge. She looked up to find him staring down at her, but then instantly he was down on his haunches right next to her.

"You can't even seem to do the safest things without getting into trouble, can you?" he said with unexpected sarcasm, clearly trying to make light of her lying on the ground in front of him, but there was worry in the tightness of his voice. It took too much effort to try to figure him out so she just let out a little laugh with a sigh. He grabbed her arm as she raised it for him to help her up before he had even asked. Out of the side of his mouth, he couldn't help the small smile that slipped out.

Finn was yelling something from the other end of the bridge, but Kaeleigh still couldn't hear him. Confused, she looked from Finn to Daegan just as Daegan glared at him over the back of his shoulder. Daegan had one arm around her waist and the other gripping her hand as he guided her the rest of the way across the bridge. All the tingles that she now associated with him—with his touch—were working their way under her skin, bringing her peace.

"Why can't I hear them?" Kaeleigh wondered out loud. "I couldn't hear you when you were over there either," she said, gesturing with her free hand to the other side of the bridge. "But I did hear you *before* I got onto the bridge."

Daegan looked down at her, slightly puzzled, but shrugged. When they were almost to the end, she paused, causing them both to stop. He didn't even look at her, just waited for her to be ready to keep going as if he could sense she needed a moment. Without looking up at him, she shyly asked, "What am I? What do I look like? I mean... do I look any different?"

"You look like you, but you also look different... I guess you do belong here," he answered with that smirk in his eyebrow that so frustrated her. He shrugged. "Ask Chel. She's waiting for you."

She knew he was changing the subject, which bothered her because well, maybe she looked bad or maybe she was some kind of freak here in this world. However, she was excited to see Chel too, so she let him walk her off the bridge. As soon as she stepped off the bridge, she heard a "pop" in her head and all her hearing was restored, as though she had been in a bubble. Kaeleigh stood for a brief second popping her ears and moving her jaw around, before she was mauled by Chel's embrace.

Daegan had to interrupt them so that they wouldn't miss Finn walking, or marching, toward the center of the bridge. He wasn't even going to stop in the center, but the mist surrounded him and held him in place. Finn's was the fastest of everyone's, as if he was somehow able to control the mist to a degree. Or the mist was disinterested in him.

Finn's transformation was the least affected. He did seem to grow a few inches and he added some muscle; more like an athlete than a moody high school student. His skin seemed to pale a little—not that he was tan to begin with. As with Daegan, he was re-clothed in more realm-appropriate clothes; soft-material pants for easy flexibility, and laced-up boots that oddly looked like a cross between something native and more modern. Ironically, he had on the same T-shirt he had on before but added a chocolate-brown buckskin vest. His hair was still sandy, but it was longer, resting just below his ears, and his eyes were a much more intense hazel than before.

As quickly as it started, it was over. He continued sauntering off of the bridge, but before he could conceal it, both the girls noticed a marking on his inner bicep that they had never seen before. It was somewhat similar to the newly visible one on Daegan's forearm. Finn's marking looked more like a sun with curved arms extending from it and surrounding it. According to the "Nice tat" comment from Chel, she too saw it. Quickly, he pulled his sleeve down, not realizing that it had crept up with the mist blowing around him. His ears were also a bit more pointed and his facial features more defined, but still Finn.

"Finn's a hottie here in Alandria," Chel mumbled under breath to Kaeleigh. Finn seemed much too intense to react to Chel's comment, if he heard it at all. He marched straight over to Kaeleigh.

"Are you all right?" he asked, focused solely on Kaeleigh and running his hands from her shoulders down to her elbows, making sure. When she nodded, he swung his head toward Daegan. "Why did that happen? I've never seen that happen before. It was trying to *kill* her!" He was shouting now.

Wow, he's intense, Kaeleigh thought, watching the show.

Daegan stepped right up in Finn's face almost nose to nose, but Finn didn't back down. "It was not trying to kill her. I wouldn't have let that happen!" he snapped. "I didn't even know I could get through the wards or I would have gotten to her sooner," he added, clearly more for Kaeleigh as he didn't feel the need to explain anything to Finn.

"Yes, why could you get through the wards?" Finn asked suspiciously.

"I do not know," Daegan replied, confused as well.

Kaeleigh stepped up right next to them and placed a hand on each of their chests, pushing them apart. Finn gently grabbed her wrist and turned it so Daegan could see the marking on her arm. "What does it mean? It shouldn't look like this." The only thing different about her marking after crossing the bridge was its shimmering iridescent quality.

Chel gasped, grabbing Kaeleigh's opposite wrist and twisting it to show her. "Look! Another one."

Surprised, Kaeleigh jerked her hand from Chel and her other from Finn, putting them both out in front of her for her own inspection. "Wow," she breathed out, half in awe and half in shock. Looking up, she sought Daegan's intensely confused and genuinely concerned eyes. Chel was intently studying the lines and curves, tracing them with a finger, trying to make some sense of it out of her own knowledge. And Finn, wide-eyed and fearful, had gone even paler, if that were possible.

"It looks similar to Finn's but not quite whole," Chel said finally, after a brief inspection.

"Enough about my wrist!" Kaeleigh frowned, frustrated. "We have a LOT to talk about." She took a deep breath, suddenly feeling weak as her arms now hung limply at her sides. "I feel like I could sleep for a week. My body feels as if it was wrung out to be hung on the line." She slouched exaggerating her point. "Could we find shelter, Daegan? Please."

It was the "please" that pulled at his heart. Daegan nodded and instantly turned and started walking. He paused briefly only to turn to Kaeleigh. "Are you able to walk a bit further?"

"I'll manage," Kaeleigh said as confidently as she could force out. Hating that she felt weak, she stood up and pulled her shoulders back, determined not to give in to the physical weakness she actually did feel. He nodded, admiring her inner strength.

Finn, Chel, and Kaeleigh all walked together, quietly assessing each other and even the smallest changes that had taken place.

"Tell me something, please?" Kaeleigh pleaded to Chel. "Do I look any different?"

Chel's eyes examined Kaeleigh from head to toe. "The changes I see are subtle and yet... more. Your hair is basically the same dark umber, but with wilder and deeper browns, reds, and even some purples—it's pretty cool!" Chel pulled a long strand in front of Kaeleigh's face so she could see the contrasts.

"What else?" Kaeleigh's eyes shone like a child's at Christmas.

"Your eyes are more defined and almost cat-like and your usual green eyes are more vivid with a golden ring at the edge of the iris." Chel inspected her friend further. "Oh! And your ears have a slightly pointed tip like Finn's." Chel bounced looking from Finn's ears to compare them to Kaeleigh's. "You seem a bit paler, but it's hard to see in this light." She paused. "Yep, that's all I can see right now."

"Thanks Chel," Kaeleigh said with a small smile. Kaeleigh touched the tips of her ears, feeling the points and traced the outline shape of her eyes, trying to visualize the changes she could feel. Other than those physical changes, she didn't feel too much different; although, she seemed more balanced and graceful, more fluid in her movements.

Kaeleigh was still weak when she walked but tried not to show it. Chel graciously held onto her arm to help support her while giving the appearance of friendly companionship. Finn remained the quietest of them all, almost as if disturbed that this part of him had been revealed.

"What does your tattoo mean, Finn?" Chel asked.

"It's the mark of the Elves."

"Do all the Elves have similar features?" Kaeleigh inquired.

"Some. Pointed ears, paler complexions, taller and athletic," he shrugged as if it was no big deal. Most his answers were short and clipped when the girls asked him about his changes or anything about Alandria in general. Eventually, they stopped talking to him directly and whispered between themselves.

Hello? It's not like too much is different. Back to moody Finn. At least you know what you look like! I need a mirror, Kaeleigh kept thinking. She knew it was vain, but she didn't really care. She could look like... well, anything. Was she an Elf like Finn? A Faerie? Was she a shifter like Chel? Kaeleigh didn't think so since she had the pointy ears and Chel didn't, but she didn't even know what her other options were in this world.

Chel helped with descriptions, but it just wasn't the same as seeing it for yourself. *Ugh! Shi....oot* Apparently being in this realm of *otherness* she felt she should watch her language, but sometimes you just needed to say something.

Kaeleigh started slowing down a bit; her breathing seemed to be strained. She couldn't understand what was causing her to feel this way. Before stepping onto the bridge, she was fine. She thought she was supposed to come off of the bridge stronger and more confident in who she learned she was, except that she wasn't and all she had were more questions that no one seemed to want to explain to her. Daegan was being his stubborn, closed-off self, and Finn had retreated to some reserved, tortured person that she hadn't known before—sure, he had always been moody and sulky, but never like this. Kaeleigh wished she could understand both of these very different men that she was with.

Chel caught Kaeleigh staring at her, looking for any difference she might find. "Do I look any different?"

Kaeleigh pursed her lips, thoughtfully. "To be honest, not really." Chel's face slightly fell. "But you seem more like the Chel I've always known was inside you." Chel beamed and Kaeleigh smiled satisfied.

"When I got off the bridge Daegan explained to me that I wasn't a were-wolf," Chel burst out, "I mean, a were-wolf... how crazy would that be?"

"But Chel you are a wolf."

"Right. But I'm not controlled by the moon or uncontrollable changes or some freak hybrid of nature," she rolled her eyes. "Anyway, there's a difference between a Shifter and the were-wolves of myth. My dad shifted in front of me before I came to The Station that day," she paused the memory brought rushing to the front of her mind, shivers ran up her arms. Kaeleigh gasped, her mouth held open with anticipation. "He changed into a wolf too, but I took off before he could fully explain things to me. I assumed he was a were-wolf and I totally freaked out," she continued. "So I guess it runs in my family. In my race, they have a dominant animal they change into, but some—with training—should be able to shift into several different animal forms." Chel had a new bounce in her step. Even though it was a lot to take in, pride in her new discovery was evident.

Kaeleigh was happy for her friend that she was coming to terms with who she really was. She was also shocked to learn Chel's parents were from here as well—that was their family secret. Finn already knew that he was an Elf; whether he was happy about that or not, at least he knew, but she still didn't know who or what *she* was. She felt a little different and she was sure that she had some physical changes even though she hadn't been able to see her face yet. Neither Finn nor Daegan seemed to want to fill her in; either that, or they really didn't know, which seemed unlikely, but perhaps they didn't.

"Daegan? I'm curious. If you're a type of Faerie, shouldn't you have wings?" Kaeleigh innocently asked.

Apparently it struck some chord with Daegan though, because he stopped in his tracks and turned back toward her, scowl in place. "We don't know. It would be prudent of you to not ask that again of a Faerie. It is a sensitive subject."

"I didn't know. I'm sor—"

Kaeleigh staggered and instantly felt life drain from her once again, as if she might faint. With a deep intake of breath, she gripped Chel's arm tighter and leaned against her. Her world was rapidly closing in around her as the darkness began to swallow her. She heard the muffled sound of Chel saying her name. The next thing she felt was her body being swept up, feet leaving the ground and strong arms holding her to a chest of solid muscle. Daegan's voice whispered into her ear for only her to hear, "Hold on, Kaeleigh, we're almost there. Don't leave me now." And Finn's hand brushing across her forehead—probing her temple—was the last thing she was aware of before she fell into the darkness of her mind.

CHAPTER THIRTY

The group approached a little cottage not far from the river and nestled in a small forest of trees unto itself. Just beyond, where the trees began to grow sparse, were sprawling fields of wild flowers of all different colors and kinds—similar to ones found in the mortal realm but much more alive, as if singing with the energies of the earth. Everything here seemed more *alive* than anything in the mortal realm. Further still were rolling hills of green in the far distance. Other than the little cottage, there were no signs of any others that might live nearby. It was secluded and hidden.

Smooth stone pavers lined their way up to the front door of the little cottage that looked like it was straight out of a fairytale that Kaeleigh remembered as a child. As a child she hadn't been read to much, but when she had the chance to read for herself, she devoured them.

Kaeleigh wasn't ready to talk to any of her group just yet, so she let her head remain buried in Daegan's chest, listening to the slow beats of his heart and his steady breathing when he walked. It was comforting. He must have felt her stir, however, because he whispered almost inaudibly for her to just stay still. So she did. She didn't have the energy to jump up and fight him on how she could walk just fine on her own; she wasn't actually sure if she could. Kaeleigh was hardly ever even sick, and this inability to do anything for herself or for her friends was infuriating. She felt Daegan rumble in his chest as he quietly shushed her. It was even more infuriating that he could sense her emotional flare-ups. She could feel him silently laugh through his chest.

Sensing something, Finn asked with a cautiously odd tone in his voice, "Daegan? Who lives here?"

Just as Daegan was about to answer him, the front door of the cottage opened. Out walked a man who might have been in his fifties. A handsome man of average height, yet appearing tall in a regal stance, with silver-white shoulder length hair—the only age-revealing feature. His goatee was sterling in color and had grown down to his mid-chest, and was held together by an opalescent bead. Points tipped his multi-pierced ears and a torque encircled one of his muscular biceps. There was a mark on his wrist that looked exactly like the one on Finn's arm with the exception of a small addition that Kaeleigh couldn't quite make out from where she was. His arms were folded across his chest in an unapproachable manner and he was holding a long walking stick, but didn't appear to actually be using it or *needing* it. He was intimidating, to say the least. Looking all of his intruders over, he stopped at Daegan with a raised eyebrow in question.

"So, *errand boy*, what errand are you on for the royal wannabes this time?" the man said with a chuckle and a half smile.

Daegan swallowed the growl in his chest, deciding to let the jab lie, he relaxed and inclined his head in deference to the older man. Holding Kaeleigh made the movement a bit awkward. With his head down he asked, "Sir, I beg forgiveness for our intrusion but we have need of some rest. Would you allow us in?"

"No need to be so formal, young Daegan. You must have traveled far. Of course you may rest in my home," the man said as he eyed Chel with curiosity and then Finn with a suspicious scowl. "Inside. We will talk," he said tersely, his gaze lingering on Kaeleigh then swinging back again at Daegan as if searching for an explanation. He brushed past them and walked expecting them to follow. Just before he went into the house, he took a sweeping gaze on all the outlying land surrounding his home. "Give her the bed in the room off to the side."

Once inside the house, Daegan helped Kaeleigh to the bed in the room as directed. But as he turned to go, Kaeleigh weakly reached for his wrist. "Am I... What's happening to me? Why am I so weak?" Her voice trembled as she tried to understand what had happened to her.

Daegan sighed and leaned down close to her face. "You ask too many questions." Then facing her half-lidded eyes, but not without a little frustration added, "I really do not know. I am hopeful this man can help us... help you." His head jerked toward the main room of the cottage.

"Now stay here and sleep." He slipped out of her grip and strode toward the door just as Finn was standing in his way blocking him. "Out of my way, Finn!" Daegan quietly grumbled.

"No," Finn fought back. "I need to feel Kaeleigh's head... I can *read* her and try to understand the problem." Finn, in frustration pushed past Daegan and into Kaeleigh's room. Then turning his head back slightly toward Daegan, he said, "I can't be here. As soon as I know that Kaeleigh is all right, I have to leave."

Daegan eyed him curiously but left the room. Almost at the same time, Kaeleigh grabbed Finn's hand and weakly pleaded. "Don't leave me, Finn. We need you."

Finn patted her hand and gently ran his hand across her forehead, probing her head and neck as if he was some kind of doctor. After several minutes, he sighed, drained from both the effort and the partial read on Kaeleigh. He had always been able to get more than that. The bridge should have stripped down her senses completely, allowing him to get a full interpretation of what her body was going through, but instead it seemed to block her further. It was a gift he had to *read* what a person was going through by the means of physical touch—almost like a healer except without the actual ability to do anything. *Except now it was useless.*

Frustrated yet satisfied that Kaeleigh had finally fallen asleep, he watched the unsteady rhythm of her breathing for a few seconds. With a heavy sigh, he stood up and straightened himself up. He had to face both the what and the *who* out in the main room of the little cottage, and despite the fact that he knew he was strong, he suddenly felt insignificant and small.

Daegan was introducing Chel to the white-haired man who methodically stoked the fire in the main room of the house. It was a very comfortable room with a couple of soft and squishy chairs and a small bench like a sofa. All very natural to the elements and nature itself. The man had rare breeds of plants and herbs growing all over the house inside and out, similar to a mortal realm's horticulturist. He didn't have many personal belongings used to decorate, but elaborate paintings of various trees and landscapes hung throughout adding splashes of vivid color. One large piece of art on the main wall was familiar to Finn. He had seen it before. *Where?* It was a scene in the clearing of a forest that he had spent much of his time growing up around—a place his parents were fond of. His heart began to hurt; it began to speed up with the haunting need for him to leave this place.

The older man looked intensely at Finn, eyes boring deep into him. He cocked his head in confusion; then the man's face took on an "aha" expression when his mind processed all that was before him. The old man looked from Finn to Daegan then back at the closed bedroom door where Kaeleigh was sleeping. He subtly clenched his fists, then took a deep cleansing breath.

"Finnlan," he said as Daegan and Chel watched with rapt attention, "I see you have failed at what seemed to be simple instructions: you were not to bring her back here. Her life depends on it." The old man paused to see if Finn would refute his statement, but all he did was hang his head in defeat. The man continued, sighing. "Just as well, it was inevitable, she would have ended up here eventually. At least you kept her safe all these years... until now," he said, more angered as he realized that she was not all right. "What is wrong with her?" The old man glared at Finn.

Daegan interrupted, "We do not know, sir, we thought you might be able to help her."

"It happened at the bridge," Finn added. "I have never seen it do what it did with her. It seemed to strip her from the inside out, not only glamour but all of her." Finn continued with a renewed strength because he had to for Kaeleigh; she needed him. "I know we shouldn't be here, and I did what I could, but if you knew her you'd know she can't be stopped when her mind is made up." He paused, pleading, "Please help her, you are the only one who can." Finn bowed his head.

Sighing, the old man—whom Finn knew to be much, much older than his appearance—put his hands on his head. "Do you know what kind of danger she is in? Do you understand what seeks her out?" He was pacing now as he seemed to be trying to weigh his options.

Daegan boldly stepped in front of him. "I do not know what is going on here, but if..."

The old man cut him off with a wave of his hand, then turned back to Finn. "Do they know?" Finn shook his head. "Does *she* know?" Again Finn shook his head.

"Does *she* know what?" Kaeleigh said, weak but stern, now standing or at least holding herself up by leaning in the doorway, looking from Finn to Daegan to the old man and back to Finn. Everyone stood silently staring at her. "Well?" she demanded. The white-haired man gave the slightest smirk at her unabashed boldness.

"It is nice to finally see you again, Kaeleighnna," the old man said as he inclined his head toward her. Finn grumbled something sounding like "not the time," obviously disapproving of what the man had said to her. He simply waved Finn off.

"Too late. She is here, no thanks to you," he said, eyeing Finn. "She must know to keep herself safe."

Taken aback by the usage of the name that the dryad priestess had used with her, she just stared at the old man, then finally remembered her manners. "I'm sorry, *who* are you?" Then she sagged a little more against the doorframe. All three of the men rushed toward her to help but the old man was surprisingly faster and even shooed them off her. Chel stood in the corner by the fire, completely confused, but eyes wide trying to take it all in.

"I beg your pardon, let me introduce myself. Many here call me 'Hunter.' Please come sit by the fire," he said as he directed her to one of the chairs.

"But that's not what you are really called, is it?" Kaeleigh asked with a small grin. "Let me guess. You aren't going to tell us who you really are... are you?" she said with a bit of snark, but she could be dying for all she knew so she didn't care.

Hunter chuckled. "No, it is not and I am not. Smart one, this girl," he said, looking over at Finn.

"Why don't you tell her who you really are, Hunter," Finn said. Hunter shot him an incredulous glare then slid his gaze over to Daegan. Finn started again, "No, let me rephrase... why don't you tell her who you are to *her*."

Kaeleigh, along with the others, watched this interaction carefully. Hunter seemed to be considering what Finn asked of him, then grinned. "Yes, I suppose I should." Turning back to Kaeleigh, he said soberly, "Kaeleighnna, or Kaeleigh, is it?" When she nodded he continued, "There is much I cannot share because of present circumstances within Alandria and the sensitivity of that which has remained hidden—"

Kaeleigh interrupted with a frustrated, "Here we go again with the 'let me tell you something but it's not the entire story and I can't tell you anything of real value because you get to go on a wild goose chase to try and figure it out for yourself.' Or is it the much used, 'It will all be revealed in due time'... whatever the heck that means," she rambled.

Chel and Finn gasped. Kaeleigh rolled her eyes. *At least I didn't swear!*

Hunter stared at her, then laughed. "You are much like him, you know?"

"No, I don't know! Because no one will tell me anything that makes any sense to me," she replied strongly.

"Your father...that is who you remind me of," he replied, waiting for her response.

Stunned and clearly not expecting what he just said, she and everyone but Finn stared at the man. "My... my father?" she stammered. "You know... knew... my father?" She sounded like a fool, not knowing whether her father was even alive or not.

"Yes, I was very close with your father once. He is alive, although many do not believe it to be true. Sadly, it must remain that way... for now," he said.

"WHAT?! I have a father?... and he's ALIVE!" she barely croaked out with what little strength she could muster with tears running down her face. Chel was crying too and holding Kaeleigh's hand.

Daegan interjected, "How do you know all this? How do you even know who she is?" It was the question that was on everyone's mind.

Hunter bowed his head, which seemed an odd thing to do in his own house, but humbly he said, looking at Kaeleigh, "Because, Kaeleighnna, I am your grandfather."

❋ ❋ ❋ ❋ ❋

Thank you for reading *Silent Orchids*! If you enjoyed the first part of Kaeleigh's journey, continue to find out what secrets her grandfather knows in book two!

VEILED SHADOWS:

Shadows linger where light is obstructed, and truth is veiled. Evil is an untreated disease in the once beautiful realm of Alandria. Kaeleigh is faced with a revelation that she must reconcile. She will decide if discovering the truth is worth the unknown consequences to both herself and her friends.

Daegan, the Ferrishyn warrior, is conflicted by more than his loyalties, and is confronted with emotions he doesn't know how to deal with. A choice must be made. A choice, that may cost him more than he ever wanted to give. The Droch-Shúil—enforcers and servants of the ancient darkness—continue to cast their shadow over Alandria, seeking those who can be turned to their side. The magic of The Orchids is growing, but not everyone will survive what is to come.

<u>One-click VEILED SHADOWS now!</u>
Or read on for an excerpt!

CHAPTER THIRTY-ONE

EXCERPT OF VEILED SHADOWS...

BOOK TWO IN THE AGE OF ALANDRIA SERIES: CHAPTER ONE

She turned back to Hunter. "I just *knew* I had family out there... somewhere. But I'm confused. Did you ever wonder where I was or how I was doing?" Kaeleigh continued, the emotion of the moment turning her tears of joy into uncontrollable sobs. "Did you...you...did you not want me? Or... Or... love me?" She ended on a hiccup.

Emotions flitted within her eyes and across her face; first heartbroken and lost, then confused and angry. A thought struck and her head snapped toward Finn, betrayal clouding her stare. "You knew all along that I had family? How could you not tell me? You knew how much I wanted...how much I *needed* to know I had family."

Finn had wanted to explain it all, but the oath, the memories, the past—all of it had kept him silent instead. He didn't dare try to defend himself, though. His eyes conveying his defeat. Finn simply hung his head.

Hunter interrupted her rant. "Yes, of course we loved you. *I* loved you, I still do... but we had to protect you." His voice became stern. "I know you can't understand yet, and I don't expect you to ever forgive me, but Finnlan was given very strict, direct orders to keep you away from this place, specifically from *us*. This all flowed out *from* our love for you."

"I'm sorry, Kaeleigh," was all Finn, her friend and guardian, could barely get out before he, too, walked out of the house, emotion dripping down his cheeks. He swiped his hand down his face as he attempted to collect himself. But before he got out the door, Hunter stopped him.

"Do not go far. I've heard rumors floating from Adettlyn that there are those searching for an intruder that broke the breach. I can only imagine that search is for you."

"What does it matter now?" Finn shot back. "They can have me. In fact, I'll turn myself in so they do not think to look further and find Kaeleigh," Finn replied dejectedly, then went out the door and possibly out of Kaeleigh's life forever. Hunter let him go, Kaeleigh's emotions needing to come full circle.

Kaeleigh began to panic. Her throat, tight with an emotion that threatened to cut off her air supply, attempted to cry out to him. She didn't know what to do or what to think. Kaeleigh was still so weak, on the verge of another collapse. She moved carefully to sit back down in the chair when she felt Chel's hand guiding her arm, assisting her.

From the time she'd come over the Bridge of Revealment to now, Kaeleigh had alternated between full of strength and bereft of the same. Her will, her eyes, her energy seemed to ebb and flow as if being controlled by some outside force or power. Chel, Daegan, Finn—all of them had noticed it, had speculated about it, but with Finn and Daegan out of the room, Chel pushed their concern out in the open. "Please, sir, Kaeleigh needs help. Is there anything you can do?"

"Am I dying?" Kaeleigh interrupted weakly, also becoming more aware of the strange ebs and flows of strength.

Taking a deep breath, Hunter looked her in the eyes and replied somberly, "Yes and no, child." He walked thoughtfully to the fireplace, gazing deeply into the embers and remembering a time long ago. "When you were two years old, your mother and father made provisions for you to be sent away to protect you from the war that was unfolding in our land should the worst happen." He sighed with great emotion. "Then it did. That is, the worst happened." He turned back to face her. "Before you left, you were heavily warded with a magic to not only glamour your outward appearance but also to internally dampen your magical energy so that you would not be discovered. The wards were some of the strongest magic ever used in our realm."

He let the words sink in a minute, then turned and faced Kaeleigh and Chel. "I believe what has happened is that when you crossed the Bridge of Revealment, the magic worked extremely hard to break down the wards... succeeding only in part. However, the strength of the wards to hide seems to have upheld against even the magic to reveal." Both girls, confused, looked back and forth from each other and back at Hunter. Attempting to break it down further, he continued, "What I am saying is, you are still part of who you *were* and part who you *are*."

"So I'm half and half?" Kaeleigh asked defeatedly.

"Well, yes, in fact, but not in the way that you are thinking. Let me explain." The older man chuckled. "Your body is experiencing internal turmoil, essentially fighting within itself." The older man sighed and gazed into the fireplace obviously deep in thought as he continued, "That is why you feel weak and drained one moment while you feel yourself gaining strength the next. Then in an ever more serious tone, he carefully added, "The answer seems to be simple: we need to either remove the remainder of the wards, allowing your full glamour to be stripped down, or replace the wards that have already been stripped to make you as whole as you were." He spoke matter-of-factly but was staring into nothing as he finished almost pondering what they should do next. He turned to look at her. Searching Kaeleigh's eyes, he spoke softly, "Kaeleighnna, the choice belongs to you."

***

Finn unintentionally found Daegan leaning against a tree, sharpening one of his small swords on a stone. His head was down, concentrating on his work, but Finn was sure he knew of his presence. Everything within Finn, wanted to run, to escape the accusation and guilt, placed upon him from himself or the others—it didn't matter. But he also made a vow to Kaeleigh and he wouldn't break it even if he had to follow behind her from a distance. He would keep his word. There was something hypnotic watching Daegan sharpen his weapon, something soothing. It called to Finn, to a part of his past that he desperately missed. Perhaps if he was able to fulfill his vow to Kaeleigh and be a part of the restoration of Alandria, he would find redemption and forgiveness.

Watching Daegan, he couldn't help but notice something familiar in the set of his shoulders and the line of his jaw. He couldn't place it, but he felt like he should know who Daegan was; it was throwing his mental balance off that he wouldn't remember him. Granted he didn't know everyone in Alandria, but someone like Daegan he was sure he would have run into especially with the company he kept.

"Do you have something to say, or will you continue to watch me?" Daegan said without looking up at Finn.

"I needed some air and to think. Oddly, the repetition of your technique and the sound of iron sharpening is relaxing to my mind," Finn said honestly in a way to distract from the real reason he had come outside to begin with.

"I, too, find it comforting," Daegan conceded to Finn's surprise. "Perhaps it would keep you from running, if you did the same."

If Finn didn't know better, he would call that an invitation, but he was sure there was more to it than that. That would be too simple.

"Do not over think it, Finn," Daegan added with keen perception. "I merely think it would not benefit Kaeleigh for you to leave during a most confusing time. She may be angry at whatever secrets you keep from her, but she will still need you in the end."

Finn sighed knowing Daegan was right, and took up a place against a tree not too close, but still in proximity to Daegan and the little cottage and began to sharpen his own knives.

***

Back inside Hunter's cottage, Kaeleigh was still puzzling through her grandfather's explanation. "So, what I hear you saying is, I can choose which *form* I want to be?"

"Yes, in a manner of speaking," Hunter answered. "But understand this: if you choose your true form, you choose *all* that identity entails, even not knowing who you are becoming; there is great responsibility and a heavy burden with this choice. You will not be able to go back to your former self once the wards are stripped. They were created with your innocence of mind when you were a small child. Only because they are still somewhat intact will I be able to recreate them." He looked her directly in her eyes. "I am sorry, but you must make your choice quickly. I fear that if your body remains in its current state for much longer, part of you will lose and the whole of you will suffer the consequences." His eyes looked pained, and yet there was a spark of hope.

Chel reached out and gripped Kaeleigh's hand and squeezed. "I'm going to give you and Hunter a little time. I won't go far, perhaps I can stop Finn from doing anything stupid." Chel's expression grew serious, she moved directly in front of Kaeleigh's face. "Kae, no matter your choice, you're stuck with me."

Kaeleigh nodded at her friend as Chel stepped backwards then slipped out the door, leaving them in a wordless silence. The only noise for several moments was the crackling of the wood that was burned slowly, if it was even burning at all. She wished she knew what he meant by "responsibility" and "burden." Why couldn't she know more before she made such an important choice, one that would change everything? But wasn't that why she had come in the first place: to find out who she was and to see if there were any answers beyond her knowledge of the mortal realm? None of this was what she had expected when she agreed to come, but it felt like pieces of a puzzle finally beginning to fit together in her soul. She had to know more, even if that meant she turned into something she would regret later. What if who she became was someone other than herself? What if she no longer wanted to remain in Alandria? What if she failed her family and her friends? Still she had more questions than answers. This was her opportunity to continue searching; either that, or she forgot it all and returned home. Did she even still have a home to go back to? She would deal with that when the time came because in her mind, she had but one choice.

Decision made, she took a deep breath.

"I choose this life." Her confident emerald gaze conveyed her intent, one that matched Hunter's own sharp green. "I came here to find out the truth and to know who I really am. I didn't expect to find any of this, but I will accept it. I choose my true identity." Relief flooded into her as the rightness of her words settled into her being.

Hunter's eyes bore deeply into her own, making sure she understood the gravity of her choice. His mouth twitched with the beginnings of a smile, and his eyes sparkled with pride. Perhaps he held the look of a grandfather. Her heart warmed, causing a single teardrop to fall from her eye and slide once again down her cheek.

Rubbing the sides of her arms, she tried shoving a shiver coming from deep within her off. The importance of this decision was not lost on her. Neither was the lack of certainty and outcome. "But do you know how to distinguish the wards from my true self?" Kaeleigh asked, nervous as she wrung her hands.

"I do," Hunter said, nodding with a knowing smile. "You see, I was the one who placed them on you in the very beginning."

One-click <u>VEILED SHADOWS</u> now!

GLOSSARY OF TERMS~

PLACES

Alandria: A realm parallel to our mortal realm inhabited by several races of magical beings and creatures. Created by the Originators also known as The Orchids.

Exhile: Another realm—a pocket realm—where the condemned souls of the non-human go to spend eternity in unrest or until they are devoured and absorbed into the land, whichever comes first.

Lenoria: The original realm from which the creators of Alandria came. The darkness destroyed it. "Old magic" comes from this realm, but not much is remembered.

Feraánmar: The territory mainly inhabited by Faeries and the Ferrishyn.

Elnye: The capital city of Feraánmar.

Lumari: The territory mainly inhabited by the Elves.

Adettlyn: The capital city of Lumari.

PEOPLE/BEINGS/CREATURES:

Ferrishyn: (fair-i-shin) They are the warrior race of Faeries, mostly male, in the territory of Feraánmar. Physically more muscular and bigger builds than other faeries. Created to fight and protect. They serve as hunters, guides, and guardians. Elite members become a part of the royal guard or for the presiding Paladin.

Earth Faeries: The most common race of Faeries. They are cultivators and growers for the lands of Alandria, their magic strengthened from the earth itself even as they give back to it. A more peaceful people.

Ehsmia: (a.k.a. The Hidden People), An ancient race of faeries that have been in hiding to protect their race from extinction—though they are already believed to be of legend, if remembered at all. Their magic is stronger as they retain a fraction of the 'old magic' from their realm of origin—Lenoria—as opposed to the magic of Earth Faeries. Though they are blessed with long life, they are cursed with slow reproduction so there are not many remaining.

Elves: At one point were the majority race in Alandria. They have a base magic as most do in Alandria, but some are gifted with more abilities than others. Their magic is strengthened from the light of the sun, moon, and stars.

Shifters: A race of beings that have the ability to shift into an animal. Those of greater strength and magic, may have the ability to shift into more than one animal form rather than just one.

The Orchids: An illusive collective of heads from various races united together, originally to create Alandria, after they fled the darkness destroying their original realm of Lenoria. Considered the "Originators" and make up the group considered the Elders—though not all Elders are Orchids. Their goal: to unite Alandria against the darkness that stirs upheaval against the kingdoms.

The Droch-Shúil: Is an evil entity. It is an ancient host collecting souls that went bad—the unforgiven dead. It grows with the strength and magic of the souls it consumes. Also considered a kind of demon. It is subservient to whichever master controls it at the time, and ultimately will forgo its purpose to fulfill its master's wishes. Can be in physical form of a hooded dark creature or most often as a intelligent mass of darkness.

Ferriers: Not quite Faeries or Elves for that matter, an ancient creature nonetheless existing in Alandria but not of it. They are neither alive nor dead, but simply exist. They are not anchored to any particular realm as they are the ferriers. They escort souls to their beyond whether it be where they are transitioned into rest, reborn, or to Exhile. They are non-partial or so it is believed. They are not to be involved other than departures.

Ónarach: A faction of Elves—mostly—that chose to go against their nature and against their race by taking the lives of Elders in order to consume their magic for their own gain transforming them into something dark, creating the Ónarach. They are an unnatural abomination who take orders from a master. Usually, they function as multiples—clones—resembling something like the walking undead or a zombie.

Paladin: The governing rulers of a territory, specifically Feraánmar territory of the Faeries, that took reign when the King and Queen died.

Sol-lumieth: A new power, a new magic, that was foretold in an ancient prophecy to return the light and life—the hope—of Alandria.

NaNai: The ancient Oak trees that were originally used to contain and protect some of the ancient magic that was transported at the inception of Alandria. They were brought into Alandria and even scattered and deposited into the mortal realm by the original Elf lords of the forest, partners with the Dryads. As the ancient magic fails, so do the great oaks.

Dryads: Many came from the origin realm of Lenoria. Previously they had been a neutral party, refusing to get involved with the politics of magical beings. In Lenoria, they were threatened to be destroyed if they didn't side with darkness, but they did not. They are an ancient race driven close to extinction. Many escaped with the Originators and refuged in Alandria—some were taken into the mortal realm for safe keeping. They are majestic beings who protect and care for the forests of Alandria, guided and cared for by Andreinna, the priestess of the forests. Some can evolve into a human form, but others choose to become "grounded" and then are unable to move.

* Several races that are present, or created, in The Age of Alandria series are inspired from various mythologies throughout history.

About the Author

Morgan Wylie is an award-winning and *USA Today* Bestselling author with several genres published from YA fantasy to adult paranormal romance and others in between. Morgan published her first novel, Silent Orchids, one year after moving across the country with her family on a journey of new discovery. After an amazing three years in Nashville, TN, and the release of two more books, Morgan and her family found their way back to the Northwest where they now reside. Still working everyday with great optimism, Morgan continues to embrace all things: "Mama", wife, teacher, host of The Lotus Bloom podcast for creatives, and mediator to the many voices and muses constantly chattering in her head... where it gets pretty loud!

You can find her and news on her books at the following:

MorganWylie.org

Morgan Wylie Books on Facebook

@MWylieBooks on IG and Twitter

The Lotus Bloom Podcast on most podcasting sites

Don't miss out! Join the Journey with Morgan today!

Newsletter of Enchanted Journeys

Or sign up at morganwylie.org

To show some love for this book, please consider leaving a review at the place of purchase or any of the locations it is sold. This means the world to an author!

THANK YOU!!

Also by Morgan Wylie

YA FANTASY:
The Age of Alandria Series:
Silent Orchids (Book 1)
Veiled Shadows (Book 2)
Daegan (Novella 2.5)
Fractured Darkness (Book 3)
Fading Light (Book 4)
Night Magic (Novella 4.5)
The Sol-Lumieth (Book 5)
The Rise of the Paladin (An Alandria Short Story Prequel)

YA PARANORMAL/SUPERNATURAL:
HAILEY: The Necromancer (A Shadow Realm Novella 1)
JAX: The Doppelgänger (A Shadow Realm Novella 2)
(A Shadow Realm Novella 3 forthcoming)
(A Shadow Realm Novella 4 forthcoming)

MISCELLANEOUS COLLECTIONS:
Dawn of The Witch Hunters (A Havenwood Falls Legends Novella)
Rise of The Witch Hunters (A Havenwood Falls Legends Novella)
Reawakened (A Havenwood Falls High Novella)
Rekindled (A Havenwood Falls Holiday Short Story Anthology 2019)
Redefined (A Havenwood Falls Novella)
Rediscovered (A Havenwood Falls High Novella)
Reunited (A Havenwood Falls Holiday Short Story Anthology 2020)
Reborn (A Havenwood Falls Holiday Short Story Anthology 2021)
Magic by Moonlight with Kallie Ross (A Havenwood Falls Spring Short Story Anthology 2022)
Remembrance (A Havenwood Falls Sunset Short Story Anthology 2022)